Jim Shepard

You Think That's Bad

Jim Shepard is the author of six novels and three previous story collections. His stories are published regularly in such magazines as *The New Yorker, The Atlantic, McSweeney's, Tin House, Zoetrope: All-Story, Playboy,* and *Vice,* among others. "The Netherlands Lives with Water," from this collection, appears in *The Best American Short Stories 2010.* "Your Fate Hurtles Down at You," also from this collection, appears in *PEN/ O. Henry Prize Stories 2011.* He lives with his wife and three children in Williamstown, Massachussets.

www.jim-shepard.com

You Think That's Bad

You Think That's Bad

STORIES

Jim Shepard

Vintage Contemporaries
Vintage Books
A Division of Random House, Inc.
New York

FIRST VINTAGE CONTEMPORARIES EDITION, MARCH 2012

The following stories were previously published: "Happy with Crocodiles" in
American Scholar; "Poland Is Watching" in *The Atlantic*; "Your Fate Hurtles Down at
You" in *Electric Literature*; "Classical Scenes of Farewell" and "The Netherlands Lives
with Water" in *McSweeney's*; "Boys Town," in *The New Yorker*; "Minotaur" in *Playboy*;
"Low-Hanging Fruit" in *Tin House*; "In Cretaceous Seas" in *Vice*; and "The Track of
the Assassins" in *Zoetrope: All-Story*.

The Library of Congress has cataloged the Knopf edition as follows:
Shepard, Jim.
You think that's bad / by Jim Shepard.—1st ed.
p. cm.
I. Title.
PS3569.H39384Y68 2011
813'.54—dc22 2010035998

Vintage ISBN: 978-0-307-74214-8

Book design by Virginia Tan

www.vintagebooks.com

Printed in the United States of America
10 9 8 7 6 5 4 3 2 1

For Shep

Contents

You Think That's Bad

Minotaur

Kenny I hadn't seen in, what, three, four years. Kenny started with me way back when, the two of us standing there with our hands in our pants right outside the wormhole. Kenny wanders into the Windsock last night like the Keith Richards version of himself with this girl who looks like some movie star's daughter. "Is that you?" he says when he spots me in a booth. "This is the guy you're always talking about?" Carly asks once we're a few minutes into the conversation. The girl's name turns out to be Celestine. Talking to me, every so often he gets distracted and we have to wait until he takes his mouth away from hers.

"So my husband brings you up all the time and then, when I ask what you did together, he always goes, 'I can't help you there,'" Carly tells him. "Which of course he knows I know. But he likes to say it anyway."

With her fingers Celestine brings his cheek over toward her, like nobody's talking, and once they're kissing she works on gently opening his mouth with hers. After a while he makes a sound that's apparently the one she wanted to hear, and she disengages and returns her attention to us.

"How's your wife?" Carly asks him.

Kenny says they're separated and that she's settled down with a project manager from Lockheed.

"Nice to meet you," Carly tells Celestine.

"Mmm-*hmm*," Celestine says.

The wormhole for Kenny and me was what people in the industry call the black world, which is all about projects so far off the books that you're not even allowed to put CLASSIFIED in the gap in your résumé afterwards. You're told during recruitment that people in the know will know, and that when it comes to everybody else you shouldn't give a shit.

If you want to know how big the black world is, go click on *COMPTROLLER* and then *RESEARCH AND DEVELOPMENT* on the DOD's Web site and make a list of the line items with names like Cerulean Blue and budgets listed as "No Number." Then compare the number of budget items you *can* add up, and subtract that from the DOD's printed budget. Now *there's* an eye-opener for you home actuaries: you're looking at a difference of forty billion dollars.

The black world's everywhere: regular air bases have restricted compounds; defense industries have permanently segregated sites. And anywhere that no one in his right mind would ever go to in the Southwest, there's a black base. Drive along a wash in the back of nowhere in Nevada and you'll suddenly hit a newish fence that goes on forever. Follow the fence and you'll encounter some bland-looking guys in an unmarked pickup. Refuse to do what they say and they'll shoot the tires out from under you and give you a lift to the county lockup.

All of this was *before* 9/11. You can imagine what it's like now.

For a while Kenny helped out at Groom Lake as an engineering troubleshooter for a C-5 airlift squadron that flew only late-night operations, ferrying classified aircraft from the aerospace plants to the test sites. They had a patch that featured a crescent moon over *NOYFB*. "None Of Your Fucking Business," he explained when I first saw it. He said that during the down time he hung with the stealth-bomber guys with their *Huge Deposit-No Return* jackets, and he told his wife when she asked that he worked in the Nellis Range, which was a little like telling someone that you worked in the Alps.

I'd met him a few years earlier when Minotaur was hatched out at Lockheed's Skunk Works. He'd been brought in for the sister program, Minion. We were developing an ATOP—an Advanced Technology Observation Platform—and even over the crapper it read: *Furtim Vigilans: Vigilance Through Stealth.*

It wasn't the secrecy as much as the slogans and patches and badges that drove Carly nuts. "Only you guys would have *patches* for secret programs," she said. "Like what're we supposed to do, be *intrigued? Guess* what's going on?"

In the old days Kenny's unit had as its symbol the mushroom, and under it, in Latin: *Always in the Dark.* The black world's big on patches and Latin. I had one for Minotaur that read *Doing God's Work with Other People's Money.* I'd heard there was a unit out at Point Mugu that had the ultimate patch: just a black-on-black circle.

"'Gustatus Similis Pullus,'" Carly said. She was tilting her head to read an oval yellow patch on Kenny's shoulder.

"You know Latin?" he asked.

"Do you know how long I've been tired of this?" she told him.

"*I* don't know Latin," Celestine volunteered.

"'Tastes Like Chicken,'" he translated.

"Nice," Carly told him.

"I don't get it," Celestine said.

"Neither does she," he told her.

"Oooh. Snap," Carly said.

"People're supposed to taste like chicken," I finally told them.

"Oh, right," Carly said. "So what're you guys doing, eating people?"

"That's what we do: we eat people," Kenny agreed. He made teeth with his forefingers and thumbs and had them bite up and down.

Carly gave him a head shake and turned to the bar. "Are we gonna order?" she asked.

It's all infowar now. Delivering or screwing up content. We can convince a surface-to-air missile that it's a Maytag dryer. Tell an over-the-horizon radar array that it's through for the day, or that it wants to play music. And we've got lookdown capabilities that can tell you from space whether your aunt's having a Diet Coke or a regular.

What Carly's forgetting is that it's not just about teasing. There's something to be said for esprit de corps. There's all that home-team stuff.

I heard from various sources that Kenny's been all over: Kirtland, Hanscom, White Sands, Groom Lake, Tonopah. "What's my motto?" he said, in front of his wife, the last time I saw him. "'A Lifetime of Silence,'" she answered back, as though he'd told her in the nicest possible way to go fuck herself.

What's it like? Carly asked me once. Not being able to tell the people you're *closest* to anything about what you care about most? She was talking about how upset I was at Kenny's having dropped right off the face of the earth. He'd gone off to his new assignment without a backwards glance some two weeks before, with not even a *Have a good one, bucko* left behind on a Post-it. She was talking about having just come home from a good vacation with her husband and watching him throw his drink onto the roof because of an e-mail in response to some inquiries that read *No can do, in terms of a back tell. Your Hansel stipulated no bread crumbs.*

The glass had rolled back off the shingles into the azaleas. By way of explaining the duration of my upset, I'd let her in on a little of what I'd risked by that little fishing expedition. I asked if she had any idea how long it took to get the kind of security clearance her breadwinner toted around or how many federales with pocket protectors had fine-tooth-combed my every last Visa bill.

"I almost said hello to you two Christmases ago," Kenny told me now. "Out at SWC in Schriever."

"You were at SWC in Schriever?" I asked.

"Oh, for Christ's sake," Carly said. "Don't talk like this if you're not going to tell us what it means."

"The Space Warfare Center in Colorado," Kenny said, shrugging when he saw my face. "Let's give the bad guys a fighting chance."

"I didn't know we *had* a Space Warfare Center," Celestine said.

"*A* Space Warfare Center?" Kenny asked her.

At our rehearsal dinner, now three years back in the rearview mirror, during a lull at our table Carly's college roommate said, "I never had a black eye, but I always kinda wished I did." Carly looked surprised and said, "Well, I licked one all over once." And everybody looked at her. "You licked a black eye?" I finally asked. And Carly went, "Oh, I thought she said 'black *guy*.'"

"You licked a black guy all over?" I asked her later that night. She couldn't see my face in the dark but she knew what I was getting at.

"I did. And it was *so* good," she said. Then she put a hand on the inside of each of my knees and spread my legs as wide as she could.

"What's the biggest secret you think I ever kept from you?" she asked during our most recent relocation, which was last Memorial Day. We had a parakeet in the backseat and were bouncing a U-Haul over a road that you would have said hadn't seen vehicular traffic in twenty-five years. I'd been lent out to Northrup and couldn't even tell her for how long.

"I don't know," I told her. "I figured you had nothing *but* secrets." Then she dropped the subject, so for two weeks I went through her e-mails.

"I don't know anything about this Kenny guy," she told me the day I threw the drink. "Except that you can't get over that he disappeared."

"You know, sometimes you just register a connection," I told her later that night in bed. "And not talking about it doesn't have to be some big deal."

"So it was kind of a romantic thing," she said.

"Yeah, it was totally physical," I told her. "Like you and your mom."

Carly had gotten this far by telling herself that compartmentalizing wasn't *all* bad: that some doors may have been shut off but that the really important ones were wide open. And in terms of intimacy, she was far and away as good as things were going to get for me. We had this look we gave each other in public that said, *I know. I already thought that.* We'd each been engaged when we met and we'd stuck with each other through a lot of other people's crap. Late at night we lay nose to nose in the dark and told each other stuff nobody else had ever heard us say. I told her about some of the times I'd been a dick and she told me about a kid she'd miscarried, and about another she'd put up for adoption when she was seventeen. She had no idea where he was now, but not a day went by that she didn't think about it. We called them both Little Jimmy. And for a while there was all this magical thinking, and not asking each other all that much because we thought we already knew.

That not-being-on-the-same-page thing had become a bigger issue for me lately, though that's something she didn't know. Which is perfect, she would've said.

What I'd been working on at that point had gone south a little. Another way of putting it would be to say that what I was doing was wrong. The ATOP we'd developed for Minotaur had been an unarmed drone that could hover above one spot like a satellite couldn't, providing instant lookdown for as long as a battlefield commander wanted it. But how long had it taken for us to retrofit them with air-to-surface missiles? And how many Fiats and Citroëns have those drones taken out because somebody back in Langley thought the right target was in the car?

There was an army of us out there up to the same sorts of hijinks and not able to talk about it. Where I worked, everything was black: not only the test flights, but also the resupply, the maintenance, the search-and-rescue. And the security scrutiny never went away. The guy who led my last project team, at home when he went to bed, after he hit the lights, waved to the surveillance guys. His wife never understood why even in August they had to do everything under the sheets.

On black-world patches you see a lot of sigmas because that's the engineering symbol for the unknown value.

"The Minotaur's the one in the labyrinth, right?" the materials guy in my project team asked the first day. When I told him it was, he wanted to know if the Minotaur was supposed to know where it was going, or if it was lost, too. That'd be funny, I told him. And we joked about the monster *and* the hero just wandering around through all these dark corridors, nobody finding anybody.

And now here I was and here Kenny was, with poor Carly trying to get a fix on either one of us.

"So what brings you to this neck of the woods?" I finally asked him once we were well into our second drinks.

"You know how *sad* he was," Carly asked, "when he couldn't get in touch with you anymore?"

"How sad?" Kenny asked. Celestine seemed curious, too.

"I thought we were gonna have to get him some counseling," Carly said.

"It's hard to adjust to not being with me anymore," Kenny told her.

"So did he ever talk to you about me?" she asked.

"You came up," Kenny answered, and even Celestine picked up on the unpleasantness.

"I'm listening," Carly said.

"Oh, he was all hot to trot whenever he talked about you," Kenny said.

"Sang my praises, did he?" Carly's face had the expression she gets when somebody's tracked something into the house.

"When he wasn't shooting himself in the foot about you, he was pretty happy," Kenny said. "I called it his good-woman face."

"As in, I had one," I explained.

"Whenever he tied himself in knots about something, I called it his Little Jimmy face," he said. When Carly swung around toward him, he said, "Sorry, chief."

"That was a comic thing for you?" Carly asked me. "The kind of thing you'd tell like a funny story?"

"I never thought it was a funny story," I told her.

"There's his Little Jimmy face now," Kenny noted. When she looked at him again, he used his index fingers to pull down on his lower eyelids and made an Emmett Kelly frown.

"We started calling potential targets Little Jimmies," he said, "whenever we were going to bring the hammer down and maximize collateral damage."

Carly was looking at something in front of her the way you try not to move even your eyes to keep from throwing up. "What is that supposed to mean?" she finally said in a low voice.

"You know," Kenny told her. "'I don't wike the *wooks* of this . . .'"

"Is that Elmer *Fudd* you're doing?" Celestine wanted to know.

And how could you not laugh, watching him do his poor-sap-in-the-crosshairs shtick?

"This is just the fucking House of Mirth, isn't it?" Carly said. Because she saw on my face just how many doors she'd been dealing with all along, both open and shut, and she also saw the We're-in-the-boat-and-you're-in-the-water expression that guys cut from our project teams always got when they asked if there was anything *we* could do to keep them onboard.

"Jesus Fucking Christ," she said to herself, because her paradigm had suddenly shifted beyond what even she could have imagined. She thought she'd put up with however many years of stonewalling for a good reason, and she'd just figured out that as far as Castle Hubby went, she hadn't even crossed the moat yet.

Because here's the thing we hadn't talked about, nose to nose on our pillows in the dark: how *I've never been closer to anyone* isn't the same as *We're so close.* That night I threw the drink, she asked why *I* was so perfect for the black world, and I wanted to tell her, How am I *not* perfect for it? It's a sinkhole for resources. Everyone involved with it obsesses about it all the time. Even what the *insiders* know about it is incomplete. Whatever stories you *do* get arrive without context. What's not inconclusive is enigmatic, what's not enigmatic is unreliable, and what's not unreliable is quixotic.

She hasn't left yet, which surprises *me*, let me tell you. The waitress is showing some alarm at Carly's distress and I've got a hand on her back. She accepts a little rubbing and then has to pull away. "I gotta get out of here," she goes.

"That girl is not happy," Celestine says after she's gone.

"Does she even know about *your* kid?" Kenny asks.

The waitress asks if there's going to be a third round.

"What'd you do that for?" I ask him.

"What'd *I* do that for?" Kenny asks.

Celestine leans into him. "Can we *go*?" she asks. "Will you take me back to the *room*?"

"So are you going after her?" Kenny asks.

"Yeah," I tell him.

"Just not right now?" Kenny goes.

I'd told Carly about the first time I noticed him. I'd heard about this guy in design in a sister program who'd raised a stink about housing the designers next to the production floor so there'd be on-the-spot back-and-forth about problems as they developed. He was twenty-seven at that point. I'd heard that he was so good at aerodynamics that his co-workers claimed he could *see* air. As he moved up we had more dealings with him at Minotaur. He had zero patience for the corporate side, and when the programs rolled out their annual reports on performance and everyone did their song-and-dance with charts and graphs, when his turn came he'd walk to the blackboard and write two numbers. He'd point to the first and go "That's how many we presold," and point to the second and go "That's how much we made," and then toss the chalk on the ledge and announce he was going back to work. He wanted to pick my brain about how I hid budgetary items on Minotaur and invited me over to his house and served hard liquor and martini olives. His wife hadn't come out of the bedroom. After an hour I asked if they had any crackers and he said no.

That last time I saw him, it was like he'd had me over just to watch him fight with his wife. When I got there, he handed me a Jose Cuervo and went after her. "What put a bug in *your* ass?" she finally shouted. And after he'd gone to pour us some more Cuervo, she said, "Would you please get outta here? Because you're not helping at all." So I followed him into the kitchen to tell him I was hitting the road, but it was like he'd disappeared in his own house.

On the drive home I'd pieced together, in my groping-in-the-dark way, that he was better at this whole lockdown-on-everybody-near-you deal than I was. And worse at it. He fell into it easier, and was more wrecked by it than I would ever be.

I told Carly as much when I got home, and she said, "Anyone's more wrecked by *everything* than you'll ever be."

And she'd asked me right then if I thought I was worth the work that was going to be involved in my renovation. By which she meant, she explained, that she needed to know if *I* was going to put in the work. Because she didn't intend to be in this alone. I was definitely willing to put in the work, I told her. And because of that she said that so was she.

She couldn't have done anything more for me than that. Meaning she's that amazing, and I'm that far gone. Because there's one thing I could tell her that I haven't told anybody else, including Kenny. At Penn my old classics professor had been a big-time pacifist—he always went on about having been in Chicago in '68—and on the last day of Dike, Eros, and Arete he announced to the class that one of our number had signed up with the military. I thought to myself: *Fuck you. I can do whatever I want.* I was already the odd man out in that class, the one whose comments made everyone look away and then move on. A pretty girl who I'd asked out shot me a look and then gave herself a pursed-lips little smile and checked her daily planner.

"So wish him luck," my old prof said, "as he commends himself over to the god of chaos." I remember somebody called out, "Good luck!" And I remember being enraged that I might be turning colors. "About whom," the prof went on, "Homer wrote, 'Whose wrath is relentless. Who, tiny at first, grows until her head plows through heaven as she strides the Earth. Who hurls down bitterness. Who breeds suspicion and divides. And who, everywhere she goes, makes our pain proliferate.'"

The Track of the Assassins

My mother liked to remind me that at the age of four I left a garden party one rainy afternoon with my toothbrush in my fist, fully intending a life of exploration, only to be returned later that afternoon by the postman. Her version of the story emphasized the boundaries that her daughter refused to accept. Mine was about the emancipation I felt when I closed the gate latch behind me and left everyone in my wake, and the world came to meet me like a wave.

On April 1, 1930, the first night of my newest expedition, I had a walled garden, overarched by thick trees, all to myself, and still was unable to sleep. I considered rousing my muleteer early but summoned just enough self-discipline to let him rest.

Orion wheeled slowly over the village roofs, and the wind stirred the wraith of a dust storm. I lay listening to the soft and granulating sound of the fall of fine particles. In the starlight I could see the mica in the sand as it gathered on my palms.

My traveler's notebook has on its oilskin cover in English, Arabic, and Persian my name, *Freya Stark,* and my mother's name and address in Asolo, and the promise of a reward should the notebook be returned. Atop the first page, I inscribed an Arab proverb that I've adopted as one of my life philosophies: *The wise man sits by the river, but the fool gets across barefoot.*

The river in this particular case is perhaps the remotest area in the entire Middle East: the Persian mountains west of the Caspian

Sea. This is country that has hardly been explored and never surveyed. The only map I had encompassed fourteen thousand square miles and featured three dotted lines and a centered *X* marking a seasonal encampment for one of the region's nomadic tribes. The rest was blank.

I'm accompanied by a guide, Ismail, and our muleteer, Aziz. The former looks like a convict, ties his trousers with string, and reeks of stale cheese. The latter has none of the former's dignity and seems perpetually gloomy, mostly because his colleague has informed him that he's almost certain to be killed. Both have long since given way to despair at the prospect of protecting a British woman traveling alone.

My plan was to locate the ruins of the mountain citadel of the Assassins, that sinister and ancient sect that for two hundred years held the entire East in its reign of terror. Their impregnable fortress, somewhere in a lost valley of the Alamut, is described by Marco Polo at length in his *Travels*. And because Schliemann discovered Troy by continually rereading the *Iliad* while he searched, I brought along my copy of the *Travels*, marked with the annotations of twenty-two years. Besides my aluminum waterbottle, when filled, Polo's account was the heaviest object in my saddlebag.

I no sooner had stepped onto a Lebanese dock before confronting the questions I'd be asked for the next three years: Why was I there? Why was I there alone? What did I intend to accomplish? Upon offering unsatisfactory answers to all three enquiries, I became a master of wrinkling customs officials' brows with perplexity and concern.

I was thirty-four and so thin from my physical travails and my sister's death that other passengers on the cargo ship began to save and wrap foodstuffs for the next time I might happen by. I was a bereaved Englishwoman who'd grown up in Italy and had only just torn free of the octopus of my mother's demands, a child of privilege who'd lived mostly hand-to-mouth, a lover of erudition who'd been mostly self-taught, and a solitary and fierce believer in independence who was prone to fixations on others. I owed everything to an aunt who'd given me a copy of *Arabian Nights* for my ninth birthday, a kind-hearted Syrian missionary who'd lived down the hill, a sister who had never lost faith in me, and those long months of illness that had left me the time to negotiate the labyrinths of Arabic and then Persian. Once I was stronger I walked an hour to the station three times a week to take the train to San Remo, where for seven years I furthered my progress with Arabic verbs in the company of an old Capuchin monk who'd lived for half his life in Beirut.

I'd arranged for temporary lodging with the monk's spinster sister in Brummana, a little village on a series of ledges above Beirut's harbor. There I continued to study the Koran, since I knew of no better way to begin to know Arabs than through the stories they knew as children, the stories their parents and nurses told them. In the spring I took the slowest train imaginable through the orchards of the Beqaa Valley to Damascus, where the spinster sister had helped me find two rooms up a steep staircase that was opened to the roof. At night I left a column of empty cans on the steps to warn me of uninvited visitors. The ascent was through a canopy of garments and saucepans and old baskets but the rooms themselves were pleasant, if exposed: in all but one nook, the entire street could see me while I dressed. But there I learned that if I didn't mind about privacy, or for that matter about cleanliness, and made myself independent of other physical needs, I could move about with astonishing freedom for next to no cost. I arranged to attend a girls' school for Arabic grammar, but was forced to leave when a classmate reminded me too powerfully of Vera. I was dumbfounded by the parade of ethnicities and sects: Chaldeans, Mandaeans, Sabaeans, Yezidi, Kurds, Armenians, Assyrians, Jews. The Sunni were persecuting the Shia and both detested the Druze, while all three loathed the Alawites as beggarly apostates. I was jolted by the visceral immediacy of their hatreds—for ancient slights!—and reminded that everyone was irrevocably marked by whatever misdeeds their predecessors had committed.

And yet on celebration days everything, from merchants' stalls to horses' tails, was overhung with bouquets of peacock-blue flowers, and petals of apricot blossoms rode the ripples in the water basins outside the shops. On my first trip alone out into the desert, I sat in the shade of a parasol until I was finally surrounded by camels, hundreds of them, their huge legs rising around me like spindly and crooked columns before the herd, in its browsing, eventually moved on.

The following year an even slower train finally brought me to Baghdad, though Scheherazade had neglected to report the seasonal temperatures of 105 degrees or the corpses of donkeys and sheep and even men alongside the river traffic on the Tigris. My mother sent aggrieved letters to the consulate which were dutifully held for me as I roamed the streets and alleys, beside myself, for Nineveh was just to the north, and the ruins of the Sumerians and Ur, with the birthplace of Abraham to the south. I'd arrived a few weeks before the stock-market crash, having expended a total of forty-five pounds on the trip, and still had ten remaining, for emergencies, in my saddlebag.

The sky at sunrise was clear, barring one pink cloud. We peered from our bedrolls at a radiant solitude and a horizon of mountain ranges. The only other sound as my companions began the breakfast fire was that of the wind on the sand, endless grains slipping into and bouncing out of equally endless hollows.

Ismail had spent his life between the Caspian passes and was to answer for my comfort and safety. For that I was paying the equivalent of three shillings per day. He'd kept a shop in Baghdad, could read and write, had completed his pilgrimage to the four Holy Cities, and projected an air of serene virtue unhindered by humility. His smile radiated benevolence until he was contradicted. He wore six bags over his white woolen tunic, including the goatskin that held the ancient cheese that made his face so trying at close quarters.

Aziz meanwhile sported for the morning chill a sheepskin cap that gave him a kind of Struwwelpeter appearance. Our lead mule allowed him to loop the water-skin over the saddle's pommel but then ceased to cooperate and, each time the muleteer approached murmuring reassurances, listened with a lack of conviction before rearing up to put the length of the halter rope between them.

I rolled my sleeping sack and tied it to my saddlebag, which carried a change of clothes and medicines on one side and my notebook and tea and sugar and Polo's *Travels* on the other. I kept a little sack of raisins tied to my saddlebow, like Dr. Johnson's lemons in the Hebrides. I thought I had little enough baggage but was still ashamed whenever I glimpsed my companions' kit.

In the distance, flocks of sheep in long processions were drawing toward a patch of green that Aziz had informed me was a renowned spring that welled up out of the stones in three pellucid streams. We were heading to its south, and now enjoyed the last good camp before a long stretch of desert. Ismail, when finally satisfied with the disposition of his bags, took the lead.

The plain opened out before us, dotted every so often with far-off low mounds that I assumed to be buried cities. For three full days we encountered no trace of human beings save the occasional heap of stones arranged days or decades ago. While we rode Ismail sang a Kurdish song whose chorus was "Because of my love / my liver is like a kabob" and whose refrain, to which Aziz joined in, was "Ai Ai Ai."

On the fourth day we shared a folded piece of bread and two pomegranates beside a compact oasis of brackish water from which a pale yellow water snake darted its head at us. And then that precinct's fertility ceased with the suddenness peculiar to the East, and we were again traversing an expanse covered with black stone that featured fossil shells and fish. For six days more we plodded on toward the sleeping hills through the inhuman emptiness and silence. Every so often Ismail related legends of buried treasure somewhere off in regions to our left or right without turning his head for my response. No one goes a mile into the Near Eastern hills without hearing such stories. I asked if some of those treasures might be burial sites and he answered, with the calm innocence of a Persian telling lies, that he'd never done anything so illegal as open a grave.

How many Europeans had ever seen this country? I knew only of Sir Henry Rawlinson, who'd led his Persian regiment across it some ninety years earlier, imagining as he rode the vanished nations that had preceded him.

The foothills when closer revealed themselves to be symmetrical rust-colored headlands akin to the upturned hulls of ships. The escarpments were long and narrow and end-on gave the impression of a fleet at anchor. The bases of the hills were white with salt and nothing, Ismail remarked, would grow on them.

I was cross-examined on the inexplicable problem of why I was not married. Where to begin, I thought later that night. With my game playing? The clumsiness of my flirtations? The continual revelations as to the scope of my ignorance? Only after four months did the young British officers in Baghdad disclose what they'd found so amusing about my blue hat with the sewn-on clock: its hands pointed to the hours of assignation—five and seven.

Aziz asked if there were any police in the area and Ismail told him that a year or so ago there had been two, and that they had been shot. He related the way robbery would work once we were in the mountains: we'd be approached and asked to allow ourselves to be looted. If we refused our interrogators would withdraw, and we would proceed until an ambush put an end to our obstinacy and to us. This region's local name, he added, translated as "the most advanced point from which one is captured." He claimed to be looking forward to reaching that part of the country in which one was less frequently murdered. During a rest break, while I stretched, he peered over at me with a mild, untrustworthy expression. And Aziz, when helping me up onto my mount, informed me in a low voice that while our guide was a bad man he would see to it that I came to no harm. Yet as I rode I understood how exhilarating it could be to climb into a country which was not considered safe.

At the gathering for my sixteenth birthday, my mother began her toast by noting that it seemed to take acquaintances about a month in my presence to overcome their first impression of my plainness. She said that she thought that it was perhaps because my face was more intelligent than pretty, though she had always held that my complexion was milky smooth. That night Vera reminded me that the only thing to do when something unpleasant happened was to pretend it hadn't, and in turn I reminded her of the fact that she was the beautiful daughter, a point to which, as always, she offered no rebuttal.

Our mother's parents had settled in Italy at the time of the Risorgimento, when Tuscany was attracting all varieties of expatriates. She liked to explain that they'd enjoyed such a thriving salon that as a little girl she had found herself at one affair accompanied on the piano by Franz Liszt. She'd had her portrait painted by Edwin Bale, and was widely admired for her winsomeness and flair. As opposed to our father, who was so reticent we might forget he was present. She described herself as more of an enthusiast for projects than for children, and would regale the room with the story of how, having brought me home from the hospital, she'd been dismayed to discover she'd made no provision for my food, my clothes, or my sleeping. By the time Vera was born, a year later, our parents had moved to the pretty hill town of Asolo, and my sister later remarked from her sickbed how much of our childhood had been spent watching adults pack or unpack great trunks. It had been only a small surprise, then, when our mother left us to join the Count di Roascio, in order, she said, to partner in his philanthropic enterprise of providing employment for the area encompassing his family's provincial seat. Later she'd had us join them in their home and, filled with happiness herself, had never noticed that our lives were heaped about in miniature ruins.

There followed a succession of Italian governesses, all erratically trained when it came to schooling, so much so that we quickly learned how to teach ourselves. We'd seen our father only when circumstances allowed. Alone in his emptied house, he gave the impression of being perpetually surrounded by seed catalogs, and as a means of conversing with him we turned ourselves into expert horticulturalists. On walks he taught us topography and geology. With animals he showed us how all of the feelings we couldn't put into words might be expressed through our hands, so that any dog or horse or child could understand, whatever our seeming reticence, how fiercely we cherished their affection. So that even today I'm still happiest just sitting and smoothing a donkey's ears in the sun.

The Assassins were a Persian sect, a branch of the Shia, and they seem to have entered history in 1071 when their founder and first Grand Master, Hassan-i Sabbah, experimented with systematic murder as a political tool, his innovation proving so successful that his ascendancy quickly spread from northern Persia all the way to the Mediterranean. Legends grew of a secret garden where he drugged and seduced his followers, and held forth on the uses of both assassination and the liberal arts, and it was the stumbling attempts of the Crusaders' chronicles to render the word for hashish users—the Hashishin—that gave the sect its name. They were the terror of their neighbors and at once inspired and intimidated the great Christian fighting orders, including the Templars, through the diabolical patience and subterfuge with which they operated. To their enemies they were ubiquitous; to their victims, invisible. Inexorably they extended their domain eastward to the Caspian, where they raised their central stronghold of Alamut, the fortress that symbolized their power until it fell to the Mongol armies some two hundred years later.

They'd become an obsession during Vera's first convalescence. In the dead of winter she had slipped out of the house and wandered off into the hills, where a search party found her lying in the snow. She'd been distraught since having learned, four years after our arrival at the Count's house, of his plan to become her suitor. It was as if we'd both been struck with a lash. Our mother when asked had replied that she knew nothing of his intentions, and that what Vera did was her own affair; but when Vera in response had begged to be sent abroad to study sculpture, she'd been sharply reminded that neither her family nor the Count possessed the funds for that sort of adventure.

The pneumonia had almost destroyed her, and as she convalesced I read to her at her bedside. We'd worked through the Greek myths and Siegfried sagas of our childhood and our mother had begun ferrying in volumes from the Count's library as well. At first Vera forbade their use but after a week or so seemed too despairing even for that, and late one night after a particularly dispiriting relapse we both found ourselves horribly engrossed by William of Tyre's chronicle, in which Henry II, Count of Champagne, considering an alliance against the Abbasid, visited the Assassin stronghold of Al-Kahf, where in order to demonstrate his authority their Grand Master beckoned to two of his adherents, who immediately flung themselves over the ramparts to their deaths.

The map was from the Survey of India series, four miles to the inch, and manifested its inaccuracy even in the few features it cited. It offered no hint of the mountains squarely before us. Polo's account, however, had thus far been borne out, its verification expedited by our use of the same method of transport. I resolved to create my own map as I went along, calling a halt three times a day to mark salient features while Ismail dipped into his cheese with an expression that suggested he was still awaiting a lull in the general perversity of my behavior.

It was gratifying to register that we were not marked on any map. For another week we negotiated naked rock rounded by the weather and without vegetation. To the southeast began some desolate and impressively dismaying salt marshes along a bitter stream that spooked the mules. For one stretch we had to unload their saddlebags and drag them by the halter ropes while Aziz shouted into their ears distressing facts about their parentage. We came upon great concentrations of Aghul and camelthorn, as well as bitter colocynth low to the ground. We saw a strange large hole whose bottom was lost to shadow. We rode in a dust storm lasting so long that after we stopped the next morning I discovered beside me two low mounds of reddish sand that revealed themselves in the gathering light to be the sleeping forms of my retainers.

We rode into the evenings, Ismail singing more Kurdish songs while we plodded along in the moonlight. I was stunned each daybreak by how the excess of light seemed to smooth away all before it.

Finally we began the ascent of a steep ravine whose shale slopes offered every few miles a smallish larkspur or some white Aethionema. What looked like yellow heather in the washes of dry gullies were disclosed to be great carpetings of thorns. Rows of flustered little birds took flight as we rode past, and circled back round and resettled once we were gone. With each day my companions' unease increased. And in the evenings they grouped themselves ever more tightly around me on the ground to guard my rest.

When I was a child, there were nights I would startle out of sleep and, in the stillness that followed, would listen to the entire house and become convinced that a flood was slowly filling the room. I heard wavelets beneath my sister's breathing. The only remedy for it was to climb into her bed and fall asleep in her arms, and our mother would scold us when she found us the next morning in our hopeless tangle with cold feet protruding from the bedcovers.

Vera and I were both outsiders who never overcame our odd and lonely upbringing or foreign accent and manner in that remote Italian hill town, and for many years we were each other's solitary playmates. Vera tied her lavish long hair back with a velvet ribbon so she could take part in my projects of rooting through brambles and bracken, and accompanied me wherever I roamed. She reassured herself with the knowledge that I had to look after her and she had to look after me. Remaining in a room once I had left it seemed to her meaningless. Once the Count took to dropping by our bedroom to chat we used for our secret conferences the kitchen's larder cupboard, which afforded space for two people if they stood without lifting their elbows. She sympathized with my desire to leave but said it was only permissible if I took her with me. While I studied and waited she chided me for brooding too much and being ungrateful for those blessings we enjoyed. One rainy March afternoon she noted I'd been peering out our window for an hour, and wanted to know at what I'd been gazing. It then occurred to me that I'd been looking at a hedge, and that a hedge was not enough at which to have been staring for so long.

We agreed on the necessity of understanding others' affections not as fixed commitments but rather as ever-changing seas, with their tides coming and going. This was of considerable service after the Count's proposal and our mother's response. He repeated his proposal some months later on the occasion of Vera's seventeenth birthday, and the previous week news had arrived that I'd be matriculating at Bedford College, London, a real school at last after all of my scuttering. Our father had agreed to pay the tuition. He himself had resolved to move to England.

Vera had been without words in my presence for a day and a half following this development, and then had slipped into my bed in the wee hours of the morning.

"See?" I whispered to her. "You do love your sister."

"Put your arms around me," she whispered back. Her nightgown's periwinkle was indigo in the darkness.

"Not without a declaration of love," I told her, and when she started to weep I gently teased, "Well, why else are you here?"

She turned so that her back was to my front and my arms could more easily encircle her. "Because I've got nowhere else to go," she finally whispered.

We awoke to a predawn aurora in the east and the cheerless and clanking procession of a small tribe descending to its winter valley. Ismail offered our greetings and informed me in a low voice that these were people of the Qazvin. The men must have gone ahead previous. There were at most fifty or sixty elders, women, and children, and even so they occupied over an hour in moving past. I went unnoticed in the low light due to the plainness of my chador and the extent of their fatigue. Mules and the occasional small ox were overhung with any number of carpets, cooking pots, poultry baskets, and tent cloths, all crisscrossed with ropes as if lashed to the frames in a windstorm. Mothers carried children on their backs. Stragglers fell out of the column and regained their feet and wavered back into it. Watching the pace they set, I began to understand why two years earlier the Lurs, when fleeing a forced resettlement, had massacred their own families to unburden themselves for the march.

After nine days' advance we were still continuing to climb, the track at times becoming so steep it was impracticable for our heavy-laden mules. We were being taken up into the joyful loneliness of the summits. Ismail's mood continued to deteriorate, and at day's end he would squat, lost in a meadow of resignation, while Aziz and I erected our poor camp. He might answer an inquiry about dinner with the comment that we still possessed some flour, and he responded to complaints by invoking the majesty of God and wondering how he was expected to produce sustenance in an uninhabited land. One evening apropos of nothing he remarked that it was no wonder England was a mighty nation, since its women did what Persian men feared to attempt.

We entered a great canyon and persisted in our ascent while

crossing and recrossing a stream tumbling down past us. Maiden-hair ferns provided a welcome green. Fish in pools at intervals swirled their wide, transparent tails. The water was altogether sweet but Ismail insisted it was known as the Eye of Bitterness. We rode until trees appeared on the high skylines of the ridges and began to spread down the slopes. We passed broom and tamarisk and terebinth, the last bearing blue berries that proved delicious.

We rode until we topped a windswept ridge of sufficient elevation that we could see for twenty miles, and there we made camp. There in that buffeting cold we looked out on Alamut country below and experienced the satisfaction of being able to glimpse, after all we had traversed, proof that the Grail of our imaginations now belonged to the tangible world.

Even as a child I had realized that in the realm of one's family, there was a weight and a drag to all things, but that even so I could walk from morning until nightfall and feel only a pleasant faint trembling in my legs at day's end. Upon receipt of one of my mother's or Vera's letters I might walk from Hyde Park to Deptford Wharf and, while walking, compose my responses. I told them about my revered new professor, William Paton Ker, who was already opening innumerable doors to me, and I conveyed my elation with the country's appetite for discoveries of every stripe: Gertrude Bell had ventured among the Jebel Druze and had reported seeing them devour their sheep raw. When Vera asked if I found Bell's success disheartening, I wrote back that the woman traveled with enough companionship and equipment for a supper club, with her dining tables and mosquito nets, and that she visited only well-charted areas, which differences would clearly distinguish my achievement from hers.

My sister asked if she might come visit, and I told her that she would always be welcome, though I had neither funds with which to entertain her nor place in which to put her. She pointed out that in roughing it she was at least my equal and offered to sleep on the floor beneath my bed. My housemistress, I observed, would be implacably unhappy with an arrangement such as this.

In subsequent letters she asked if I'd been so very discontented in Italy and if living alone had brought me any more fulfillment. I answered that the discontented were the least capable of living with only themselves, since the same goad that drove them to isolation would spoil their solitude as well. The true traveler left not to renounce but to seek. And while to be given a cold bath was not a merit in itself, to take one voluntarily might be.

A month later my mother wrote that my sister had accepted the Count's proposal, and that Vera was sorrowful she would not be able to realize her dream of a wedding in England. My mother's tone was brisk. For the first time she referred to the Count as Mario. My sister herself wrote that she hoped to become a good friend to him, but also that she felt she'd wasted years in just learning how to live, knowledge that now was going to be locked away. She noted, apropos of another breakdown, that she was so wretched it pleased her to make everyone else wretched as well. And that what attractiveness she ever possessed had deserted her, and that I was now the beautiful one. And I'm disconcerted still by the potency of the thrill I experienced at my escape, amid all of my misery on her behalf. She wrote that our mother had taken her to Venice on holiday, and I read and reread the letter and castigated myself during my circumnavigations of the city, because this was how competitive I could be: once, at the age of eight, when my father had beaten me at chess, I became so enraged that I buried his white queen in the garden.

The descent to the valley was hair-raising. It was as if the entire range on which we'd been perched was a giant breaking wave, and having ascended the gentle backslope, we next had to negotiate down the much steeper face. We made camp that night at its base and then for five days traversed untracked and seared reaches of red, hardened earth. This country Ismail believed to be inhabited by heretics capable of eating, or at least sitting in, fire. He mentioned with some concern that he didn't think they were Moslem at all.

On the sixth day we encountered, just as Polo's account recorded, a stepped and crooked valley rising to our left. The path of its dried riverbed the Italian called the Track of Thieves. As it narrowed, its walls radiated heat. We could feel our elevation. In the winter, Ismail speculated, a bitter wind must scour out this funnel. Aziz responded from ahead that winters in his village were so cold that even the wolves stayed home.

Eventually we reached the willows and sanjid trees of the Badasht oasis, smaller than Polo described it, and had our bread and raisins by a stream while white-and-black magpies stalked to and fro before us. On either side the cliffs were so high we were untouched by the sun. When Ismail smeared his cheese on his lips as a kind of balm, I found myself longing for the minor relief of some mealtime companionship that didn't involve spitting or mashing food with one's fingers.

We were joined in the late afternoon by a shepherd with crossed eyes and his two sons. They afforded us the standard greeting, polite without effusion, and for a time we sat in a circle in silence that in the East is good manners. Upon seeing the whiteness of my arms they pulled up their own sleeves in order to demonstrate the contrast. Finally the shepherd informed Ismail that they had never seen a European woman. Or man. They seemed pleased with us for having been brave enough to come among them.

They laid out their meal before them and shared what they had with great hospitality. This meant less for them, and when I partook at their insistence, the father looked off downstream with a comfortable kind of sadness and the smaller boy's eyes followed every mouthful I took.

While the boys filled the family goatskin with water and Aziz gathered straw for the mules, the shepherd asked Ismail to explain my presence, glancing over every so often to see if my appearance corroborated the outlandish story he was receiving. He told us that Alamut was the name not of the fortress but of the valley itself. He said that people often came in search of the fortress but when pressed on that point clarified that to his knowledge only two men had done so in the last seven years. Later, as we made our arrangements for sleep, the boys exclaimed over a wandering tortoise. And then we retired to the tremolo of water running nearby, the sweetest of sounds in the night.

A priest counseling Philip VI of France against the hazards of an exploratory campaign in the East wrote of the Assassins that they were thirsty for human blood, contemptuous of life and salvation, and could, like the devil, encloak themselves in radiance. If encountered they were to be cursed, then fled. They had turned *taqiyya,* the Shia tradition of concealment in the face of persecution, back against the Sunni in the most lethal of configurations. When not disguised they were said to have worn white gowns with red headcloths, the colors of innocence and blood. This and more came from Von Hammer-Purgstall's history of the sect in the London School of Oriental Studies, and when I wrote Vera excitedly of my find, she wrote back, "Wolves in sheep's clothing: of course it would excite you."

Ismail warned that we should travel as much by night in this region as we could manage, for safety's sake, and the shepherd when taking his leave of us seemed to agree. The path above the oasis after a short stretch led us through a long defile of dark stone the shepherd had called the Black Narrows and in which he had warned us not to linger. When that ended we found our track clinging to a cliff that fell away below us a thousand feet. Each slip by our mules occasioned a curse from Ismail, tired and furious at being forced to navigate such a passage. So narrow that our outside feet hung out over the abyss, it continued for miles with no widening that might allow us to take our ease, and after nightfall the darkness grew so total that even my mule's ears were lost to sight. I entrusted the edge, step by step, wholly to him.

Mid-morning the next day, round a particularly terrifying corner, the track finally opened out onto an ancient road and the ruins of an old bridge over a cataract plunging away into the valley below: the Alamut stream, I was certain, whose spring provided water for the fortress. From anywhere but this spot, the great ridge and headland of rock seemed to close off with a wall any upward access. We still had a thousand feet to climb, along that thin thread of water which near the top dispersed its spray to the wind, but even so we knew how close we were. After an uncomfortable cliffside night's rest, a morning's ascent brought us in searing sunlight onto the knife-edge of a ridge. And before us, like the prow of a great ship, was what had to be the western redoubt of the Rock of the Assassins.

Around its northern flank appeared a path tilted on a frighteningly steep gradient through white limestone that powdered like salt beneath the mules' hooves. The scree was sufficiently treacherous that Ismail and I ascended as much with our hands as our feet, Aziz behind us leading the mules. At the summit we scrambled over a low outer wall made of a few loose stones and into a cold wind, sweat-soaked as we were. The height was such that we could plainly see the roundness of the Earth. On the northwestern side a granite pillar adjoining an even higher cliff face formed a natural citadel and revealed itself as the site of the spring, the conduits of which were still visible as grooves running south to rectangular cisterns dug into the solid rock.

The site had long since been pumiced clean by the wind, although traces of the outer walls emerged here and there, as well as half the central keep, still upright and brandishing an iron loophole at its highest point. On all sides the natural walls fell away sheer. From the southern end we looked down two thousand feet of stone. To the east, in huge stone slabs, were round holes four inches deep and eight in diameter that may have held the doorposts for giant gates. Out of one hole I fished a piece of blue-glaze pottery pictured in von Hammer-Purgstall's history, and sank to my knees with a cry. "It is Polo's fortress!" I shrieked to Aziz, who smiled back in terror at my agitation.

I was streaming sweat despite the cold. I retrieved the map from my saddlebag and took some bearings with numbed fingers. To the east we could see the great semicircle of a mountain range covered with snow, and through its passes northward a hint, in the haze, of the Caspian jungle and the sea. We were so high that by late afternoon the sunlight had lost its force and our bones seemed to absorb the mountains' frigidity. Ismail, alarmed, wrapped my bedroll about my shoulders, where it flailed and thrashed. I sank to a sitting position while I wept, and the wind felt as I did about the map, buffeting it to pieces.

The next morning I woke to clouds from the Caspian Sea pouring like a wave over the distant watershed to the northeast. They sailed toward us and melted away in the sun's heat before reaching our valley. I had lost the energy to raise my arms and pitched from dehydration to floods of perspiration, and knew immediately that it must be malaria. Ismail examined me and diagnosed that as well as dysentery, two diseases he assured me he was well used to seeing. He prescribed a soup of rice, milk, and almonds that would scrub me out like soap. I reminded him that we had none of those ingredients and he answered that we would make use of them once we did. I instructed him to fetch the quinine from my saddlebag and gave myself a double dose. How far were we from the nearest motor road, or doctor? It was all another world.

They arranged some of their bedding in a kind of awning to shade me from the sun. I spent the day slipping in and out of consciousness in the wind. Cloud shadows came and went on the iron loophole of the keep. I was given some tea to which the goatskin water had imparted a nauseating smell. My mule gave me a fright when she snuffled beneath my head for my toiletries.

I woke to a fire and twilight, and an even more bitter cold. Ismail's eyes wandered from my face to my extra bedding, and he made no effort at conversation. Aziz beside him gazed at my aluminum water bottle. When able to speak I offered it to him, and he seemed alarmed and said he wouldn't think of depriving me.

By morning the awning was down and I could see the sky. My companions' expressions were full of pity and they kept fanning the flies from my face. Where had the flies come from? And on what at this altitude did they live? The sun every so often managed to erase everything from my sight. I remembered myself on the train to San Remo dreaming of owning a little shop somewhere in a Near Eastern town, for its possibilities for observation and meditation. I remembered myself at sixteen, dressed for a dinner party and murmuring that what I should *really* have liked was to have been pretty.

The wind seemed to have subsided and round us the white rock grew unbearable in the afternoon heat. Ismail pressed my temples between his palms with a slowly increasing pressure I found to be amazingly restful.

The August before I first set foot on that Lebanese dock, our mother had taken my sister on another holiday, this time to the seashore at Varazze, and there Vera had had her miscarriage and developed septicemia. My mother and I had sat at her bedside for the five weeks she suffered. The night before she died, I told her I couldn't help but believe that if she wanted life more, she could hold on to it, and she reassured me that in her time alone with our mother and Mario she had developed certain resources and that she'd been far from only miserable. She had become bright enough through her reading, for example, that he had never grown bored with her. "All you do is *weep,*" she complained with some weariness and anger later that night. "Aren't you ever happy to be with me?"

A family friend at the funeral confided he'd been so appalled at the news of the marriage that he'd refused my mother's request to use his villa for the reception. Her own eulogy asserted that she and Vera had grown so close that when they were reunited in the next world she doubted Saint Peter would be able to determine one from the other. When I was packed and ready to leave for the station, Mario remarked that my mother and I had only barely spoken and hardly looked at each other. My mother responded at the piano by commencing Berlioz's "Le Dépit de la bergère."

When her note arrived in Brummana deploring my decision to abandon her so soon after our loss, I wrote back that Vera had died bowing to the agendas of others. In response, after some months, she sent the letter from London in which I'd informed Vera that I could not take her in.

Reading it once more, I recalled another letter to my sister in which I'd enthused about the way my notebooks, with a single word, could save an experience from oblivion, and her response, in which she expressed a lack of surprise that I'd choose the notebook over the diary, since in the former one's emotions were largely omitted in favor of their causes.

In those last few nights with her, I spent what time we had left trying to recover the irrecoverable with only my presence. I wanted to believe that nothing had been lost of what we had shared so many years before. But we look on everyone's transformations as fluid except our own. "Dress them up as you like, but they will always run away," the King of Naples is reported to have said of his inadequate soldiers. The mother I trusted, the Vera I loved, the woman I imagined myself to be: all of those phantoms have clip-clopped away into limbo.

I told my mother the last time I wrote her that no crime short of murder was comparable to destroying in another the capacity to love. Her silence in response constituted yet another instance of her having behaved with more honor than her surviving daughter had achieved.

The main thing the traveler carries about with her is herself. There's my home, and then the world: the sea is much stronger than the anchor. I've acted wherever I've alighted like a guest for life, or, when at my best, as in that line from the *Purgatorio:* "We are pilgrims, as you are."

Over the horizon to the east, the weather that's heading toward us lies in a dark line at the end of the world. Ismail washes my face with water from the goatskin while Aziz attends to the mules straying in the dusk. "I have more with which to pay you, once we return," I manage to tell them. Ismail makes a brief gesture as if to clarify that it needn't be discussed. "God give you strength," he murmurs as we exchange smiles: fellow travelers. Aziz appears beside him. My eyes close under the weight of so much sadness and gratitude. And out of courtesy we say goodnight to one another with our hands upon our breasts.

In Cretaceous Seas

Dip your foot in the water and here's what you're playing with: Xiphactinus, all angry underbite and knitting-needle teeth, with heads oddly humped and eyes enraged with accusation, and ribboned bodies so muscular they fracture coral heads when surging through to bust in on insufficiently alert pods of juvenile Clidastes, who spin around to face an oncoming maw that's in a perpetual state of homicidal resentment. The smaller Xiphactinus are three times your length and swallow their prey whole. They're gill-to-gill with Cretoxyrhina, great white sharks fifty feet long with heads the size of Mini Coopers and twelve-inch nightmare triangles of teeth. Mosasaurs big and small, the runts weighing in at two tons and the alphas like tylosaur a stupefying sixty feet. Under the surface, they're U-boats with crocodiles' heads. Pliosaurs in their hunting echelons, competing to see who's the more viciously ill-tempered. Kronosaurs whose jaws provide the kind of leverage that can snap whales' spines. Thalassomedons, the biggest of the elasmosaurs, with twenty-foot watersnake necks that allow the Venus-flytrap teeth to be everywhere at once. Dakosaurs gliding through the murk of fish parts spewed by their initial thrashing attacks.

And rising out of the blue gloom like the ridged bottom itself easing up to meet you, Lipleurodon, holdover from the Jurassic, the biggest predator that ever lived. Families could live in its skull. On the move it's like the continental shelf taking a trip. It feeds everywhere, even in shallow water with the surf breaking over it like a sandbar. Its earth-moving front flippers keep it from stranding. If some of the bigger land predators stand around the shallows trolling for what floats in, that's their mistake. It takes them off their feet like fruit off a tree.

This is the Tethys Ocean, huge, shallow, and warmed by its position locked between the world's two giant supercontinents. This is the place where the *prey* could kill a sperm whale. This is all this one guy's bed. This guy—we'll call him Conroy, because that's his fucking name—whose insomnia every night is beyond debilitating, teeming, epic with hostile energy, oceanic. What's his problem? Well, where to begin? Kick your feet and watch something else surface from below. He's been a crappy son, a shitty brother, a lousy father, a lazy helpmate, a wreck of a husband. As a pet owner he's gotten two dogs and a parakeet killed. Some turtles and two other dogs died without his help.

His daughter won't speak and wears a ski hat in the house and writes stories in which family members are eviscerated as the narrator laughs. She's an isolate, watched but not approached. *We don't want to make the problem into more than it is.* His brother's alone in Florida, an older version of the same pain, just a phone call away. Whenever Conroy makes his hangup indications in their once-in-a-blue-moon conversations, his brother says it was great talking to him. His father's ignoring the doctor's advice—most of that advice having to do with meds, his Dilantin, his Prozac, his everything else—and going downhill because of it, and still they rehearse the same conversational rituals, as though time is standing still instead of vortexing down a drain. His career involves assuring people he's got the answers and he's got their back when he doesn't have the answers and he's all about craven self-interest: he's part of the team rolling out a major new pharmaceutical, one of the accomplished tyros vouching for one of the eminences who did the science, and in that capacity he didn't so much invent his data as cherry-pick it. Will it kill anyone? He hopes not. Because he *means* well.

He always *means* well. He tells himself this, treading water in bed.

The good news is who's in this bed with him. His wife, the person he loves most in the world. Here's the thing about his wife: she travels a lot, in her role as headhunter for the Center for American Progress, and she's concerned about him, and the conversational form her concern has lately taken has been to suggest, half-jokingly and half-kindly, that he should have a fling. And to him this sounds like "You should get yourself some tenderness somewhere. Because you ain't getting it here."

He could *ask* if that's what she means. But he's the kind of guy given to building tall towers of self-pity and then watching them sway. So he speculates instead.

In bed he hints around. His wife is all psychological acuity and knows him like she knows her childhood bedroom, but she's always been impatient with hinting and her requests for clarification sound like demands. Exasperation makes him close up shop like a night-blooming flower.

Think of the good you've done, he counsels. Think of the good you continue to do. A breeze blows over the water's surface.

But here's this letter in which a Sri Lankan says he's all but sure he's found some major links between the product and miscarriage. The Sri Lankan wants to know if Conroy didn't review the same data. And here's this journal entry from his daughter: *My Throat = the Shit Pit.* And here's this dream he keeps having of himself as ringmaster with no acts performing, just a guy holding a hoop looking at him and waiting, and with everyone he's ever let down scattered in the uncomfortable stands, eager to tell him that all of his forays into selflessness have only made clearer what they're not, like a thimbleful of cola after a trek across the Kalahari.

His mode on such nights is the circuit between bed and bathroom and lamplit magazines. But tonight he's heard his daughter downstairs ahead of him, and the delicate hiccups of the little breath-intakes that are her version of crying when it's crucial she not be heard. Her favored position is to wedge herself into the wingbacked chair with her knees by sitting Indian-style. He holds himself still, listening, then throws open the sash on their upper-story bedroom window and climbs out on the roof. And his wife stirs and, sleeping, is sad for his unsettlement. The grit stings his knees. Gravity wants to welcome him forward in a rush. The breeze cools his butt. In the moonlight he's just a naked guy, most of his weight on his hands, his hands bending the front edge of the aluminum gutter, the grass two stories below a blue meridian, zenith and nadir at once.

How do we help? Throw him a life preserver? How long *should* anyone survive in that ocean?

He's Tethys Man, superhero and supervillain all in one. How much does he sweat at night? His sheets smell mildewy in the morning. If you saw him padding to the toilet, stepping naked in place, and waving off the bad images like the world's least fetching drum majorette, would you imagine that "inauthenticity" was a term that haunted him? If you saw him bare-assed on his roof, gauging the distance from the sloping dormer to the strain insulators and primary cables of the telephone wires, would you imagine that once he jumped he'd ferry himself hand over hand from house to house? Would you imagine that if he did, he would have proved something to himself, in his own inchoate way, about his desire for change? Would you imagine that he then hated himself less?

Would you imagine that when he confronted his loved ones' sadnesses, his vanity knew no bounds? Would you imagine that he thought his problems would solve themselves? Would you imagine that he fancied himself the prey when he was really the apologetic predator? Would you imagine that he'd last very long, much less get through this alive? Would you imagine that his kind should die out once and for all? Would you imagine that even now he was telling you the truth?

The Netherlands Lives with Water

A long time ago a man had a dog that went down to the shoreline every day and howled. When she returned the man would look at her blankly. Eventually the dog got exasperated. "Hey," the dog said. "There's a shitstorm of biblical proportions headed your way." "Please. I'm busy," the man said. "Hey," the dog said the next day, and told him the same thing. This went on for a week. Finally the man said, "If you say that once more I'm going to take you out to sea and dump you overboard." The next morning the dog went down to the shoreline again, and the man followed. "Hey," the dog said, after a minute. "Yeah?" the man said. "Oh, I think you know," she told him.

"Or here's another one," Cato says to me. "Adam goes to God, 'Why'd you make Eve so beautiful?' And God says, 'So you would love her.' And Adam says, 'Well, why'd you make her so stupid?' And God says, 'So she would love you.'"

Henk laughs.

"Well, he thinks it's funny," Cato says.

"He's eleven years old," I tell her.

"And very precocious," she reminds me. Henk makes an overly jovial face and holds two thumbs up. His mother takes her napkin and wipes some egg from his chin.

We met in the same pre-university track. I was a year older but hadn't passed Dutch, so I took it again with her.

"You failed Dutch?" she whispered from her seat behind me.

She'd seen me gaping at her when I came in. The teacher had already announced that's what those of us who were older were doing there.

"It's your own language," she told me later that week. She was holding my penis upright so she could run the edge of her lip along the shaft. I felt like I was about to touch the ceiling.

"You're not very articulate," she remarked later, on the subject of the sounds I'd produced.

She acted as though I were a spot of sun in an otherwise rainy month. We always met at her house, a short bicycle ride away, and her parents seemed to be perpetually asleep or dead. In three months I saw her father only once, from behind. She explained that she'd been raised by depressives who'd made her one of those girls who'd sit on the playground with the tools of happiness all around her and refuse to play. Her last boyfriend had walked out the week before we'd met. His diagnosis had been that she imposed on everyone else the gloom her family had taught her to expect.

"Do I sadden you?" she'd ask me late at night before taking me in her mouth.

"Will you have children with me?" I started asking her back.

And she was flattered and seemed pleased without being particularly fooled. "I've been thinking about how hard it is to pull information out of you," she told me one night when we'd pitched our clothes out from under her comforter. I asked what she wanted to know, and she said that was the kind of thing she was talking about. While she was speaking I watched her front teeth, glazed from our kissing. When she had a cold and her nose was blocked up, she looked a little dazed in profile.

"I ask a question and you ask another one," she complained. "If I ask what your old girlfriend was like, you ask what anyone's old girlfriend is like."

"So ask what you want to ask," I told her.

"Do you think," she said, "that someone like you and someone like me should be together?"

"Because we're so different?" I asked.

"Do you think that someone like you and someone like me should be together?" she repeated.

"Yes," I told her.

"That's helpful. Thanks," she responded. And then she wouldn't see me for a week. When I felt I'd waited long enough, I intercepted her outside her home and asked, "Was the right answer no?" And she smiled and kissed me as though hunting up some compensation for diminished expectations. After that it was as if we'd agreed to give ourselves over to what we had. When I put my mouth on her, her hands would bend back at the wrists as if miming helplessness. I disappeared for minutes at a time from my classes, envisioning the trancelike way her lips would part after so much kissing.

The next time she asked me to tell her something about myself I had some candidates lined up. She held my hands away from her, which tented the comforter and provided some cooling air. I told her I still remembered how my older sister always replaced her indigo hair bow with an orange one on royal birthdays. And how I followed her everywhere, chanting that she was a pig, which I was always unjustly punished for. How I fed her staggeringly complicated lies that went on for weeks and ended in disaster with my parents or teachers. How I slept in her bed the last three nights before she died of the flu epidemic.

Her cousins had also died then, Cato told me. If somebody even just mentioned the year 2015, her aunt still went to pieces. She didn't let go of my hands, so I went on, and told her that, being an outsider as a little boy, I'd noticed *something* was screwed up with me, but I couldn't put my finger on what. I probably wasn't as baffled by it as I sounded, but it was still more than I'd ever told anyone else.

She'd grown up right off the Boompjes; I'd been way out in Pernis, looking at the Caltex refinery through the haze. The little fishing village was still there then, huddled in the center of the petrochemical sprawl. My sister loved the lights of the complex at night and the fires that went hundreds of feet into the air like solar flares when the waste gases burned off. Kids from other neighborhoods never failed to notice the smell on our skin. The light was that golden sodium vapor light, and my father liked to say it was always Christmas in Pernis. At night I was able to read with my bedroom lamp off. While we got ready for school in the mornings, the dredging platforms with their twin pillars would disappear up into the fog like Gothic cathedrals.

A week after I told her all that, I introduced Cato to Kees. "I've never seen him like this," he told her. We were both on track for one of the technology universities, maybe Eindhoven, and he hadn't failed Dutch. "Well, I'm a pretty amazing woman," she explained to him.

Kees and I both went on to study physical geography and got into the water sector. Cato became the media liaison for the program director for Rotterdam Climate Proof. We got married after our third International Knowledge for Climate Research conference. Kees asked us recently which anniversary we had coming up, and I said eleventh and Cato said it was the one hundredth.

It didn't take a crystal ball to realize we were in a growth industry. Gravity and thermal measurements by GRACE satellites had already flagged the partial shutdown of the Atlantic circulation system. The World Glacier Monitoring Service, saddled with having to release one glum piece of news after another, had just that year reported that the Pyrenees, Africa, and the Rockies were all glacier-free. The Americans had just confirmed the collapse of the West Antarctic ice sheet. Once-in-a-century floods in England were now occurring every two years. Bangladesh was almost entirely a bay and that whole area a war zone because of the displacement issues.

It's the catastrophe for which the Dutch have been planning for fifty years. Or, really, for as long as we've existed. We had cooperative water management before we had a state. The one created the other; either we pulled together as a collective or got swept away as individuals. The real old-timers had a saying for when things fucked up: "Well, the Netherlands lives with water." What they meant was that their land flooded twice a day.

Bishop Prudentius of Troyes wrote in his annals that in the ninth century the whole of the country was devoured by the sea; all the settlements disappeared, and the water was higher than the dunes. In the Saint Felix Flood, North Beveland was completely swept away. In the All Saints' Flood, the entire coast was inundated between Flanders and Germany. In 1717 a dike collapse killed fourteen thousand on Christmas night.

"You like going on like this, don't you?" Cato sometimes asks.

"I like the way it focuses your attention," I told her once.

"Do you like the way it scares our son?" she demanded in return.

"It doesn't scare me," Henk told us.

"It *does* scare you," she told him. "And your father doesn't seem to register that."

For the last few years, when I've announced that the sky is falling she's answered that our son doesn't need to hear it. And that I always bring it up when there's something else that should be discussed. I always concede her point, but that doesn't get me off the hook. "For instance, I'm still waiting to hear how your mother's making out," she complains during a dinner when we can't tear Henk's attention away from the Feyenoord celebrations. If its team wins the Cup, the whole town gets drunk. If it loses, the whole town gets drunk.

My mother's now at the point that no one can deny is dementia. She's still in the little house on Polluxstraat, even though the Pernis she knew seems to have evaporated around her. Cato finds it unconscionable that I've allowed her to stay there on her own, without help. "Let me guess," she says whenever she brings it up. "You don't want to talk about it."

She doesn't know the half of it. The day after my father's funeral, my mother brought me into their bedroom and showed me the paperwork on what she called their Rainy Day Account, a staggering amount. Where had they gotten so much? "Your father," she told me unhelpfully. When I went home that night and Cato asked what was new, I told her about my mother's regime of short walks.

At each stage in the transfer of assets, financial advisors or bank officers have asked if my wife's name would be on the account as well. She still has no idea it exists. It means that I now have a secret net worth more than triple my family's. What am I up to? Your guess is as good as mine.

"Have you talked to anyone about the live-in position?" Cato now asks. I'd raised the idea with my mother, who'd started shouting that she never should have told me about the money. Since then I'd been less bullish about bringing Cato and Henk around to see her.

I tell her things are progressing just as we'd hope.

"Just as we'd hope?" she repeats.

"That's it in a nutshell," I tell her, a little playfully, but her expression makes it clear she's waiting for a real explanation.

"Don't you have homework?" I ask Henk, and he and his mother exchange a look. I've always believed that I'm a master at hiding my feelings, but I seem to be alone in that regard.

Cato's been through this before in various iterations. When my mother was first diagnosed, I hashed through the whole thing with Kees, who'd been in my office when the call came in. And then later that night I told Cato there'd been no change, so as not to have to trudge through the whole story again. But the doctor had called the next day, when I was out, to see how I was taking the news, and she got it all from him.

Henk looks at me like he's using my face to attempt some long division.

Cato eats without saying anything until she finally loses her temper with the cutlery. "I told you before that if you don't want to do this, I can," she says.

"There's nothing that needs doing," I tell her.

"There's plenty that needs doing," she says. She pulls the remote from Henk and switches off the news. "Look at him," she complains to Henk. "He's always got his eyes somewhere else. Does he even know that he shakes his head when he listens?"

Pneumatic hammers pick up where they left off outside our window. There's always construction somewhere. Why not rip up the streets? The Germans did such a good job of it in 1940 that it's as if we've been competing with them ever since. Rotterdam: a deep hole in the pavement with a sign telling you to approach at your own risk. Our whole lives, walking through the city has meant muddy shoes.

As we're undressing that night she asks how I'd rate my recent performance as a husband.

I don't know; maybe not so good, not so bad, I tell her.

She answers that if I were a minister, I'd resign.

"What area are we talking about here," I wonder aloud, "in terms of performance?"

"Go to sleep," she tells me, and turns off the lamp.

If climate change is a hammer to the Dutch, the head's coming down more or less where we live. Rotterdam sits astride a plain that absorbs the Scheldt, Meuse, and Rhine outflows, and what we're facing is a troika of rising sea level, peak river discharges, and extreme weather events. We've got the jewel of our water defenses—the staggeringly massive water barriers at Maeslant and Dordrecht, and the rest of the Delta Works—ready to shut off the North Sea during the next cataclysmic storm, but what are we to do when that coincides with the peak river discharges? Sea levels are leaping up, our ground is subsiding, it's raining harder and more often, and our program of managed flooding—Make Room for the Rivers—was overwhelmed long ago. The dunes and dikes at eleven locations from Ter Heijde to Westkapelle no longer meet what we decided would be the minimum safety standards. Temporary emergency measures are starting to be known to the public as Hans Brinkers.

And this winter's been a festival of bad news. Kees's team has measured increased snowmelt in the Alps to go along with prolonged rainfall across Northern Europe and steadily increasing windspeeds during gales, all of which lead to increasingly ominous winter flows, especially in the Rhine. He and I—known around the office as the Pessimists—forecasted this winter's discharge at eighteen thousand cubic meters per second. It's now up to twenty-one. What are those of us in charge of dealing with that supposed to do? A megastorm at this point would swamp the barriers from both sides and inundate Rotterdam and its surroundings—three million people—within twenty-four hours.

Which is quite the challenge for someone in media relations. "Remember, the Netherlands will always be here," Cato likes to say when signing off with one of the news agencies. "Though probably under three meters of water," she'll add after she hangs up.

Before this most recent emergency, my area of expertise had to do with the strength and loading of the Water Defense structures, especially in terms of the Scheldt estuary. We'd been integrating forecasting and security software for high-risk areas and trying to get Arcadis to understand that it needed to share almost everything with IBM and vice versa. I'd even been lent out to work on the Venice, London, and Saint Petersburg surge barriers. But now all of us were back home and thrown into the Weak Links Project, an overeducated fire brigade formed to address new vulnerabilities the minute they emerged.

Our faces are turned helplessly to the Alps. There's been a series of cloudbursts on the eastern slopes: thirty-five centimeters of rain in the last two weeks. The Germans have long since raised their river dikes to funnel the water right past them and into the Netherlands. Some of that water will be taken up in the soil, some in lakes and ponds and catchment basins, and some in polders and farmland that we've set aside for flooding emergencies. Some in water plazas and water gardens and specially designed underground parking garages and reservoirs. The rest will keep moving downriver to Rotterdam and the closed surge barriers.

"Well, 'Change is the soul of Rotterdam,'" Kees joked when we first looked at the numbers on the meteorological disaster ahead. We were given private notification that there would be vertical evacuation if the warning time for an untenable situation was under two hours, and horizontal evacuation if it was over two.

"What am I supposed to do," Cato demanded to know when I told her, "tell the helicopter that we have to pop over to Henk's school?" He now has an agreed-upon code; when it appears on his iFuze, he's to leave school immediately and head to her office.

But in the meantime we operate as though it won't come to that. We think we'll come up with something, as we always have. Where would New Orleans or the Mekong Delta be without Dutch hydraulics and Dutch water management? And where would the U.S. and Europe be if we hadn't led them out of the financial panic and depression, just by being ourselves? EU dominoes from Iceland to Ireland to Italy came down around our ears but there we sat, having been protected by our own Dutchness. What was the joke about us, after all? That we didn't go to the banks to take money out; we went to put money in. Who was going to be the first, as economy after economy capsized, to pony up the political courage to nationalize their banks and work cooperatively? Well, who took the public good more seriously than the Dutch? Who was more in love with rules? Who tells anyone who'll listen that we're providing the rest of the world with a glimpse of what the future will be?

After a third straight sleepless night—"Oh, who gets any sleep in the water sector?" Kees answered irritably the morning I complained about it—I leave the office early and ride a water taxi to Pernis. In Nieuwe Maas the shipping is so thick that it's like kayaking through canyons, and the taxi captain charges extra for what he calls a piloting fee. We tip and tumble on the backswells while four tugs nudge a supertanker sideways into its berth like puppies snuffling at the base of a cliff. The tanker's hull is so high that we can't see any superstructure above it.

I hike from the dock to Polluxstraat, the traffic on the A4 above rolling like surf. "Look who's here," my mother says, instead of hello, and goes about her tea-making as though I dropped in unannounced every afternoon. We sit in the breakfast nook off the kitchen. Before she settles in, she reverses the pillow embroidered "Good Night" so that it now reads "Good Morning."

"How's Henk?" she asks, and I tell her he's got some kind of chest thing. "As long as he's healthy," she replies. I don't see any reason to quibble.

The bottom shelves of her refrigerator are puddled with liquid from deliquescing vegetables and something spilled. The bristles of her bottle scraper on the counter are coated with dried mayonnaise. The front of her nightgown is an archipelago of stains.

"How's Cato?" she asks.

"Cato wants to know if we're going to get you some help," I tell her.

"I just talked with her," my mother says irritably. "She didn't say anything like that."

"You talked with her? What'd you talk about?" I ask. But she waves me off. "Did you talk to her or not?"

"That girl from up north you brought here to meet me, I couldn't even understand her," she tells me. She talks about regional differences as though her country's the size of China.

"We thought she seemed very efficient," I reply. "What else did Cato talk with you about?"

But she's already shifted her interest to the window. Years ago she had a traffic mirror mounted outside on the frame to let her spy on the street unobserved. She uses a finger to widen the gap in the lace curtains.

What else should she do all day long? She never goes out. The street's her revival house, always showing the same movie.

The holes in her winter stockings are patched with a carnival array of colored thread. We always lived by the maxim that things last longer mended than new. My whole life, I heard that with thrift and hard work I could build a mansion. My father had a typewritten note tacked to the wall in his office at home: *Let those with abundance remember that they are surrounded by thorns.*

"Who said *that*?" Cato asked when we were going through his belongings.

"Calvin," I told her.

"Well, you would know," she said.

He hadn't been so much a conservative as a man whose life philosophy had boiled down to the principle of no nonsense. I'd noticed even as a tiny boy that whenever he liked a business associate, or anyone else, that's what he said about them.

My mother's got her nose to the glass at this point. "You think you're the only one with secrets," she remarks.

"What's that supposed to mean?" I ask, but she acts as though she's not going to dignify that with a response. Follow-up questions don't get anywhere, either. I sit with her a while longer. We watch a Chinese game show. I soak her bread in milk, walk her to the toilet, and tell her we have to at least think about moving her bed downstairs somewhere. The steps to her second floor are vertiginous even by Dutch standards, and the risers accommodate less than half your foot. She makes an effort to follow what I'm saying, puzzled that she needs to puzzle something out. But then her expression dissipates and she complains she spent half the night looking for the coffee grinder.

"Why were you looking for the coffee grinder?" I ask, a question I have to repeat. Then I stop, for fear of frightening her.

Henk's class is viewing a presentation at the Climate campus—"Water: Precious Resource and Deadly Companion"—so we have the dinner table to ourselves. Since Cato's day was even longer than mine, I prepared the meal, two cans of pea soup with pigs' knuckles and some Belgian beer, but she's too tired to complain. She's dealing with both the Americans, who are always hectoring for clarification on the changing risk factors for our projects in Miami and New Orleans, and the Germans, who've publicly dug in their heels on the issue of accepting any spillover from the Rhine in order to take some of the pressure off the situation downstream.

It's the usual debate, as far as the latter argument's concerned. We take the high road—it's only through cooperation that we can face such monumental challenges, etc.—while other countries scoff at our aspirations toward ever more comprehensive safety measures. The German foreign minister last year accused us on a simulcast of acting like old women.

"Maybe he's right," Cato says wearily. "Sometimes I wonder what it'd be like to live in a country where you don't need a license to build a fence around your garden."

Exasperated, we indulge in a little Dutch bashing. No one complains about themselves as well as the Dutch. Cato asks if I remember that story about the manufacturers having to certify that each of the chocolate letters handed out by Santa Claus contained an equal amount of chocolate. I remind her about the number-one download of the year turning out to have been of *fireworks sound effects,* for those New Year's revelers who found real fireworks too worrisome.

After we stop, she looks at me, her mouth a little slack. "Why does this sort of thing make us horny?" she wonders.

"Maybe it's the pea soup," I tell her in the shower. She's examining little crescents of fingernail marks where she held me when she came. Then she turns off the water and we wrap ourselves in the bedsheet-sized towel she had made in Surinam. Cocooned on the floor in the tiny, steamy bathroom we discuss Kees's love life. He now shops at a singles' supermarket, the kind where you use a blue basket if you're taken and a yellow if you're available. When I asked how his latest fling was working out, he said, "Well, I'm back to the yellow basket."

Cato thinks this is hilarious.

"How'd *we* get to be so lucky?" I ask her. We're spooning and she does a minimal grind that allows me to grow inside her.

"The other day someone from BBC1 asked my boss that same question about how he ended up where he did," she says. She turns her cheek so I can kiss it.

"What'd he say?" I ask when I've moved from her cheek to her neck. She's not a big fan of her boss.

She shrugs comfortably, her shoulder blades against my chest. I wrap my arms tighter so the fit is even more perfect. The gist of his answer, she tells me, was mostly by not asking too many questions.

My mother always had memory problems and even before my sister died my father said that he didn't blame her; she'd seen her own brothers swept away in the 1953 flood and had been a wreck for years afterward. On January 31, the night after her sixth birthday, a storm field that covered the entire North Sea swept down out of the northwest with winds that registered gale force 11 and combined with a spring tide to raise the sea six meters over NAP. The breakers overtopped the dikes in eighty-nine locations over a 170-kilometer stretch and hollowed them out on their land sides so that the surges that followed broke them. My mother remembered eating her soup alongside her two brothers listening to the wind increase in volume until her father went out to check on the barn and the draft from the opened door blew their board game off the table. Her mother's Bible pages flapped in her hands like panicked birds. Water was seeping through the window casing, and her brother touched it and held out his finger for her to taste. She remembered his look when she realized that it was salty: not rain but spray from the sea.

Her father returned and said they all had to leave, now. They held hands in a chain and he went first and she went second, and once the door was open, the wind staggered him and blew her off her feet. He managed to retrieve her but by then they couldn't find the others in the dark and the rain. She was soaked in ice and the water was already up to her thighs and in the distance she could see breakers where the dike had been. They headed inland and found refuge inside a neighbor's brick home and discovered that the back half of the house had already been torn away by the water. He led her up the stairs to the third floor and through a trapdoor onto the roof. Their neighbors were already there, and her mother, huddling against the wind and the cold. The house west of them imploded but its roof held together and was pushed upright in front of theirs, diverting the main force of the flood around them like a breakwater. She remembered holding her father's hand so their bodies would be found in the same place. Her mother shrieked and pointed and she saw her brothers beside a woman with a baby on the roof of the house beyond them to the east. Each wave that broke against the front drenched her brothers and the woman with spray, and the woman kept turning her torso to shield the baby. And then the front of the house caved in and they all became bobbing heads in the water that were swept around the collapsing walls and away.

She remembered the wind finally dying down by mid-morning, a heavy mist in the gray sky, and a fishing smack off to the north coasting between the rooftops and bringing people on board. She remembered a dog lowered on a rope, its paws flailing as it turned.

After their rescue, she remembered a telegraph pole slanted over, its wires tugged by the current. She remembered the water smelling of gasoline and mud, treetops uncovered by the waves, and a clog between two steep roofs filled with floating branches and dead cattle. She remembered a vast plain of wreckage on the water and the smell of dead fish traveling on the wind. She remembered two older boys sitting beside her and examining the silt driven inside an unopened bottle of soda by the force of the waves. She remembered her mother's animal sounds and the length of time it took to get to dry land, and her father's chin on her mother's bent back, his head bumping and wobbling whenever they crossed the wakes of other boats.

We always knew this was coming. Years ago the city fathers thought it was our big opportunity. Rotterdam no longer would be just the ugly port, or Amsterdam without the attractions. The bad news was going to impact us first and foremost, so we put out the word that we were looking for people with the nerve to put into practice what was barely possible anywhere else. The result was Waterplan 4 Rotterdam, with brand-new approaches to storage and safety: water plazas, super cisterns, water balloons, green roofs, and even traffic tunnels that doubled as immense drainage systems would all siphon off danger. It roped in Kees and Cato and me and by the end of the first week had set Cato against us. Her mandate was to showcase Dutch ingenuity, so the last thing she needed was the Pessimists clamoring for more funding because nothing anyone had come up with yet was going to work. As far as she was concerned, our country was the testing ground for all high-profile adaptive measures and practically oriented knowledge and prototype projects that would attract worldwide attention and become a sluice-gate for high-tech exports. She spent her days in the international marketplace hawking the notion that we were safe here because we had the knowledge and were using it to find creative solutions. We were all assuming that a secure population was a collective social good for which the government and private sector alike would remain responsible, a notion, we soon realized, not universally embraced by other countries.

Sea-facing barriers are inspected both by hand and by laser imaging. Smart dikes schedule their own maintenance based on sensors that detect seepage or changes in pressure and stability. Satellites track ocean currents and water-mass volumes. The areas most at risk have been divided into dike-ring compartments in an attempt to make the country a system of watertight doors. Our road and infrastructure networks now function independently of the ground layer. Nine entire neighborhoods have been made amphibious, built on hollow platforms that will rise with the water but remain anchored to submerged foundations. And besides the giant storm barriers, atop our dikes we've mounted titanium-braced walls that unfold from concrete channels, leviathan-like inflatable rubber dams, and special grasses grown on plastic-mat revetments to anchor the inner walls.

"Is it all enough?" Henk will ask, whenever there's a day of unremitting rain. "Oh, honey, it's more than enough," Cato will tell him, and then quiz him on our emergency code.

"It's funny how this kind of work has been good for me," Cato says. She's asked me to go for a walk, an activity she knows I'll find nostalgically stirring. We tramped all over the city before and after lovemaking when we first got together. "All of this end-of-the-world stuff apparently cheers me up," she remarks. "I guess it's the same thing I used to get at home. All those glum faces, and I had to do the song-and-dance that explained why they got out of bed in the morning."

"The heavy lifting," I tell her.

"Exactly," she says with a faux mournfulness. "The heavy lifting. We're on for another simulcast tomorrow and it'll be three Germans with long faces and Cato the Optimist."

We negotiate a herd of bicycles on a plaza and she veers ahead of me toward the harbor. When we cross the skylights of the traffic tunnels, giant container haulers shudder by beneath our feet. She has a beautiful back, accentuated by the military cut of her overcoat.

"Except that the people you're dealing with now *want* to be fooled," I tell her.

"It's not that they want to be fooled," she answers. "It's just that they're not convinced they need to go around glum all the time."

"How'd that philosophy work with your parents?" I ask.

"Not so well," she says sadly.

We turn on Boompjes, which is sure to add to her melancholy. A seven-story construction crane with legs curving inward perches like a spider over the river.

"Your mother called about the coffee grinder," she remarks. "I couldn't pin down what she was talking about."

Boys in bathing suits are pitching themselves off the high dock by the Strand, though it seems much too cold for that, and the river too dirty. Even in the chill I can smell tar and rope and, strangely, fresh bread.

"She called you or you called her?" I ask.

"I just told you," Cato says.

"It seems odd that she'd call you," I tell her.

"What *was* she talking about?" Cato wants to know.

"I assume she was having trouble working the coffee grinder," I tell her.

"Working it or finding it?" she asks.

"Working it, I think," I suggest. "*She* called *you?*"

"Oh my God," Cato says.

"I'm just asking," I tell her after a minute.

All of Maashaven is blocked from view by a giant suction dredger that's being barged out to Maasvlakte 2. Preceded by six tugs, it looks like a small city going by. The thing uses dragheads connected to tubes the size of railway tunnels and harvests sand down to a depth of twenty meters. It'll be deepening the docking areas out at Yangtzehaven, Europahaven, and Mississippihaven. There's been some worry that all of this dredging has been undermining the water defenses on the other side of the channel, which is the last thing we need. Kees has been dealing with their horseshit for a few weeks now.

We rest on a bench in front of some law offices. Over the front entrance, cameras have been installed to monitor the surveillance cameras, which have been vandalized. Once the dredger has passed, we can see a family of day campers on the opposite bank who've pitched their tent on a berm overlooking the channel.

"Isn't it too cold for camping?" I ask her.

"Wasn't it too cold for swimming?" she responds, reminding me of the boys we'd passed.

She says Henk keeps replaying the same footage on his iFuze of Feyenoord's MVP being lowered into the stadium beneath the team flag by a V/STOL. "So here's what I'm thinking," she continues, as if that led directly to her next thought. She mentions a conservatory in Berlin, fantastically expensive, that has a chamber-music program. She'd like to send Henk there during his winter break, and maybe longer.

This seems to me to be mostly about his safety, though I don't acknowledge that. He's a gifted cellist, but hardly seems devoted to the instrument.

With her pitchman's good cheer she repeats the amount it will cost, which to me sounds like enough for a week in a five-star hotel. But she says money can always be found for a good idea, and if it can't, then it wasn't a good idea. Finally she adds that as a hydraulic engineer, I'm the equivalent of an atomic physicist in technological prestige.

Atomic physicists don't make a whole lot of money, either, I remind her. And our argument proceeds from there. I can see her disappointment expanding as we speak, and even as my inner organs start to contract I sit on the information of my hidden nest egg and allow all of the unhappiness to unfold. This takes forever. The word in our country for the decision-making process is the same as the one we use for what we pour over pancakes. Our national mindset pivots around the word "but": as in "This, yes, but that, too." Cato puts her fingers to her temples and sheaths her cheeks with her palms. Her arguments run aground on my tolerance, which has been elsewhere described as a refusal to listen. Passion in Dutch meetings is punished by being ignored. The idea is that the argument itself matters, not the intensity with which it's presented. Outright rejections of a position are rare; what you get instead are suggestions for improvement that if followed would annihilate the original intent. And then everyone checks their agendas to schedule the next meeting.

Just like that, we're walking back. We're single-file again, and it's gotten colder.

From our earliest years, we're taught not to burden others with our emotions. A young Amsterdammer in the Climate campus is known as the Thespian because he sobbed in public at a co-worker's funeral. "You don't need to eliminate your emotions," Kees reminded him when the Amsterdammer complained about the way he'd been treated. "You just need to be a little more economical with them."

Another thing I never told Cato: my sister and I the week before she caught the flu had been jumping into the river in the winter as well. That was my idea. When she came out, her feet and lips were blue and she sneezed all the way home. "Do you think I'll catch a cold?" she asked that night. "Go to sleep," I answered.

We take a shortcut through the sunken pedestrian mall they call the Shopping Gutter. By the time we reach our street it's dark, raining again, and the muddy pavement's shining in the lights of the cafes. Along the new athletic complex in the distance, sapphire-blue searchlights are lancing up into the rain at even intervals, like meteorological harp strings. "I don't know if you *know* what this does to me, or you don't," Cato says at our doorstep, once she's stopped and turned. Her thick brown hair is beaded with moisture where it's not soaked. "But either way, it's just so miserable."

I actually *have* the solution to our problem, I'm reminded as I follow her up the stairs. The thought makes me feel rehabilitated, as though I've told her instead of only myself.

Cato always maintained that when it came to their marriage, her parents practiced a sort of apocalyptic utilitarianism: on the one hand they were sure everything was going to hell in a handbasket, while on the other they continued to operate as if things could be turned around with a few practical measures.

But there's always that moment in a country's history when it becomes obvious the earth is less manageable than previously thought. Ten years ago we needed to conduct comprehensive assessments of the flood defenses every five years. Now safety margins are adjusted every six months to take new revelations into account. For the last year and a half we've been told to build into our designs for whatever we're working on features that restrict the damaging effects *after* an inevitable inundation. There won't be any retreating back to the hinterlands, either, because given the numbers we're facing there won't be any hinterlands. It's gotten to the point that pedestrians are banned from many of the sea-facing dikes in the far west even on calm days. At the entrance to the Haringvlietdam they've erected an immense yellow caution sign that shows two tiny stick figures with their arms raised in alarm at a black wave three times their size that's curling over them.

I watched Kees's face during a recent simulation as one of his new configurations for a smart dike was overwhelmed in half the time he would have predicted. It had always been the Dutch assumption that we would resolve the problems facing us from a position of strength. But we passed that station long ago. At this point each of us understands privately that we're operating under the banner of lost control.

The next morning we're crammed together into Rotterdam Climate Proof's Smartvan and heading west on N211, still not speaking. Cato's driving. At 140 km/hr the rain fans across the windshield energetically, racing the wipers. Gray clouds seem to be rushing in from the sea in the distance. We cross some polders that are already flooded, and there's a rocking buoyancy when we traverse that part of the road that's floating. Trucks sweep by backwards and recede behind us in the spray.

The only sounds are those of tires and wipers and rain. Exploring the radio is like visiting the Tower of Babel: Turks, Berbers, Cape Verdeans, Antilleans, Angolans, Portuguese, Croatians, Brazilians, Chinese. Cato managed to relocate her simulcast with her three long-faced Germans to the Hoek van Holland; she told them she wanted the Maeslant barrier as a backdrop, but what she really intends is to surprise them, live, with the state of the water levels already. Out near the barrier it's pretty dramatic. Cato the Optimist with indisputable visual evidence that the sky is falling: can the German position remain unshaken in the face of that? Will her grandstanding work? It's hard to say. It's pretty clear that nothing else will.

"Want me to talk about Gravenzande?" I ask her. "That's the sort of thing that will really jolt the boys from the Reich."

"That's just what I need," she answers. "You starting a panic about something that might not even be true."

Gravenzande's where she's going to drop me, a few kilometers away. Three days ago geologists there turned up crushed shell deposits seven meters higher on the dune lines inland than anyone believed floods had ever reached, deposits that look to be only about ten thousand years old. If this ends up confirmed, it's seriously bad news, given what it clarifies about how cataclysmic things could get even before the climate's more recent turn for the worse.

It's Saturday, and we'll probably put in twelve hours. Henk's getting more comfortable with his weekend nanny than with us. As Cato likes to tell him when she's trying to induce him to do his chores: "Around here, you work." By which she means that old joke that when you buy a shirt in Rotterdam, it comes with the sleeves already rolled up.

We pass poplars lining the canals in neat rows, a canary-yellow smudge of a house submerged to its second-floor windows and, beyond a roundabout, a pair of decrepit rugby goalposts.

"You're really going to announce that if the Germans pull their weight, everything's going to be fine?" I ask. But she ignores me.

She needs a decision, she tells me a few minutes later, as though tired of asking. Henk's winter break is coming up. I venture that I thought it wasn't until the twelfth, and she reminds me with exasperation that it's the fifth, the schools now staggering vacation times to avoid overloading the transportation systems.

We pass the curved sod roofs of factories. The secret account's not a problem but a solution, I decide, and as I model to myself ways of implementing it as such, Cato finally asserts—as though she's waited too long already—that she's found the answer: she could take that Royal Dutch Shell offer to reconfigure their regional media relations, they could set her up in Wannsee, and Henk could commute. They could stay out there and get a bump in income besides. Henk could enroll in the conservatory.

We exit N211 northwest on an even smaller access road to the coast, and within a kilometer it ends in a turnabout next to the dunes. She pulls the car around so it's pointed back toward her simulcast, turns off the engine, and sits there beside me with her hands in her lap.

"How long has this been in the works?" I ask. She wants to know what I mean, and I tell her that it doesn't seem like so obscure a question; she said no to Shell years ago, so where did this new offer come from?

She shrugs, as if I'd asked if they were paying her moving expenses. "They called. I told them I'd listen to what they had to say."

"They called you," I tell her.

"They called me," she repeats.

She's only trying to hedge her bets, I tell myself to combat the panic. Our country's all about spreading risk around. "Do people just walk into this conservatory?" I ask. "Or do you have to apply?"

She doesn't answer, which I take to mean that she and Henk already have applied and he's been accepted. "How did Henk feel about this good news?" I ask.

"He wanted to tell you," Cato answers.

"And we'd see each other every other weekend? Once a month?" I'm attempting a version of steely neutrality but can feel the terror worming its way forward.

"This is just one option of many," she reminds me. "We need to talk about all of them." She adds that she has to go. And that I should see all this as being primarily about Henk, not us. I answer that the Netherlands will always be here, and she smiles and starts the van.

"You sure there's nothing else you want to talk to me about?" she asks.

"Like what?" I say. "I want to talk to you about everything."

She jiggles the gear shift lightly, considering me. "You're going to let me drive away," she says, "with your having left it at that."

"I don't want you to drive away at all," I tell her.

"Well, there is that," she concedes bitterly. She waits another full minute, then a curtain comes down on her expression and she puts the car in gear. She honks when she's pulling out.

At the top of the dune I watch surfers in wetsuits wading into the breakers in the rain. The rain picks up and sets the sea's surface in a constant agitation. Even the surfers keep low, to stay out of it. The wet sand's like brown sugar in my shoes.

Five hundred thousand years ago it was possible to walk from where I live to England. At that point the Thames was a tributary of the Rhine. Even during the Romans' occupation, the Zuider Zee was dry. But by the sixth century B.C. we were building artificial hills out of marsh grass mixed with manure and our own refuse to keep our feet out of the water. And then in the seventeenth century Hulsebosch invented the Archimedes screw, and water wheels could raise a flow four meters higher than where it began, and we started to make real progress at keeping what the old people called "the Waterwolf" from the door.

In the fifteenth century Philip the Good ordered the sand dike that constituted the original Hondsbossche Seawall to be restored, and another built behind it as a backup. He named the latter the Sleeper Dike. For extra security he had another constructed behind that, calling that one the Dreamer Dike. Ever since, schoolchildren have learned, as one of their first geography sentences, that "Between Camperduinen and Petten lie three dikes: the Watcher, the Sleeper, and the Dreamer."

We're raised with the double message that we have to address our worst fears but that nonetheless they'll also somehow domesticate themselves. Fifteen years ago Rotterdam Climate Proof revived "The Netherlands lives with water" as a slogan, the accompanying poster featuring a two-panel cartoon in which a towering wave in the first panel is breaking before its crest over a terrified little boy, and in the second it separates into immense foamy fingers so he can relievedly shake its hand.

When Cato told me about that first offer from Shell, I could *see* her flash of feral excitement about what she was turning down. Royal Dutch Shell! She would've been fronting for one of the biggest corporations in the world. We conceived Henk a few nights later. There was a lot of urgent talk about getting deeper and closer and I remember striving once she'd guided me inside her to have my penis reach the back of her throat. Periodically we slowed into the barest sort of movement, just to further take stock of what was happening, and at one point we paused in our tremoring and I put my lips to her ear and reminded her of what she'd passed up. After winning them over, she could have picked her city: Tokyo, Los Angeles, Rio. The notion caused a momentary lack of focus in her eyes. Then as a response she started moving along a contraction, and Shell and other options including speech evanesced away.

If she were to leave me, where would I be? It's as if she was put here to force my interaction with humans. And still I don't pull it off. It's like that story we were told as children, of Jesus telling the rich young man to go and sell all he has and give it to the poor, but instead the rich man chose to keep what he had, and went away sorrowful. When we talked about it, Kees said he always assumed the guy had settled in Holland.

That Monday, more bad news: warm air and heavy rain has ventured many meters above established snowlines in the western Alps, and Kees holds up before me with both hands GRACE's latest printouts about a storm cell whose potential numbers we keep rechecking because they seem so extravagant. He spends the rest of the morning on the phone trying to stress that we've hit another type of threshold here; that these are calamity-level numbers. It seems to him that everyone's saying they recognize the urgency of the new situation but that no one's acting like it. During lunch a call comes in about the hinge-and-socket joint, itself five stories high, of one of the Maeslant doors. In order to allow the doors to roll with the waves, the joints are designed to operate like a human shoulder, swinging along both horizontal and vertical axes and transferring the unimaginable stresses to the joint's foundation. The maintenance engineers are reporting that the foundation block—all 52,000 tons of it—is moving.

Finally Kees flicks off his phone receptor and squeezes his eyes shut in despair. "Maybe our history's just the history of picking up after disasters like this," he tells me. "The Italians do pasta sauce and we do body retrieval."

After waiting a few minutes for updated numbers, I call Cato and fail to get through and then try my mother, who says she's soaking her corns. I can picture the enamel basin with the legend "Contented Feet" around the rim. The image seems to confirm that we're all naked in the world, so I tell her to get some things together, that I'm sending someone out for her, that she needs to leave town for a little while.

It's amazing I'm able to keep trying Cato's numbers, given what's broken loose at every level of water management nationwide. Everyone's shouting into headpieces and clattering away at laptops at the same time. At the Delta stations the situation has already triggered the automatic emergency procedures with their check-lists and hour-by-hour protocols. Outside my office window the canal is lined with barges of cows, of all things, awaiting their river pilot to transport them to safety. The road in front of them is a gypsy caravan of traffic piled high with suitcases and furniture and roped-down plastic bags. The occasional dog hangs from a car window. Those roads that can float should allow vehicular evacuation for six or seven hours longer than the other roads will. The civil defense teams at roundabouts and intersections are doing what they can to dispense biopacs and aquacells. Through the glass everyone seems to be behaving well, though with a maximum of commotion.

I've got the mayor of Ter Heijde on one line saying he's up to his ass in ice water and demanding to know where the fabled Weak Links Project has gone when Cato's voice finally breaks in on the other.

"Where are you?" I shout, and the mayor shouts back "Where do you *think*?" I kill his line and ask again, and Cato answers, "What?" In just her one-word inflection, I can tell she heard what I said. "Is Henk with you?" I shout, and Kees and some of the others around the office look up despite the pandemic of shouting. I ask again and she says that he is. When I ask if she's awaiting evacuation, she answers that she's already in Berlin.

I'm shouting other questions when Kees cups a palm over my receptor and says, "Here's an idea. Why don't you sort out all of your personal problems now?"

After Cato's line goes dead I can't raise her again, or she won't answer. We're engaged in such a blizzard of calls that it almost doesn't matter. "Whoa," Kees says, his hands dropping to his desk, and a number of our co-workers go silent as well, because the windows facing west are now rattling and black with rain. I look out mine, and bags and other debris are tearing free of the traffic caravan and sailing east. The rain curtain hits the cows in their barges and their ears flatten like mules and their eyes squint shut at the gale's power.

"Our ride is here," Kees calls, shaking my shoulder, and I realize that everyone's hurriedly collecting laptops and flash drives. There's a tumult heading up the stairs to the roof and the roar of the wind every time the door's opened, and the scrabbling sounds of people dragging something outside before the door slams shut. And then, with surprising abruptness, it's quiet.

My window continues to shake as though it's not double pane but cellophane. Now that our land has subsided as much as it has, when the water does come, it will come like a wall, and each dike that stops it will force it to turn, and in its churning it will begin to spiral and bore into the earth, eroding away the dike walls, until the pressure builds and that dike collapses and it's on to the next one, with more pressure piling up behind, and so on and so on until every last barrier falls and the water thunders forward like a hand sweeping everything from the table.

The lights go off, and then on and off again, before the halogen emergency lights in the corridors engage, with their irritated buzzing.

It's easier to see out with the interior lights gone. Along the line of cars a man carrying a framed painting staggers at an angle, like a sailboat tacking. He passes a woman in a van with her head against the headrest and her mouth open in an *Oh* of fatigue.

I'm imagining the helicopter crew's negotiations with my mother, and their fireman's carry once those negotiations have fallen through. She told me once that she often recalled how long they drifted in the flood of 1953 through the darkness without the sky getting any lighter. When the sun finally rose they watched the navy drop food and blankets and rubber boats and bottles of cooking gas to people on roofs or isolated high spots, and when their boat passed a small body lying across an eave with its arms in the water, her father told her that it was resting. She remembered later that morning telling her mother, who'd grown calmer, that it was a good sign they saw so few people floating, and before her father could stop her she answered that the drowned didn't float straightaway but took a few days to come up.

And she talked with fondness about how tenderly her father had tended to her later, after she'd been blinded by some windblown grit, by suggesting she rub one eye to make the other weep, like farmers did when bothered by chaff. And she remembered, too, the strangeness of one of the prayers her village priest recited once they were back in their old church, the masonry buttressed with steel beams and planking to keep the walls from sagging outwards any further: *I sink into deep mire, where there is no standing; I come into deep waters, where the floods overflow me.*

The window's immense pane shudders and flexes before me from the force of what's pouring out of the North Sea. Water's beginning to run its fingers under the seal on the sash. Cato will send me wry and brisk and newsy text updates whether she receives answers or not, and Henk will author a few as well. Everyone in Berlin will track the developments on the monitors above them while they shop or travel or work, the teaser heading reading something like *The Netherlands Under Siege.* Some of the more sober will think, *That could have been us.* Some of the more perceptive will consider that it soon might well be.

My finger's on the Cato icon on the screen without exerting the additional pressure that would initiate another call. What sort of person ends up with someone like me? What sort of person finds that *acceptable,* year to year? We went on vacations and fielded each other's calls and took turns reading Henk to sleep and let slip away the miracle that was there between us when we first came together. We hunkered down before the wind picked up. We modeled risk management for our son when instead we could have embraced the freefall of that astonishing *Here, this is yours to hold.* We told each other *I think I know* when we should've said *Lead me farther through your amazing, astonishing interior.*

Cato was moved by my mother's flood memories, but brought to tears only by the one my mother cherished from that year: the Queen's address to the nation afterwards, her celebration of what the crucible of the disaster had produced, and the return, at long last, of the unity the country had displayed during the war. My mother had years ago purchased a vinyl record of the speech, and later had a neighbor transfer it to a digital format. She played it once while we were visiting, and Henk knelt at the window spying on whoever was hurrying by. And my mother held the weeping

Cato's hand and she held mine and Henk gave us fair warning of anything of interest on the street, while the Queen's warm and smooth voice thanked us all for working together in that one great cause, soldiering on without a thought for care, or grief, or inner divisions, and without even realizing what we were denying ourselves.

Happy with Crocodiles

Her envelope had hearts where the *o*'s in my name should have been and I tore it open and read her letter right there in the sun. The V-Mail was like onionskin and in the humidity you spent all your time peeling sheets apart and flapping them dry. Two guys who'd been waiting behind me for their mail passed out and fell over. Our CO had orders to keep everyone under some sort of shade until further notice. That was it in terms of his responsibilities for the day. But the mail hadn't caught up to us since Port Moresby so even this one load pulled most of us out around the truck.

The guy next to me spat on the back fender just to watch it sizzle. As far as we could tell, we were the only four companies not getting any beach breezes, and we'd been sitting through this for two weeks and were pretty much wiped out to a man. Guys just lay in the bush with their feet sticking out onto the trail. The Bren gun carrier already looked like a planter, it was so overgrown. Almost nothing was running because the lubricating oils ran off or evaporated. We'd lost half our water when the heat dissolved the jerry cans' enamel lining. Two unshaded shells farther down the trail had exploded. The tents accumulated heat like furnaces. The midday sun raised blisters on an arm in ten minutes. One of the medics timed it. Everybody lost so much fluid and salt that we had ice-pick headaches or down-on-all-fours dry heaves and cramping. Turning your head wasn't worth the effort. Pickets got confused and shot at anything. A few facing the afternoon sun on the water went snowblind from the glare and didn't bother to report it until relieved.

At least the Japs were lying low, too. I had a palm-frond bush hat but even through that the sun beat on my head like a mallet.

The first paragraph was all about how good it was to hear I was okay. It made her whole day easier, apparently. The second said "To answer your question, no, I didn't see your brother when he was home on leave." But he'd already written that she had. And then he'd left it at that.

"Get out of the *sun,* Foss," the CO called.

One of the guys who'd passed out came to and staggered back to his tent. The other guy just lay there. The guy behind me got handed a Christmas package, but whatever was in it was smashed flat and melted besides. He picked over it standing in the truck cab's shadow.

The PFC dishing out the mail was clearly hacked off that he had to do it right there on the trail. There was one good patch of shade from a clump of coconut palms and no one was budging out of it to let him park his truck. He called a name and if someone didn't answer right away he pitched the letter or package over the side and went on to the next one. He was wearing a bush helmet and on the back of it someone had drawn a woman with her legs spread and written "Your Mother Says Hi" across the brim.

The third paragraph went on to something else as though that was the end of it. So-and-so said such-and-such about a friend of hers, could I believe that?

"What do you need, a road map?" my friend Leo said when I asked him about it.

"What?" I asked, like I already knew. "What do you think you think is going on?"

"What do I *think* I think is going on?" he asked, and the rest of Dog Company, a little ways farther off the trail, laughed. We'd heard that Baker and Fox Companies had been bombed with daisy cutters the night before, so we were working on two-man slit trenches, and in the close quarters entrenching tools kept whipping by people's ears. "I think the two of them spend a lot of time agreeing on what a great guy you are. I think it makes them sad for you and they cry together in their beer. And then I think he's sticking his dick in her."

"What's wrong with *him*?" our staff sergeant asked Leo while we redug our slit trenches the next morning. As if everybody else was the picture of contentment. If it rained at all during the night we lost like a foot and a half of depth to the mud.

"He's jealous of his brother," Leo told him.

"His brother better-lookin' than him?" the staff sergeant asked, amused.

"I've seen knotholes better-lookin' than him," Leo told him.

"Why would he think it was about looks?" I asked him later. "Why wouldn't he think I was jealous of something else?"

"Where the heck is *chow*?" Leo wondered. Guys were milling around the bivouac, waiting. You could always tell when a hot meal was late, because everybody started acting like zoo animals.

We were the Second Battalion, 126th Infantry, 32nd Division, Michigan and Wisconsin National Guard, here in New Guinea all of fourteen days and—leave it to the Army—apparently the spearhead of General MacArthur's upcoming drive to dislodge what everyone agreed were two divisions of the world's most fearsome jungle fighters from one of the world's most impenetrable jungles.

Two of us hadn't hit puberty yet. Three of us couldn't see without our glasses, and our hygiene officer couldn't see *with* them. Before this, only one of the Wisconsin guys had been out of the state. We were fifteen miles from the nearest hut and a hundred and fifty from the nearest civilization, in the form of the mostly uninhabited northeastern Australian coast. We were ten thousand miles from home.

We'd trained in South Carolina, which didn't prepare us much for jungle fighting but did its bit in getting us ready for the humidity. Any number of us couldn't keep up during the double-time drills, which meant we had to run around the entire battalion area three times with knapsacks full of grenades. At one point our unit was first in the entire camp in hospitalizations.

We just weren't crackerjack soldiers. Guys who panicked every morning about climbing into full field dress and getting their beds made in time for reveille and inspection started sleeping already dressed and under their beds. We were each scored on particular skills and then all classified as riflemen anyway and herded onto transports and shipped out. Once we got through the Panama Canal the ships were under orders to never stop moving, so anybody who fell overboard would have to take care of himself. We slept in the holds in canvas hammocks slung in tiers of four from the support beams. The top slot was so close to the metal ceiling that if you tried to see your feet you cracked your head. Everything smelled of socks or farts or armpit. Weapons were stowed in baggage racks and anything else got dumped on the floor. In the exact middle of the trip everyone was issued five dollars, a huge morale builder with the dice and card players. Some guys slept on deck because of the smell or because they figured they'd have a better shot of getting off if the boat was torpedoed. Like that would've mattered: all the cargo was high explosives. The whole stern hold was mostly gasoline in seventy-gallon drums.

We had one fifty-caliber mounted aft for protection. If we'd been attacked by three guys in a motor launch, we would've been A-OK.

We were only in Australia a week when we were told to pack up for New Guinea. We were playing baseball with some Kiwis when we heard. Leo was in the batter's box when they called the game. He dropped his bat in the dirt and said, "Shit. I can hit this guy."

When we got within range of the coast, the smell of everything rotting was so strong that we could pick it up before the shore was even in sight. "What *is* that?" Leo asked. We were all hanging on the cable railings. "That's the jungle," one of the LCT pilots told him. "What's *wrong* with it?" Leo asked, and the guy laughed. It was like you could taste the germs in the air. Nobody on deck wanted to open his mouth.

It took our pathfinders an hour just to locate the trailhead that supposedly led inland. If you stepped five yards into the wall of leaves, you disappeared completely. All the barracks bags had to be left behind for the hump, so we carried only our weapons and ammo, knives, quinine tablets, mosquito lotion, canteens, and canvas water buckets. Everything else was left to the bearers. Our first night was spent in an old Aussie camp that was mostly a supply dump, camouflaged. Since Leo and I couldn't sleep we watched the natives file in carrying everything on poles on their shoulders. They looked scrawny, but judging by the loads they were plenty strong. I tried out some sign language on one. "You need something?" the guy asked when I finished.

They made their own pile and then went off the trail to sleep by themselves. Fifteen of them took like three steps and disappeared. Leo fell asleep too, finally. Then it was just me, listening to the bugs.

I got Leo's advice about everything. He was older, twenty-one, and had been in the Army for three years and Dog Company for two. We'd been friends since stateside. Or at least we'd gone off on passes together. He liked to say I spent the whole war surprised. Sometimes he enlarged it to life instead of just the war. "You know I ain't got a single friend?" he told me, like it had just hit him, the night we came ashore.

"What do you mean?" I asked him. "You got me."

"Yeah, that's right," he said after a minute, looking at me. Then he let it go.

The week we met he asked if I was a virgin, and when I told him no that's how Linda came up. He said, "So you've really done everything with her?" and for some reason I told him about all four nights. This was on the chow line and at one point I looked up and the guy ladling out the creamed chipped beef had just frozen in mid-pour. "You did all that?" Leo asked as we found a table. And I told him yes. Because I had.

Linda was in my high-school geography class and my brother was two years ahead. We all drove around in her older brother's car and argued about whether Mineral Point was the deadest place in Wisconsin or the deadest place on earth. We did our drinking at the turnoff for the abandoned quarry and her brother always said you could do human sacrifice there and nobody would find it for a year and a half. One night after I got my permit he let us have the car and we drove out there thinking about what he'd told us. "I want to show you something," she said in this low voice once I'd turned off the headlights, then took my head with one hand and leaned me over and kissed me as if she was looking for something really carefully with her mouth and it was all the same to her if she never found it. "Like this," she whispered a few times, showing me how to make it even better.

"I think I need to show you something else," she whispered later, and pushed me back again and unbuckled my pants and pulled them down past my hips. She brought her head down to where my pants were. "Where's your brother?" she asked, like she was making conversation.

"*I* don't know," I said, not even sure how I managed to say that. "What're you *doing*?" I asked her, holding her shoulders and her hair.

She laughed a little and let me go. I could feel the wetness and the cold air. "Mmm," she said, and the warmth came all around me again.

I didn't know what to say. "Would you *marry* me?" I finally called out, with my eyes closed, and she laughed again.

The next time we went back I got protection from my brother and we did everything else. The third time I pushed her up against her door and she started making noises, too.

"Why'd you ask about my brother when we were out here that other night?" I said afterwards, when we were just resting.

"When?" she wanted to know. "With my brother?"

I had my face on her shoulder and she had a foot up on the dash. "No, alone," I told her.

"I don't know," she said. "I don't remember." She sighed and shifted around and pulled me with her. The car seat underneath us felt soaked.

"So how'd it go, sport?" my brother asked when I got back. "Don't even tell me. I can see."

"So I hear you guys are going steady," he told me the next day after school.

"Where'd you get that?" I asked, though I was happy to hear it.

"Linda wants to know all about you," he said.

"Why doesn't she ask me?" I said. She'd given me a wave in geography, then disappeared with her friends at the bell.

"I guess because she wants the truth," he said.

"So what'd you tell her?" I asked.

"What do you think?" he said. "That she jumped the wrong Foss."

"What're you boys talking about?" our mom said, coming into the kitchen. She had a bowl of hard-boiled eggs to slice and she was going to line the bottom of her vegetable pie with them.

"Your son's talking about his new hobby," my brother said.

"Sounds like he's talking about a girl," our mom told him, shelling the eggs into a bowl.

"Where did you find time to talk to her?" I asked him.

"I like to think I don't wait for life to come to *me*," he said, hefting one of the peeled eggs and dropping it back into the bowl.

"Which one did you just touch?" our mom demanded.

"All of them," he said. He used both hands to smooth back his hair.

"She's my girl," I reminded him.

"I'm the one who just told *you* that," he said.

"So you *are* talking about a girl," our mom said. "What's her name?"

The cat wandered into the room and nosed at his dish. He sat down and we watched his tail do a few slow curls.

"I guess it's none of my business," she finally said to herself after looking back and forth at the two of us.

"Your mom's funny," Linda told me the next time we were alone.

"How do you know *that*?" I asked her. I put her brother's keys up under the sun visor so they wouldn't jingle when we moved around the steering wheel. I had a little pillow she'd brought for the armrest on the door, and the car was making ticking noises in the quiet.

"I have my sources," she said, smoothing her cheek along mine.

"How often do you *see* my brother?" I asked.

"Every single minute of every single day," she murmured. Then she asked if I could do something for her, and explained what it was. While she waited for me to register what she was talking about, she pointed out that one part of me really wanted to, anyway.

It rained for a full day and everything that could come crawling up out of a hole did: mosquitoes, sand flies, black flies, and leeches. Leo went to clean out his mess kit and found a spider in the bowl clenched like a fist. Nothing got put on without first having been shaken and reshaken. Most mornings something fell out and we all did the stamping dance before it got away.

We took to using smoke pots and head nets for the mosquitoes. But then we couldn't eat. On one side of the trail the ants were so small that the only kind of netting that could keep them out would have also kept out the air. Ticks clustered in the pinch points in our clothes. In one slit trench, what we thought was smoke one morning turned out to be a cloud of fleas. Little pelletlike bugs even got into the C-rations. Cockroaches ate the glue in the field manuals. Termites collapsed the CO's field table and cot. We were told to splash or make noise when crossing the creek, because the aborigines said it was happy with crocodiles. By that, we were told, they meant lousy with them.

"So *noise* scares crocodiles?" Leo wanted to know while they were telling us this.

"No, not really," the guy giving the briefing confessed.

Some guys were so bored and hot that they sat in the water anyway. "I'm hoping one comes by," Doubek, our radioman, said when we teased him about it. "Crocodile takes a piece of this ass, I got my ticket home."

Everywhere you went, if you asked somebody how it was going, he said, "Sweatin' it out, boy. Sweatin' it out." After a while that changed to, "Well, it won't be long now!" Some of the officers thought the guys who said that were serious.

We had reason to be a little shaky in terms of morale when it came to the big picture. All during basic and the long boat ride over, there'd been nothing but bad news from this part of the world: we were told at least we had Rabaul and its naval base, though none of us knew where Rabaul was, and by the time we found out it had surrendered. They showed us a newsreel called *Singapore the Impregnable* the week before the Japs took it. Darwin was bombed. Jap submarines shelled Newcastle. "Isn't that in *England*?" Leo asked.

"The other Newcastle," a swabbie told him. We were on deck mid-ocean, lounging near the garbage dump on the stern. "Well, tell the Aussies help is on the way," Leo said, picking through a crate of wrinkled oranges from the officers' mess.

Apparently things had looked so bleak that the Aussies figured they'd just *give up* the northern half of their country, planning to draw their defensive line just above their southern cities. MacArthur supposedly talked them out of it.

Part of his argument, we were told, was that the Japs didn't even have total control of New Guinea. Though it was only the terrain that left Moresby in our hands. No one could get over the mountains and through the jungle in any kind of fighting shape. All we had holding that side of the island was a Wirraway, two Catalina flying boats, and a Hudson minus its wing. When we came ashore some guys were working on the wing. They had one anti-aircraft gun. In the event of a Jap attack, they said, their orders were to hold out for at least thirty-six hours. When we exclaimed at that, they looked insulted and snapped that Rabaul had only held out for four. The news wasn't all bad, though: it turned out that if they depressed their anti-aircraft gun to its minimum elevation, they could also use it against landing craft.

When our barracks bags finally arrived they showed up slit open and looted. The CO said he wasn't going to report it because we'd only seem like a bunch of crybabies. I dropped my rifle into the creek and pulled it out full of sand and water, then spent two nights cleaning it while everybody else was sleeping. Leo found the hammock he'd shanghaied from the boat in the bottom of his barracks bag, and tried to rig it up to a tree and pulled the tree down. The tree was sixty feet high and as thick as he was. The rain forest was so dense it only fell a third of the way before it got hung up on the other trees. The whole thing was swarming with red ants. He said after he got out of the creek and started putting his clothes on again that the bites were like getting stuck with hat pins.

The aborigines came and went. When they wanted something, they did some work. They kept saying "Dehori." It was pretty much the main word of their language. It meant "Wait a while."

We got moved farther off the trail into denser jungle. Under the canopy, night fell so fast it was like you'd gone blind. Every so often some of us got to hike to the beach to pick up rations and lug water. Each trip we passed the same noncom from Graves Registration, just sitting around. That's how we knew there was a lot of fighting going on somewhere: he'd run out of forms.

Offshore, one of our old freighters had been bombed in half and waves were breaking over the bow, which was lying on its side. There was a wrecked Bren gun carrier at the low-tide mark, already half buried by the sand. There was no real harbor so the natives had to ferry all the supplies in on their outriggers, hollowed-out logs with two little poles connected to pontoons on both sides. Everything came in wet because the slightest weight shift capsized the hulls. The quartermaster running the show sat in a folding chair in shorts and a sleeveless sweater way too big for him. The last time we saw him he was trying to open a can of apricots with a bayonet. That night at sundown we hung around before heading back because they were supposed to be showing a movie on the side of the hospital tent, but the projector got bollixed up and the picture kept getting the jiggers.

My brother was in the Air Corps. He wasn't a pilot, but still.

"It's not like he's a pilot," I told Leo.

"Ever see their uniforms?" he asked me. "They got *wings* on their chest. They walk into a bar and the girls are all, 'What's it like to be up that high in the *air*?' What do they ask *us*? What's it like to dig a hole?"

He also got twice as many leaves as me. Every time he was reassigned, I heard about another one. And every last time, he went home.

"He's a homebody," Leo shrugged. "He misses his ma."

"You're not helping," I told him.

"I don't see that as my job," he answered.

I only signed up because Linda was in tears one day and wouldn't talk about it. "So your brother enlisted, huh?" her best friend said when I asked what was wrong.

"Linda's upset about *that*?" I asked her.

"I'm just saying I heard, is all," she said, offended.

I tried for the Air Corps too, but washed out on account of my eyes. Even though I hardly ever wear glasses.

The next day I signed up for the Army National Guard, just in case there was a chance to stay stateside. "I'm goin' away," I told Linda outside of school.

"I know. Everybody is," she said. Then she gave me a huge hug, pulled back to look at various parts of my face, and kissed me, right there in front of everybody.

That was at the beginning of the summer. I had a few weeks before I had to report, but for most of them her family was off at their house on the lake in Michigan.

"So have you brought up marriage?" my brother asked me the

night before he left. I was due to report two weeks after him. You couldn't talk to our mom about it. She was so upset the cat refused to come out of the cellar.

"Marriage?" I said.

"I didn't think so," he said.

"You think I should bring up marriage?" I asked him later that night, out on the porch. It wasn't so much a porch as two steps, but we called it the porch.

"That's all your mother needs to hear," he said.

Our father was trying to calm her down in the living room. That's how he spent most nights at that point. He wasn't happy about it. Whenever she stopped for a minute you could hear the radio.

"I don't think I'm ready to get married," I said. But the minute I said it I thought, *But I do want to be* buried *with her.*

Clouds came over and turned black and it rained for three straight weeks. "Where're all the *birds* going?" our medic asked right before it started. The trail washed out. They started calling the turnoff to the beach the Raging Rapids. The main forward-supply depot was a lake. The first downpour was like a train coming through and beat at our shoulders and bounced in huge sprays off our helmets. Four days into it our clothes started rotting. Whatever we carried in waterproof bags was soaked. Whatever we carried in watertight containers was mildewed. Tent supports collapsed, trenches filled in, bridges were washed away. The mud got into mess kits and stewpots and underwear and eyes. Guys walked through some areas by holding on to ropes tied tree-to-tree. Everywhere you put your boot you sank in. Every so often someone would pitch into a flooded slit trench. Shoes were gardens of green mold around the insoles. Field telephones corroded. Insulating material rotted. Batteries ruptured and leaked. Rifle cartridges rusted. Ration cans when opened already stank.

We had one day when it was cloudy and then thirty-six more

days of rain. Everybody was covered with rashes, sores, blisters, bubbles, boils, and bites. Guys got tropical ulcers, dysentery, pneumonia, and scrub typhus. The skin under married guys' rings got infected with fungus. Our toes turned black and looked fused. The medics called it jungle rot. The rule was that only a temperature over 103 moved you to the rear. The mud sucked the soles off our boots. Everybody just squatted or sat in the rain and shook. Guys with dysentery tried to stay on sloping ground.

On the thirty-seventh day we got the news we were moving up. Doubek, sitting up to his neck in his flooded slit trench, cheered.

"What do you think, we're going somewhere where it *isn't* raining?" Leo asked.

"Who knows when it comes to this screwy country?" Doubek said.

About sixty percent of us were still fit to walk somewhere. Everybody had given up on raingear a long time before. Nobody carried packs but a lot of guys stuffed C-ration cans into their hip pockets. On a little patch of high ground we dumped in a pile everything we wanted carried and the native in charge divided the loads among the bearers while we watched. When the rain was at its worst he sometimes cupped his hands around his mouth and chin and just drank.

Our jumping-off point was apparently six miles away. The sooner we got there, the more time we'd have to hunker down and get a hot meal before moving forward.

Most of the way we had to march alongside the trail, a knee-deep river of glue. Every so often you'd see guys working together to try and pull something loose from the middle of it, like it was flypaper.

By an hour in we were stumbling along blind, just trying to keep our bodies focused on the next step. Other companies with nothing to do came out of their bivouacs to watch us go up the line. By two hours in, those of us in the back of the column started passing guys up front who'd fallen out. We'd started at first light and by nighttime we still weren't there and a third of the unit was back behind us. For dinner they handed around boxes of cold canned hash and hard biscuits. When you took a spoon of hash the space in the tin filled with rainwater. Everybody slept where they came to a halt. The CO slogged around for a head count and figured we'd lost forty-five percent of those who'd been able to march. The next morning the major he reported to told him that we'd ended up with the best mark of the battalion.

There were a lot of units around us, packed into not much space. I recognized the PFC who'd been dishing out the mail. While we were waiting, more and more of our stragglers stumbled in. A trail in front of us ran up a hill and disappeared. From the other side, even over the rain, we could hear the occasional small-arms fire. People were cleaning their guns as best they could and hoarding clips. A couple guys threw up and it washed away as soon as it hit the ground. I upended my helmet for a drink. While it filled I threw in a few halazone tablets just to be safe. "Think there are germs in this water?" I asked Leo.

"About nine fucking million," he said. He did this thing with his hand like he was wringing it in the rain to dry it off. The mud was so fine it outlined his fingerprints. He cupped his hands and splashed himself. Cleaning his face seemed to make him feel better.

Twenty minutes, the CO announced. We were to be the first assault group. We didn't know where we were headed besides that hill, but our platoon leaders apparently did.

Everyone was sitting cross-legged with his rifle in his lap. The mess sergeant went around with a C-ration stack and guys took what they wanted for breakfast. I had a cold can of beans and sat there mashing them between my molars. Leo chewed on his thumb. We could see G for George, the battalion's heavy-weapons company, trying to find stable spots on the slope for their mortars. Whatever we picked up—our spoons, our bloc clips, everything covered in mud—got even greasier from all the cleaning oil.

We were National Guard recruits from Wisconsin. Our uniforms were rags, our boots sponges, our rifles waterlogged. We'd never been so tired in our lives. Everybody was sick. No one was talking. All of us were crouched over our weapons. I remembered how amazing it had been to think, when I first saw this place, that some of us were going to stay on it, dead.

"Biggest drunk of your lives, all of it on me, once we're off the line," the CO called out. He and the lieutenant shared a little waterproof map and kept looking up the slope and then back at the map.

"Drinks on the CO," the lieutenant agreed. Our staff sergeants went from group to group, checking weapons and whacking shoulders.

When I was a kid my dad was always off working for the CCC, mostly putting up power lines around the southern part of the state. He did some fence construction and tree planting, too. He was one of the oldest guys there. He worked forty hours a week for thirty dollars a month, with twenty-five of it sent home to the family. He had to wear a uniform and live in a camp during the week. He got up to a bugle at sunrise and only came home on weekends. He said the sign over the main gate read "We're Here to Lick Old Man Depression." "Lick him where?" he said when my mom quoted it to some friends they had over. She shushed him. After that he got a job building roads, but didn't get home much more often. And one night around Christmastime he came home late with frostbite on his feet. Just a little bit, but he was still mad about it. I was seven and my brother was nine. Our dad was sitting with his feet in a pan of water while we sat there watching him. Our mom was somewhere else, staying out of the way. There were Christmas carols on the radio. He looked at us from top to bottom and bottom to top like he hadn't found anything yet that looked the way it was supposed to.

"What's the matter?" my brother finally asked him. I was amazed he'd found the guts to do that.

My dad sat there and didn't say anything. We all listened to my mom empty the pan from under the icebox.

"What's the matter?" my brother asked again.

"What's the matter?" my dad said, exactly the same way. It made my brother tear up. One of the Christmas carols ended and another one started. Finally we couldn't stand how he was looking at us. My brother left first, but I hung around for a minute, to see if it was just my brother or the both of us he hated.

With five minutes left we were told we weren't going yet. There was some softening up that was supposed to have happened ahead of our attack, but all we could hear was the rain and the *kekekekek* sound that the geckos made. Word was that the mortar shells were still stuck somewhere down the trail and nobody knew what was up with our artillery. We weren't happy about waiting but were even less happy about going.

"So what are you going to do about this Linda-and-your-brother thing?" Leo said. "I mean if you're not dead."

My stomach was barely keeping itself together. I was taking deep breaths to help with that. "You know what I sometimes wonder?" I finally asked him. "How does she know so much about doing it? Where did that information come from?"

"Oh," Leo said, raising his hand, "I think *I* know."

While we sat there the CO told us we were headed for a foot track over the Owen Stanley Range through the Gap. This range was one of the steepest in the world and divided the island in half. The staff sergeants told us to dump anything nonessential because whatever we took was going to be on our backs the whole way. Doubek inverted his pack and it turned out he'd collected twenty-eight cans of sliced peaches. He figured he could carry six and started trying to eat the rest right there. "One thing the American Army's never going to run out of," Leo said, watching him. "Canned fruit."

We finally got the go-ahead even though the rain hadn't let up and there'd been no artillery. "What happened to the softening up, sir?" Leo asked the CO as he passed our position.

"The thinking now is that we're going to take 'em by surprise," the CO called back. He got everybody moving and we all climbed a preliminary hill, slipping and sliding. No one could keep his head up without losing his footing.

At the top everyone was already beat, but on the other side of a little swale we could see our path climbing up into the clouds. The occasional scout was slithering down the slope in our direction. Where the trail went was cut off by the same clouds that were raining all over us.

It took us about an hour to get organized at the base and ready to climb. Three porters were coming along to hump the extra ammunition until we came under fire. The CO let us rest for a half an hour and then got us going again. The slopes kept sliding out from under us and the porters got a bang over how bad we were at keeping our feet. In places where the mud was covered with leaves a guy would manage maybe one step before falling and taking the next three guys down with him. "Heads up" meant "Catch whoever's sliding down at you." We took breaks on our hands and knees with water streaming over our wrists.

I started throwing up and tried to do it on the side of the trail. We passed abandoned emplacements so well camouflaged that a couple guys fell into them. A little farther up was a switchback and a curtain of jungle that came down like a wall. We came across some sulfa packs and morphine needles scattered in the mud. A boot.

From below Leo tugged at my pant leg. "Hang back," he said quietly. I stepped a foot and hand off the trail and rested, chest heaving, and let a couple guys go by. Leo stopped behind me.

"How far's this fucking thing go on?" Doubek panted, climbing past. He lifted his head to see and the jungle up above us went nuts. The wall of leaves jittered and blurred and the noise of all the fire at once was a pandemonium.

Doubek's shirt came alive from the inside and he spread-eagled out past me and pinwheeled down the slope, crashing through the undergrowth. His helmet sailed off in another direction. We all gripped the mud, hugging the slope. Leaves, sticks, bark, and splinters flew and spun, popping from trees. The noise sucked the air out of us. It stopped my ability to think. I was under a little lip of overhang with Leo below me. My boots kicked through a mat of stems. Thorns tore at my cheek. I was clawing and looking to burrow. Some guys were firing back but I wasn't one of them. The firing went on and then it stopped in front of us and after a minute you could hear the CO screaming to cease fire.

When the last of our guys did, the sound of the rain came back. And some whimpering and cursing. The CO and one of the staff sergeants shouted orders. Leo had to crawl up and over me before I could bring myself to move. He thought I was dead.

"How is he?" the CO called up to him.

"Untouched," Leo called back down.

"What about the other guys?" the CO wanted to know. I could see him twenty feet below us, one shoulder dug in, his outer arm cradling his carbine. Every so often he had to stick a heel back in the mud to keep from sliding. He meant the guys ahead of me. There'd been about six of them.

Leo told him none of them was calling for a medic, which he took to be a bad sign.

We could hear the clatter of new clips being fed into guns up above us.

"Should we fall back, sir? Sir?" Leo called.

"Form on me! Form on me!" a sergeant called out below.

"Fall *back*?" the CO called. "What's the problem? We ran into Japs?" I think he thought he was funny.

We were flattened against the muck, the mud and rainwater pouring straight through our clothes.

"Keep an eye out, you two," the CO called. Then he called a meeting on the slope right below us: him and the lieutenant and a couple of the staff sergeants. He asked for suggestions. Nobody had any. Could we spread out? one of them finally asked. Could we provide any covering fire? Was there any room anywhere to maneuver?

"This is depressing," Leo finally said to me, after they'd all gone quiet.

"That might be the one trouble spot, though," we heard the CO venture to guess. "It could be that we only have to get past that."

"You all right?" Leo asked me. His nose was next to mine.

"You guys *watchin'*?" the CO called.

We both looked up at the switchback. Even in the rain the mists were creeping around the bottoms of the trees. We still hadn't seen a Jap.

"They're not going to let us go back down, are they?" I asked Leo. I'd never been so cold in my life and started shivering the minute the shooting stopped. I hadn't meant to be crying but I was.

"Think of it this way," Leo said. "Linda'll be taken care of."

"*Fuck* this place," I told him.

"Yeah," he told me back.

The third or fourth night we all drove around in Linda's brother's car, I'd walked over to her house but her mom said she was still getting dressed. I was welcome to wait, she told me, there in the parlor or out back with Glenn. Glenn was the older brother. Glenn it turned out was in the shed. "How're you doin'," I said to him.

"What's it *look* like I'm doing?" he said back.

Stuff like that happened every single place I went. "Marble mouth," my dad would say to my mom at the dinner table when I asked a question. "I understood him perfectly," she sometimes said, but then he'd be mad at *her* the rest of the night.

"Leave those alone," Glenn said.

I didn't see what he was talking about. There wasn't a lot of light in the shed. "You been *trapping*?" I asked when my eyes adjusted.

"Those are cat skins," he said. "I'm drying cat skins."

"Your brother's drying cat skins," I told Linda the first night we had the car to ourselves.

"What are you *talking* about?" she said. And I decided it was the last time I'd ever bring up something that would make her move her hand away.

"What do you think, *your* brother's Mister Normal?" she asked.

She told me I could ride in front with Glenn and we'd gotten a block from her house when she asked what my brother was up to. "Let's go get him," she said, before I answered.

"Yeah, let's go get the brother," Glenn said.

When we got to my house my brother was already sitting on the front steps. "Well, this is a surprise," he said, and got in the back with Linda.

"Eyes front, buddy," Glenn said when I turned to look back at them. The whole way to the quarry, if I started to turn around he jiggled the steering wheel and we all rocked and swayed. Linda told him to stop and he told her it wasn't him, it was me, so she told *me* to sit still.

"I want to look at you," I said.

"That's sweet," my brother said.

"It *is*," Linda told him.

When we got to the quarry, she said she had to pee.

"I better go with you," my brother told her. "It's pretty dark out there."

"No, thank you," she said. "I can handle this myself."

She was gone a long time. I sat in the car with my brother and Glenn and thought of her poking around in the dark, feeling for a safe place.

Glenn had his arm along the top of the seat so his fingers were at my shoulder. My brother whistled to himself the same two notes that went up and down, up and down.

"What I wouldn't give to be a little flower right now," Glenn said.

"Two little flowers," my brother said.

"I should go look for her," I told them.

They both snorted. "She knows this place better than we do," Glenn said.

"Or at least as well," my brother told him.

I tried a few sentences in my head and then said, "So you guys have been here before."

There was a pause like they were deciding who was going to answer.

"We been here before," my brother confirmed.

Linda finally appeared out of the dark, wet-eyed, and opened the door and climbed in.

"You okay?" I said.

"Absolutely," she said.

"Shouldn't *I* be in the back with you?" I asked.

"Yeah, absolutely. *Move*, you," she said to my brother.

"Absolutely," my brother said.

"Absolutely," Glenn said.

In the light when the car door opened again I could see Linda flinch.

"We gotta give these two some time alone," my brother told Glenn.

"Absolutely," Glenn said.

"But first I have to show you something," my brother said, meaning me.

"Now?" I asked him. I had one foot in the backseat.

"Don't go now," Linda said. She had her back to her door and was holding out some fingers to me.

"C'mon, chief, this'll only take a minute," my brother said. "I need to *ask* you something."

"This doesn't feel right," I said.

"It'll feel right once you're back," my brother said. "Five minutes. Then we'll clear out and it's all you and her."

Linda had lowered her arm and was looking out the back.

"*Five minutes*," my brother repeated.

I got out. He led me down a trail. I looked over my shoulder before we went around some rocks and saw Glenn opening his door.

It wasn't five minutes. It was more like twenty. What my brother wanted to ask was if I thought our dad was getting worse. If I thought he was drinking again. "I didn't know he was drinking in the first place," I told him. "You dragged me out here to tell me that?"

Linda was alone in the car when we got back. "Where's Glenn?" I asked.

"I don't know," she said.

"How long have you been here by yourself?" I asked.

"He just left," she said.

"I'll go hunt him down," my brother said. "You two behave while I'm gone."

I got in next to Linda but her face was wet and she didn't shove over so half of me was still hanging out the open door. I braced myself with a foot in the dirt. "What's the matter?" I asked. "What happened?"

She nodded and smiled and wiped her eyes and said she was okay, that sometimes she got happy and sad at the same time. I was going to ask her again what happened but she scooched over and patted the seat where she'd just been and told me to shut the door. She brought her face closer and wiped her mouth with her finger-tips and said, "Do something for me. Show me how much you want to kiss me."

"What are you *sad* about?" I asked her later.

"If I thought you really wanted to know, I'd tell you," she finally whispered. And we lay there for a little while, me holding on to her, her holding on to me.

"See what I mean?" she finally said.

"Why do you think Linda was crying tonight?" I asked my brother after they dropped us off. He and Glenn had given us a half hour, then hopped in the front seat and driven off without even asking us if we were ready.

It looked like the question bothered him and I had to ask him again before he answered me. "I think she feels lucky to be with you," he said.

"I don't think that's it," I told him.

"Don't you feel lucky to be with her?" he asked.

I do, I thought that night, lying there in bed. *I do,* I thought, every miserable night on the troop ship, and in the slit trenches, and listening to Leo talking to himself as soon as he thought I'd fallen asleep.

We waited the rest of the afternoon for the artillery support. I spent an hour watching rainwater pour off vines and creepers alongside the trail. In the rain we only knew the sun had gone down when we realized we couldn't make out each other's expressions. Word came up the line to dig in, so Leo slid back below me to his old spot and started going at it with his entrenching tool. He was always the first man in the company to finish his hole. He had it easier than I did because he was shaking less and was more off to the side. With all the water coming down the trail it was like rerouting a waterfall. By the time I was finished I was sheltered enough from the main flow that it missed my head and shoulders.

The rain started to let up and every so often the clouds and mist cleared and I could see black peaks high above us. I'd shake and then settle down, shake and settle back down.

Pretty soon it would be dark. Anything we tried to do besides sit tight would be blind and probably of no use. I would be the perimeter. Maybe Leo would be too. When they came down the trail they'd be coming over us first.

We'd all heard the stories of how quiet they could be, creeping through the timber, easing over rocks drenched in rain. They had special rubber boots with separate big toes. They had night-camouflaged bayonets with serrated top edges.

They could see where we couldn't. Once they were on top of me they'd see bodies all the way down the hillside. Guys who were all mud, bearded to the eyes. Guys who could barely move. Guys who hadn't asked to be there but if left alive the next day would get to their feet and follow the artillery in and try to kill as many Japs as they came across. Guys who'd think, *The way they are, they deserve it.* Like the Japs who'd crouch over Leo and me. When they rolled us over they'd be shocked to see what we'd come to. Shocked to see what they'd done. Shocked to feel the ugliness we felt every single day, even with those—especially with those—we cherished the most.

Your Fate Hurtles Down at You

We call ourselves *die Harschblödeln:* the Frozen Idiots. There are four of us who've volunteered to spend the coldest winter in recent memory in a little hut perched on a wind-blasted slope of the Weissfluhjoch 3,500 meters above Davos. We're doing research. The hut, we like to say, is naturally refrigerated from the outside and a good starting point for all sorts of adventures, nearly all of them lethal.

It's been seven years since the federal government in Berne appointed its commission to develop a study program for avalanche defense measures. Five sites were established in the high Alps, and as Bader likes to say, we drew the short straw. Bader, Bucher, Haefeli, and I wrap ourselves in blanket layers and spend hours at a time given over to our tasks. The cold has already caused Haefeli to report kidney complaints.

He's our unofficial leader. They found him working on a dam-building project in Spain, the commission having concluded correctly that his groundbreaking work on soil mechanics would translate usefully into this new field of endeavor. Bucher's an engineer who inherited his interest in snow and ice from his father, a meteorologist who in 1909 led the second expedition across Greenland. Bader was Professor Niggli's star pupil, so he's our resident crystallographer. And I'm considered the touchingly passionate amateur and porter, having charmed my way into the group through the adroit use of my mother's journals.

It might be 1939 but this high up we have no heat and only kerosene lanterns for light. Our facilities are not good. Our budget is laughable. We're engaged in a kind of research for which there are few precedents. But as Bader also likes to say, a spirit of discovery and a saving capacity for brandy in the early afternoon drives us on.

We encounter more than our share of mockery down in Davos, since your average burgher is only somewhat impressed by the notion of the complexities of snow. But together we're now approaching the completion of a monumental work of three years: our *Snow and Its Metamorphism,* with its sections on crystallography, snow mechanics, and variations in snow cover. My mother has written that the instant it appears, she must have a copy. I've told her I'll deliver it myself.

Like all pioneers we've endured our share of embarrassment. Bader for a time insisted on measuring the hardness of any snowpack by firing a revolver into it, and his method was discredited only after we'd wasted an afternoon hunting for his test rounds in the snow. And on All Hallows' Eve we shoveled the accumulation from our roof and started an avalanche that all the way down in Davos destroyed the church on the outskirts of town.

I'm hardly alone in being excessively invested in our success. At the age of eighteen Haefeli lost his father in what he calls a scale 5 avalanche. As to be distinguished from, say, a scale 1 or 2 type, which obliterates the odd house each winter but otherwise goes unnoticed.

His scale 5 was an airborne avalanche in Glärnisch that dropped down the steeper slopes above his town with its blast clouds mushrooming out on both sides. His father had sent him to check their rabbit traps on a higher, forested slope and had stayed behind to start the cooking pot. The avalanche dropped two thousand vertical meters in under a mile and crossed the valley floor with such velocity that it exploded upward two hundred feet on the opposite hillside, uprooting spruces and alders there with such force that they pinwheeled through the air. The ensuing snow cloud obscured the sun. It took ten minutes to settle while Haefeli skied frantically down into the debris. Throughout the next days' search for survivors, there were still atmospheric effects from the amount of snow concussed into the upper atmosphere.

The rescuers found that even concrete-reinforced buildings had been pile-driven flat. When he finally located a neighbor's three-story stone house, he mistook it for a terrazzo floor.

Fifty-two homes were gone. Seventeen people were dug out of a meeting house the following spring, huddled together in a circle facing inward. Three hundred meters from the path of the snow, the air blast had blown the cupola off a convent tower.

But when it came to a good night's sleep I had my own problems.

In my childhood it was general practice for Swiss schools around the Christmas holidays to sponsor Sport Week, during which we all hiked to mountain huts to ski. My brother Willi and I were nothing but agony for our harried teachers every step up the mountains and back. He was a devotee of whanging the rope tows once the class hit an especially steep and slippery part of the hillside. I did creative things with graupel or whatever other sorts of ice pellets I could collect from under roof eaves or along creek beds.

We were both in secondary school, and sixteen. I'd selected the science stream and was groping my way into physics and chemistry, while he'd chosen the literary life and went about fracturing Latin and Greek. Even this surprised me: when had he become interested in Latin and Greek? But given the kind of brothers we were, the question never arose.

I claimed to be interested in university; he didn't. Our father, to whom such things mattered, called us his happy imbeciles, took pride in our skiing, and liked to say with a kind of amiability during family meals that we could do what we pleased as long as it reflected well on him.

He styled himself an Alpine guide, though considering how he dressed when in town, he might as well have been the village mayor, complete with watch fob and homburg. He always spoke as though a stroke of fate had left him in the business of helping Englishmen scale ice cliffs, and claimed to be content only at altitudes over 3,000 meters, but we knew him to be unhappy even there. The sole thing that seemed to please him were his homemade medicines. Willi considered him reproachful but carried on with whatever he wished, secure in our mother's support. I followed his moods minutely, even as disinterest emanated from him like a vapor. We had one elder sister who found all of this distasteful and whose response was to do her chores but otherwise keep to her room, awaiting romances that arrived every few months via subscription.

Willi's self-absorption left him impatient with experts. On our summer trek on the Eiger glacier the year before, we'd been matched for International Brotherhood Week with a hiking group from Chamonix. They spoke no German and we spoke no French, so only the teachers could converse. At one point the French teacher brought the group to a halt by cautioning us that any noise where we stood could topple the ice seracs looming above us.

Willi and I had been on glaciers since we were eight. While everyone watched, he scaled the most dangerous-looking of the seracs and, having established his balance at the top, shouted loud enough to have brought down the Eiger's north face. "What's French for 'You don't know what you're talking about'?" he called to our teacher as he climbed back down.

We were to base our day around one of the ski huts above Kleine Scheidegg. The village itself, on a high pass, consists of three hotels for skiers and climbers and the train station and some maintenance buildings serving the Jungfraubahn, but our group managed to lose one of our classmates there anyway—a boy from the remote highlands where a cowherd might spend the entire summer in a hut, with his cows and family separated only by a waist-high divider—and by the time he was located we were already an hour behind schedule. We were led by one of the schoolmistresses who held a ski instructor's certificate and her assistant, a twenty-year-old engineering student named Jenny. They had as their responsibility fourteen boys and ten girls.

In summer, the ski run to which we were headed involved a steep climb along the edge of a dark forest broken by occasional sunlit clearings, before the trees thinned out and there were meadows where miniature butterflies wavered on willowherbs and moss campion. Immediately above sheep and goats found their upland pastures. Above that were only rocks and the occasional ibex. An escarpment above the rocks was ideal for wind-sheltered forts. We'd discovered it on our ninth birthday. Willi said it was one of those rare places where nothing could be grown or sold, that the world had produced exclusively for someone's happiness. In winter storms the wind piled snow onto it, the cornices overhanging the mountain's flanks below. And the night before our Sport Week outing brought strong westerly winds and a heavy accumulation on the eastern slopes. Avalanche warning bulletins had been sent to the hotels an hour after our departure.

We spread ourselves out around the bowl of the main slope. Some of us had climbed in chaps for greater waterproofing and were still shedding them and checking our bindings when our schoolmistress led the others down into the bowl. The postmaster's daughter, Ruth Lindner, of whom Willi and I both retained fantasies, waited behind with us while we horsed about, setting her hands atop her poles in a counterfeit of patience. She had red hair and pale smooth skin and a habit, when laughing with us, of lowering her eyes to our mouths, and this we found impossibly stirring.

The skiers who'd set off were already slaloming a hundred yards below. We'd been taught from the cradle that however much we thought we knew, in winter there were always places where our ignorance and bad luck could destroy us. A heavy new snowmass above and an unstable bowl below: in this sort of circumstance our father would have cautioned us, if uncertain, to back away.

"Race you," I said.

"*Race* me?" Willi answered. And he nosed his ski tips out over the bowl edge.

"See if you can stay on your feet," I teased him from above, flumphing my uphill ski down into a drift.

There was a deep cutting sound, like shears tearing through heavy fabric. The snowfield split all the way across the bowl, and the entire slab, half a kilometer across, broke free, taking Willi with it. He was enveloped immediately. Ruth shrieked. I helped her pole herself farther back. The tons of snow roaring down caught the skiers below and carried them away in seconds. One little girl managed to remain upright on a cascading wave but then she too was upended and buried, the clouds of snowdust obscuring everything else.

Guides climbing up from the hotels spread the alarm and already had the rescue under way when Ruth and I reached the debris field. The digging went on for thirty-six hours and fifteen of our classmates, including Willi and the schoolmistress, were uncovered alive. The young assistant Jenny and seven others were dug out as corpses. Two were still missing when the last of their family members stopped digging three weeks later.

My brother had been fifteen feet deep at the very back edge of the run-out. They found him with the sounding rod used for locating the road after heavy snowfalls. He'd managed to get his arm over his face and survived because of the resulting air pocket. A shattered ski tip near the surface had aided in his location. One of the rescuers who dug him out kept using the old saying "Such a terrible child!" for the difficulties they were encountering with the shocking density of the snowmass once it had packed in on itself. Not even sure if he was down there, we called for Willi to not lose heart. Ruth dug beside me and I was taken aback by the grandeur of her panic and misery. "*Help* us!" she cried at one point, as if I weren't digging as furiously as the rest.

He was under the snow for two hours. When his face was finally cleared, it was blue and he was unconscious but the guides revived him with a breathing tube even as he still lay trapped. And when someone covered his face with a hat to keep the snow from falling into his mouth and eyes, he shouted for it to be taken away, that he wanted air and light.

He was hurried home on a litter and spent the next two days recovering. I fed him oxtail soup, his favorite. His injuries seemed slight. He asked about Ruth. He answered our questions about how he felt but related nothing of the experience. When we spoke in private he peered at me strangely and looked away. On the third night, when I put out the lamp, he seemed suddenly upset and asked not to be left alone. "You're not alone," I said. "I'm right here." He cried out for our mother and began a horrible rattling in his throat, at which he clawed, and I flew down the stairs to get her. By the time we returned he was dead.

The doctor called in another doctor, who called in a third. Each tramped slush through our house and drank coffee while they hypothesized and my mother trailed from room to room in their wake, tidying and weeping until she could barely stand. Their final opinion was contentious but two favored delayed shock as the cause of death. The third held forth on the keys to survival in such a situation, the most important being the moral and physical strength of the victim. He was thrown bodily out of the house by my father.

The inquiry into the tragedy held that the group leaders—the schoolmistress and her dead assistant—were blameless, but the parents of the children swept away decided otherwise, and within a year the miserable and ostracized schoolmistress was forced to resign her post.

How could our mother have survived such a thing? She had always seemed to carry within herself some quality of calm against which adverse circumstances contended in vain, but in this case she couldn't purge her rage at the selfishness of those whose blitheness had put the less foolhardy at risk. She received little support from my father, who refused to assign blame, so she took to calling our home "our miserable little kingdom," and at the dinner table mounting what questions she could as if blank with fatigue.

By May, scraps from the two missing children poked through the spring melt like budding plants, and in the course of a day or two a glove, a scarf, and a ski pole turned up. Renewed digging recovered one of the little girls, her body face-down, her arms extended downhill, her back broken and her legs splayed up and over it.

Our mother talked to everyone she considered knowledgeable about the nature of what had happened, and why. From as early as we could remember, she'd always gathered information of one kind or another. I'd never known anyone with a more hospitable mind. My sister often complained that no one could spend any time in our mother's company without learning something. She was the sort of woman who recorded items of interest in a journal kept in her bedroom, and she joked to our father when teased about it that it represented a store of observations that would someday be more systematically confirmed as scientific research. Why did one snowfall of a given depth produce avalanches when another did not? Why was the period of maximum danger those few hours immediately following the storm? Why might any number of people cross a slope in safety only to have another member of their party set the disaster in motion? She remembered from childhood a horrible avalanche in her grandmother's village: a bridge and four houses had been destroyed and a nine-year-old boy entombed in his bed, still clutching his cherished stuffed horse.

She spent more time with me as her preoccupation intensified. There was no one else. Her daughter had grown into a long, thin adult with a glum capacity for overwork and no interest in the business of the world. We had few visitors, but if one overstayed his welcome my sister would twist her hair and wonder audibly, as if interrogating herself, "Why doesn't he leave? Why doesn't he *leave*?"

Early one morning I found my mother on my bed. When she

saw I was awake, she remarked that Willi's shoulders had been so broad that it made him appear shorter than he was. "And mine, too," I said. "And yours, too," she smiled. Somewhere far away a dog was barking as if beside itself with alarm.

I told her I thought I might have started the avalanche. She said, "You didn't start the avalanche." I told her I might have, though I hadn't yet explained how. She reminded me of the farmers' old saying that *they* didn't make the hay, that the sun made the hay.

"I think *I* made the avalanche," she finally suggested. When I asked what she was talking about, she wondered if I remembered the Oberlanders' tale of the cowherd whose mother thought he'd gone astray and, enraged by having been offered only spoiled milk by his new wife, called on ice from the mountain above to come bury them both and all of their cows.

How old was I then? Seventeen. But even someone that young can be shocked by his own paralysis in the face of need. My mother sat on my bed picking her heart to pieces and I suffered at the spectacle and accepted her caresses and wept along with her and fell back asleep comforted, never offering my own account of what might have happened, whether or not it would have helped. The subject was dropped. And that morning more than anything else is what's driven me to avalanche research.

Bucher's a good Christian but even he gave up the long ski down to services after a few weeks, and instead we spend our Sabbaths admiring the early-morning calm of the mountains. The sun peeps over the sentinel peaks behind us and the entire snow-covered world becomes a radiance thrown back at the sky. The only sounds are those we make. On our trips to Davos for supplies, Bader and I for a few months held a mock competition for the affections of an Alsatian widow, who negotiated the burden of her sexual magnetism with an appealing modesty. Then, in February, I slipped on an ice sheet outside a bakery and bounced down two flights of steps. "So much for the surviving Eckel brother," Ruth Lindner said in response from across the street.

What was she doing in Davos? She'd trained as a teacher and been reassigned to a new school district. How did she like teaching? She hoped the change of scene would help. What did her parents make of the move? They'd been against it, but lately she'd felt home was more like prison. We arranged to meet for coffee the following weekend, and back at the hut the group made much of my announcement of my withdrawal from the Alsatian sweepstakes.

I'd lost track of Ruth after Willi's memorial service. My last words to her had been "I blame myself," and her response had been, "I blame everyone." Then she'd gone on holiday to her maternal grandparents' farm near Merligen. That visit had extended itself, and my two letters to that address were returned unopened. When I'd pressed her father for an explanation, he said that the postmaster must have found them undeliverable. When I'd protested that he was the postmaster, he lost his temper. My parents had been no more help. Her few friends claimed to be equally mystified.

Over coffee she asked how I was finding Davos and then moved on to Willi: his poor grades and how he liked to present himself as indisposed to exertion indoors, and how outside he had no time for anything except his skis. She became misty-eyed. She asked if he'd ever told me that the high summits were like giants at their windows looking down at us.

"No," I said. She wore a beeswax-and-aloe mixture on her lips to protect them, and the effect was like a ceramic glaze I longed to test with my finger.

"He told me that," she said, pleased.

She asked if I remembered a winter camping trip some of our classmates had taken a month before the Sport Week outing. I told her I remembered it better than she imagined. I'd worked up the courage to ask if she was going and she'd said no, so I'd dropped out. Later I discovered that both she and Willi had gone.

"Had that always been the plan?" I wanted to know, pained even after all these years.

"I need you to listen," she told me.

"What do you suppose I'm doing?" I answered.

"This is not easy for me," she went on to say.

"Does it seem so for me?" I asked.

She told me that the first afternoon they'd pitched camp in a little squall of butterflies blown above the snowline by an updraft. That night a full moon had risen above their tents and their breath vapor had frozen onto the canvas above them. It had broken off in a sheet when in the predawn stillness she'd lifted the flap to slip into Willi's tent.

"I don't need to hear this," I told her. But it was as if I'd claimed I did. She said that once they'd shed their clothes and embraced inside his sleeping sack, she'd felt the way she had years earlier during an electrical storm when her hair had lifted itself into the air and her hands, holding a rake, had sung like a kettle with the discharge.

We sat across from each other and our coffees. Why does anyone choose one brother and not another? I wanted to ask.

"You have his facial expressions," she said instead.

"Twins are like that," I answered.

"He told your mother when he got back," she added, addressing my silence. That part of the story seemed to affect her most of all.

"Told her what?" I asked.

"That we were in love," she said.

A truck outside the window ground its gears. "And you got pregnant," I suggested.

"And I got pregnant," she said. She seemed to be considering our hands.

Carousers clattering skis and poles came and went. "Did my mother find out?" I wanted to know.

"I assume she guessed," Ruth said.

"I have to get back," I told her.

At the door, while I bundled against the weather, she said she was sorry, and had so much more to tell me. She asked if I would see her again. When at first I didn't respond, she removed one of my mittens and placed my hand against her cheek. But she already knew what I wanted. She already knew what I felt. It was as if there'd never been any point in pretending otherwise.

The position in which she left me brought to mind the subject that Haefeli insists should be absorbing our every waking moment. The American W. A. Bentley was the first to have photographed snow crystals, having recorded over six thousand different forms before conceding that he'd only scratched the surface, given the number of types that must exist. Such crystals are formed when water vapor in the cooling air condenses onto particulate matter in the atmosphere and then freezes, the ice particles growing as more vapor attaches itself in a process called sublimation: that small miracle, Bader reminds us, as we dig cores, in which a substance transforms itself from gas to solid without having passed through its liquid state. The variations in design are as infinite as the conditions that govern the crystals' development, but each as it reaches the ground is subject to a change of environment: from having been a separate entity, it becomes a minute part of the mass and begins to undergo a series of changes in its nature, all of which will reflect on the stability of the area of which it's a part. When new snow alights, its crystals interlock by means of their fine branches and spikes, but the strength of this cohesion is undermined by destructive metamorphism as the branches and spikes regress under the pressure of rising temperatures or the snow's weight. It was Professor Paulcke of Innsbruck who first observed a particular kind of degraded crystal that because of its shape constituted a noncohesive mass in the snow cover: such crystals were excessively fragile and ran like loose pebbles; they formed, wherever they were found, a hugely unstable base for the other layers above. He called them "depth hoar" or "swim-snow." My mother recorded the same phenomenon in her journals and called it "sugar snow" because it refused to bond even when squeezed tightly in the hand. Haefeli loved the term. A stratum of such crystals is like a layer of ball bearings under the tons of more recently fallen snow on a slope, requiring only the slightest jar to set the mass in motion.

We spend the afternoon, after my coffee with Ruth, cutting blocks of snow out of various slopes and tapping the tops to test the frequency of layer fracture and collapse. Bader wears an out-sized dinner jacket over his cardigan, claiming it's the only material he's discovered to which snow doesn't cling. He looks as young as I do, in his beardlessness reminding everyone of a cleric or a shepherd. Before Professor Niggli found him, he'd lived a life circumscribed by the peaks at either end of his valley.

I'm teased for being love-struck because of my silence, then teased further for failing to react. But throughout the day, my heart roams in and out of my chest as though tethered to its own misery. Of course my mother knew—that was the source of her Oberlander remark—and in my newly reconfigured map of that time, everyone knew everything, except Willi's endlessly oblivious brother. Had she had the baby? Of course, but how could I have left without asking if she'd had the baby?

"I need to go back down," I finally told Haefeli as we hiked back from a northeastern ice wall. We'd been sampling under a nine-meter cornice.

"Not right now you don't," he answered.

"Now he's pouting," Bucher informed the group, half an hour later.

"What are you going to settle today?" Haefeli wants to know once we're all back in the hut for the night. The sun's a vermilion line along the western ridge. "Are you going to go down there and profess your undying love? Haul her back up here for your wedding night?"

He's working by lantern light on what he calls a penetrometer: a pointed steel tube a meter long for measuring the firmness of strata. He has the two virtues perhaps most important to such a place as this: presence of mind and affability. In his own casual way he combines for us the functions of priest, guide, and hotelier. Once, during a rockfall in a narrow gully, he stepped between me and a head-sized stone that appeared out of the snowcloud, and deflected it with the handle of his shovel much like a cricketer bats a ball.

"Go if you have to," he finally tells me later that night, in exasperation, into the frigid darkness above our hammocks and blankets. "Go. Go. Go. God knows we don't need you up here."

Of course it occurs to me only as I finally reach Davos the next morning that she's in school and will be for most of the day. I have little money to spare but waste some anyway on coffee and a sweet roll to get in out of the cold. The lunch rush comes and goes. My nose to the window, I man the chair farthest from the door with the unsettled vacancy of an old dog left home alone.

At the awaited hour I'm outside her school, the dismissal bell ringing, and shouting and happy children stream past, looking no different than we were. "What are you doing here?" she wants to know. Somehow she's come out another door and come up to me from behind.

"So you had the baby?" I ask.

"This is my supervisor, Frau Döring," she tells me.

Frau Döring and I exchange greetings, and she appears to be hoping that whatever I'd just asked will be repeated.

"This is the brother of my late fiancée," Ruth informs her. It's as if the world's been filled with unexpectedly painful things.

Once back at the coffee shop she asks, "Why do you think you're so in love with me? What is it that you think you love?"

"You never answered about the baby," I tell her.

She looks at me, gauging my reaction, and makes a let's-get-on-with-it face.

"You gave it to an orphanage," I tell her. "Some convent or other. The Sisters of Perpetual Help."

She continues to consider me. I'm not weeping, but I might as well be.

"What is it you want?" she finally asks. "You want me to say that you're as nice a boy as Willi?" After a silence she adds, "I always thought of you as the sort of boy who pinned the periodic table over his bed, instead of pictures of girls from magazines."

An older couple at an adjacent table has grown quiet, eavesdropping.

"I thought about you more than Willi did," I finally tell her. "That camping trip when you were *with* him, I thought about you more than he did."

It angers her, and that's at least something between us.

The eavesdropping couple resumes its conversation.

She talks a little about her work. She remarks how her loneliness has been exacerbated by her fondness for children. At least here she slept better, though. Maybe that's what relocation was: a balm for the faint-hearted.

"You said you had more to tell me," I remind her.

She puts a hand around my coffee cup. "I've always liked you," she says. "I'll put the question to you. Do *you* think you were Willi's equal?"

She's sympathetic and tender and would sleep with me if she weren't sure it would lead to further tediousness. She'd like to help but she's also sure of the justice of this injustice, just as the English believe the poor to be poor and the rich rich because God has decreed it so.

"You're not really still unable to get over this, are you?" she asks.

"What we're doing on the mountain is more important than any of this," I tell her, and she's relieved to hear it.

"How's your mother?" she wants to know.

Outside she turns and steps close and presses her mouth to my cheek and then lets it drift across my lips. "There's no reason for us to stay angry with one another," she says, as though confiding this to my mouth. The couple from the adjacent table emerges, fixing their collars and hats, and excuse themselves to get by.

My mother and I had both dealt with our devastation in the months after Willi's death by devoting our free time to the library at Lauterbrunnen. We seemed to have arrived at this attempted solution independently. We went mostly after chores on Saturdays. Sometimes I'd take the bus and discover, having arrived, that my father had driven my mother in the car. Sometimes I'd search for a book in the card catalog and discover that she'd already signed it out and was leafing through it on the other side of the reading room. There was very little written, then, about the properties of snow, and we were continually driven back to geographies and histories of the high Alps, there to glean what we could. We encountered Strabo's accounts of passes subject to the collapse of whole snow-mountains above them that swept his companions into abysmal chasms: passes he described as "places beyond remedy." We found Polybius's account of Hannibal's having had to witness the eruption of a slope that took with it his entire vanguard. Saint Bernard's of having stepped out of a chapel to relieve himself when his fellow pilgrims inside were scoured away by a roaring river of snow, and his prayer, having been saved downslope in the branches of a pine, that the Lord restore him to his brethren so he might instruct them not to venture into this place of torment. Early one rain-swept evening my mother set before me a memoir in which one of Napoleon's generals related an anecdote of a drummer boy swept into a gorge who drummed for several days in the hope of attracting rescue before he finally fell silent. The librarians, intrigued by our industry and single-mindedness, helped out with sources. We read how in ancient days avalanches were so omnipotent and incontestable that they were understood to be diabolic weapons of the powers of darkness. How else to explain an entire village smashed flat while a china cupboard with all its contents remained undamaged? A single pine left upright on the roof of a pastor's house, as if it had grown there? A house so shattered that one of the children had been found in a meadow three miles away, tucked up into her bed as if by human hands? Each of these stories caused my mother pain. Each of them drove us on.

If one house was spared and others destroyed, it was because that house had been favored by the spirits. When I first came across that claim, I closed the book and circled the library before returning to it. And those spirits rode astride such calamities as they thundered down the slope. Erstfeld's town history recorded a spinster blown from her house who, still in her rocking chair, negotiated a wave of snow into the center of her village, and who, as she was giving thanks to Providence for her life, was carried to a clearing by her enraged neighbors, surrounded by a pyre, and burned alive.

How was my mother? I answered Ruth's question before I left to return to my hut mates. My mother wasn't doing so well. My mother, like everyone else in this drama, seemed determined to blame herself. My mother used to believe that we all could call the thunder down onto anyone's head whenever we wanted.

"You're just like Willi," Ruth said in response, after a moment. And it was the first time that I saw something in her look like the admiration he must have enjoyed.

Those were the sorts of histories, reiterated for Haefeli and Bucher, that insured my success when I interviewed to join the group. Haefeli believes there's much to be learned from such narratives, particularly when the phenomena described have been confirmed elsewhere. He collects his own and recounts them for us when he's in the mood, once we're swinging in our hammocks in the dark. They're especially compelling when we reflect that we're hearing them in an area that itself is an avalanche zone. "I think our friend Eckel *wants* to be blown out of his hammock," Bader complains about my appetite for them.

As a compromise, Haefeli promises us just one more for the

time being. A sixteenth-century avalanche just below us in Davos was recorded to have generated such force that it smashed through the ice of the lake—measured at a meter in thickness—and scattered an abundance of fish killed by the concussion out onto the snow. But then he can't resist adding two more: one of a porter he knew, an Austrian, who stepped momentarily off his line of ascent to adjust a shoulder harness and saw his three companions blasted out of their skis by a snowcloud moving with such velocity that its sound seemed behind it. And another of an infamous pass called Drostobel, above Klosters, that came to be known as a deathtrap because of an extraordinarily large and steep catchment area that fed into a single gully. Drostobel, the French liked to say, was German for "Your fate hurtles down at you."

The following weekend we all ski down to Davos to resupply. I'm responsible for the sausage, bread, lemons, raisins, prunes, sugar, and raspberry syrup. The entire way down I'm determined not to call on Ruth and the instant I hit the valley floor I go to the rooming-house address she provided. I'm ushered into the breakfast room and watch her butter both sides of a biscuit before she glances toward me.

The breakfast room has a view of the Jakobshorn. Filaments of snow and vapor stream from its summit in the wind. It's foreshortened here, as opposed to how it appears from 3,500 meters. Under overcast conditions the peak splits the clouds that pass over as a boulder does a stream.

"I was always jealous of your mother," Ruth remarks, once I've settled into my chair. The wicker seat's seen better days and every movement occasions fusillades of pops and cracks.

"She and Willi had this tradition of summer walks," I tell her, though she probably knows. "She called them revivifying. She told me a neighbor said to her once, 'You have twin sons, yet I always see you with only the one.'"

"It was kind of your mother to have passed that along to you,"

Ruth responds. No one's come out of the kitchen to see if there's anything I require.

"When I've dreamed of him, he's always been with your mother and you," she adds. She says that in the last one, he had a hold of her ear.

"Been with us in what way?" I want to know.

She smiles at the practicality of my question. "Could you be any more Swiss?" she asks.

"You think I'm not forthcoming," I tell her.

"I think some people don't seem to *want* information," she tells me. She's crimping the lacework under the creamer and it reminds me how, even back at school, her brain and fingers were always at work.

"So do you know where the baby is now?" I ask.

"I should hope so," she says, and more comes into focus with a jolt.

"You didn't give it away," I tell her.

"Her," she says. "Marguerite. Why would I give her away? She's with her grandmother. Probably napping."

We both take a few moments to ponder this. The housemistress brings a filled coffeepot.

"Are you bringing the baby here?" I ask.

"I'm going to try my hand at homemaking," she tells me. "Don't the French have a word for a cow that at the end of the day just gives up on its own desires and returns, without being herded, to the stable?"

"A little girl," I say to myself.

"Maybe I'll end up as one of those women you see tossing hay in the upper fields," she jokes.

"Willi's little girl," I say.

"Your mother and father both have met her," she tells me.

"Of course they have," I tell her back. One of Haefeli's most insistent bromides concerning snow safety describes how at certain altitudes, nothing might be less like a particular location than that same location under different conditions.

Everyone's all bustle and efficiency in the hut when I finally labor up to it in midafternoon. While I unpack the provisions, Bader informs me that we're going on a rescue. Down in town the group discovered that a pair of Germans have gotten themselves in a fix on the south face of the Rinerhorn, just over the ridge. From below it was apparent that they were in some sort of distress and that the easiest route to them was from our hut. Haefeli's and Bucher's silence while he relates all of this is unsettling.

Once we're ready we set out. Haefeli straps onto each of us one of his innovations: what he calls avalanche cords, thin red ropes eight meters long that will trail behind us like long tails. Each has a fisherman's float on the end and the hope is that those, at least, would be visible on the surface should the slope let go. They've never been tested. He still hasn't spoken and now he's taken the lead. Bader, who tends to chatter when frightened, is behind me in the column and tells me more than I want to know. The south face is a vast bowl that catches the sun from all angles and channels avalanches from each side into its middle. Climbing that bowl in heavy snow will be like climbing up into a funnel. Haefeli has in Bader's presence called that face "self-cleaning" because it avalanches so often. In the summer smashed trees and boulders spread out from its base like a river delta. Bader's from the flatlands and not one to panic easily—for some weeks he thought the White Death the villagers referred to was a local cheese—but even his eyes are glittery with apprehension. And the sudden rise of temperature around midday will have softened the snow.

We follow Haefeli's thigh-deep track through the heavy drifts and enter from our ridge halfway up the bowl. The Germans are lodged on the face only a couple of hundred meters above us. One waves and the other has perhaps broken his leg. None of us speak. Who knows why the Germans do what they do.

We keep a gap of fifteen meters between each of us. We put our boots only in one another's tracks. With each step we listen for the sound that indicates our weight has broken the layer between strata and that the ball bearings of the depth hoar are about to start into motion. It never comes. Haefeli has us traverse laterally, once we've reached the Germans, across the face to get out of the bowl as quickly as possible. Bucher and I take the injured boy's shoulders and Bader his good leg. His broken one we bind with his snowshoe.

The sun is setting by the time we return from having guided them down to a part of the slope from which a sledge can carry them to Davos. We'd traded off hauling the boy but we're all still exhausted and fall into our hammocks after barely stripping off our outer garments. No one's even lit the lamp.

"We should have stayed down in the village," Haefeli says out of the darkness, thinking of the slopes around and above us. Twenty centimeters have fallen in snowstorms in the last three days, and temperatures have dipped and climbed with a kind of cheerful incoherence. Bader was the last one in, and on almost his last step before regaining the hut he triggered a slab release that carried away below us a piece of the slope the breadth of a city block. It swept off an outcropping to the southwest and then was lost to sight.

Now everything has settled into a quiet. The night is windless and no one stirs in their hammocks. There's no sound of snoring.

Eventually I hear Bader's breathing, and then Bucher's. A hammock eyelet creaks. The mountain makes subtle, low-frequency sounds, like freight shifting.

I ask Haefeli if he's awake. He responds so as not to disturb the others. He says that an avalanche's release depends on a system of factors so complicated that prediction involves as much divination as science. I offer as rebuttal that we do know some things, and he says of course: we know that gravity and temperature fluctuations together propel the settling and creep that create the stress within the layers. And that those stresses are greater or smaller depending on the slope's steepness and the snowpack's weight and viscosity. And that the snow's ability to resist that stress is measured by its cohesion, or the friction between its crystals.

For an avalanche to occur, then, he murmurs, something has to either increase the stress or decrease the cohesion. The process by which the ratio changes can be gradual, or some kind of incident.

And then we're silent. Does he know I'm weeping? I do my best to remain discreet, and he makes no indication that he's heard.

A boy makes a happy gesture in the snow that's meant to signal *We're so close.* Fractures streak away from his ski at the speed of sound, find the stress lines beneath the surface, and generate the ruptures that cause the release.

I once refused to sit still for one of my mother and brother's walks. I was twelve. He explained I wasn't invited. I once again was baffled and once again unwilling to explain that I was upset. "Leave him alone," my father counseled, indicating me. He felt as left out of my mother's plans as I was. In his last letter to me, after I arrived at the hut, he wrote *My memory is going! I'll devote the rest of my energies to digging potatoes and other pursuits suitable to a second childhood.* My sister wrote soon after *Your mother now has nothing to do with him, or with me. I've always been the one ignored. You always were the one who shed suffering and went off to your life.* I wanted to write back that in our family the most exacting labor had been required to obtain the bleakest of essentials. I wanted to confide to her my devotion to Ruth. I wanted to ask her what it meant when women did the sorts of things Ruth had done outside the coffee shop. I wanted to tell her our father's story about how old Balmat, having conducted Empress Eugenie around a glacier, kept for the rest of his life the piece of chocolate that, upon their return, she'd broken in half to share with him. I wanted to tell her that I was like the man who after a cataclysm tethered his horse in the snow to an odd little hitching post that revealed itself the next morning to be the top of a church steeple.

But in the end I wrote nothing. Because mostly I wanted to write to Ruth. Because my sister was right: I had what I thought I required. I had my resentments, and my work, and I made my choices with even more ruthlessness than the rest of my family.

Haefeli, too, is asleep now, his breathing uncertain, as though awaiting that offstage tremor. We've learned more than any who've come before us what to expect, and it will do us no more good than if we'd learned nothing at all. Tonight, or tomorrow night, or some night thereafter, the slopes above us will lose their patience and sound their release. We'll be overwhelmed with snow as if in a flume of water, the sensation of speed fantastic. We'll none of us cry out, for our leader has instructed us, in or out of an avalanche, to keep our mouths shut, whatever our impulses to open ourselves to the snow's power. We'll be uncovered, months later, gingerly, because no one likes to touch the faces when recovering the bodies. Bucher will appear as if he's come to rest in mid-somersault. Bader as though he were still swimming freestyle, downhill. Haefeli will have his arms extended, as if having embraced what the mountain would bring. And I'll be discovered petrified as though lunging forward, flung far from my companions' resting place, my eyes open, my shoulders back, my expression that familiar one of perpetual astonishment.

Low-Hanging Fruit

When I was twelve my father bought me a sailboat, nothing America's Cup–ish, just something he thought even I couldn't get into trouble with—like a Sunfish, only tubbier and slower. The first day I owned it I dragged it to Long Island Sound in a thunderstorm. People were sprinting from the beach and here I was hauling this low trailer through the wet sand the other way. The rain was so heavy it knocked me to my knees. Lightning stripped the color away and left the afterimage of dune grasses and their individual shadows. It occurred to me that I should let go of the metal mast. When I did, it started this low *keening* and my hair lifted, as if in celebration, and even I knew something amazing was transpiring on a *very* fundamental level. My father, in his raincoat, dragged me off the beach by the collar. He wondered aloud then and later if his son had the brains of a walking doorknob. He was at that point interrupting his son's first stirrings as a theorist. His son had been modeling something in his head, thinking that maybe there was *already* lightning *inside* the mast and inside his *head*, trying to connect with some kind of energy in the air.

It wasn't the stupidest idea I've ever had. As my father and wife would be the first to point out.

I'm a particle physicist. Most of us here could be dumped into that hopper, in terms of category, though of course there's the specializations-within-specializations: don't tell the *accelerator* physicists that they're particle physicists.

By "here" I mean in the general vicinity of the Large Hadron Collider; or, in my case, this room with that screen, that chair, and that locker for my coat. My coat doesn't fit in it. It's not like they didn't warn me. When I'd wandered, stunned, out of grad school and into the job market, I'd been thinking mostly about Fermilab. And it's not like the CERN people gave me the hard sell. They told me: you come here, your office'll be a closet. *Everyone's* here.

They weren't kidding. Three thousand physicists, all roaming through how many little Swiss and French towns in their off-hours? Every one of them slopping food around and breaking things. Every one of them with a different idea of what constitutes collegiality. And as for all of the different project groups: well, let's just say we've got some *rivalries* going. Even the engineers seem well adjusted next to us, and they spend their every waking hour petrified of system failures.

What are they worried about? Well, what could go wrong? They've only cobbled together the most massive and expensive and complicated piece of scientific equipment ever built. Never mind the collider itself; some of these *detectors* are so big that working on them requires climbing gear. Everybody's triple- and quadruple-checked everybody else's numbers, but so what? Tell that to the people on the *Challenger*. There've already been double-digit serious breakdowns.

But for us—the theory people—that's neither here nor there. We're all like, C'mon, let's get this thing going. We only have so much data to work with. As far as we're concerned, an ideal world is a place where experiments happen faster.

All of us have kids and spouses and pets and hobbies, but that's not where we *live*. Where we live is that part of the cortex where we do our model building, what my advisor liked to call Adventure Travel Through Concepts. And that's an ongoing whipsaw between exhilaration and despair. Welcome aboard, loved ones. Strap in. We call this one the Widowmaker.

First you hope you come up with something. Then you hope that it leads to something else. Then that that something else doesn't bore you. Then that you're not just entertaining yourself. Theorist friends when they get uppity tell me they do *real* theory, not phenomenology. Me, I think that whatever's in my intellectual playground *better* connect to the outside world, because I'm not doing too well there, otherwise. I have the sort of life where even computational work makes me feel closer to the human race.

"You got *that* right," my wife said when I made that joke in her presence.

She was talking about my capacity for certain kinds of curiosities and my apparent *in*capacity for others. Did I *notice* when she barely came out of her room all weekend? Did it *strike* me that dinners had been a little quieter those last few weeks before I left? Those questions, among others, hadn't seemed to have crossed my desk.

She claims I have a dad thing going with my old advisor. She had some training in psychology and comes out with stuff like that every so often.

She complains that theorists *say* they have all the ambition, but really what they've got is vanity. But I say: when *that* curiosity's gone, what do you have left?

Some stuff you come across and *bam,* you drop to your knees right there: that's it, you think; *that* shifts the paradigm. Other stuff, you're like, Why is *this* taking up everybody's time? Some of the bigger-name theorists, they're just out there hustling. They're better salesmen.

The key is to go after the major stuff. Otherwise, you're one of those guys who's looking for what we call low-hanging fruit: the questions that are the easiest to answer.

I'm not the world's worst husband but there's a whole lot I'd walk away from to be a part of something even one-third as cool as this. The kind of collisions we're going to generate should knock all sorts of stop-the-presses particles onto our screens, the way two torpedoes colliding head-on should knock some spray out of the Atlantic.

Imagine what it's like for us most of the time. We spend our days in front of chalkboards. Progress is slow. The tea gets cold. Our only idea of the last three weeks fizzles out.

Anything that just confirms the standard model—as in "Oh, look, there's a Higgs boson"—that'd be the most depressing result. We've been sleepwalking through the last thirty years waiting for what's going to *shake us up.*

My wife was crying next to me in bed the night before I flew to Geneva, and I put my hand on her forehead in the dark. She said, "Remember when you told me that the one thing physics teaches you is that the reality you *think* you observe doesn't have much to do with the reality that's out there?"

We're not entirely well matched emotionally. When I told my dad we were getting married, his way of putting it was, "Well, it could work for a short while, if everything breaks right."

She had a miscarriage and felt like I wasn't entirely on board for the stunned-by-grief thing. She's also been blindsided by my refusal to try again.

The overarching lesson from science in the last century, I tell her, is that *my* experience isn't going to help all that much, not in terms of providing a guide to *yours.*

It's like when she heard me sparring with an old friend who's a string theorist about how some of the follow-up discoveries about the likelihood of the Higgs field were redefining the meaning of empty. She'd snorted. "What was *that?*" the string theorist asked, long-distance from Berkeley.

They think this is even bigger for them than it is for us. This gives what they do the chance to make contact with observable physics and become an experimental science. If strings are as large as some of them think—a billionth of a billionth of a meter—that's within reach of the LHC, and we'll see new particles whose masses line up like harmonics in a choral piece. We'll all be notes from a universal melody, patterns from the same object: a string. These people will go nuts with joy. As he puts it, they'll hear the shrieks over in the humanities buildings.

Every time you turn a corner, something gets defamiliarized.

This is the elevator that's going to take us to the next floor. *Some* of those nuts that have been too hard to crack are about to get pried open. "What are you *really* looking for?" my wife said to me, last thing, before I left. What we're *all* looking for. That saving thing, I think: something that right now is beyond our ability to even imagine.

Gojira, King of the Monsters

Once again he weathered an afternoon of unease and little progress. He'd forgotten that today was the Star Festival, one of his wife's favorites, and was beginning to wonder at which he was more adept: hurting Masano inadvertently or intentionally. He'd settled into the backseat that morning and spread onto his lap his section of the production board, glued on heavy stock and color-coded, when the driver had reminded him about the festival. The driver had noticed the paper cows and kimonos Masano had hung in their potted bamboo out front. They had to have been there when Tsuburaya had come home the night before.

The driver at that point had already turned onto the main street and Tsuburaya had considered asking to be returned to his home, but then had finally said, "Oh, keep going." Immediately he'd understood how that compounded his offense. He imagined himself telling Masano, "I forgot. And when I remembered, I kept going anyway."

She had signed the first love note she'd ever sent to him "Shokujo," the name of the Weaver Princess Star, the central figure of the festival. It had been a reference to the extent to which their discipline for work had suffered in the face of their feelings. According to the legend, the princess had fallen in love with a cow-herder; and as a reward for their diligence and industry, the king had allowed them to marry, but their lovemaking had become for them such a delirium that she had neglected her weaving, and the herder had allowed his cows to stray, so in his exasperation the king had forced them to remain on opposite sides of the Milky Way, to approach each other only once a year. Every July Masano had celebrated the festival, in recent years more and more often with only Akira, their youngest child. The previous July, while Tsuburaya had looked on, she had shown Akira through his toy telescope how on this night and this night alone the Weaver Princess Star and the Herdboy Star were allowed to meet on the banks of the river of heaven. Tsuburaya had watched as if she were having this conversation with her son in order to have it with him. And if it rained? Akira had asked. If it rained, his mother told him, the two stars had to wait an additional year.

He was falling behind everywhere: in his wife's affections and his work's responsibilities. But in the case of the latter, whether he put in fourteen- or sixteen-hour days, each evening left his production team with still more to accomplish, with principal photography set to commence one way or the other on August first.

He told his staff whenever they protested that there was no sense in blaming Tanaka, since he hadn't misled anyone. "Well, then he's the first producer who hasn't," one of his assistants grumbled. But it was true, Tsuburaya reminded them: at the meeting at which Tsuburaya had agreed to come aboard, Tanaka had begun by saying, "The good news is: do you want to make this movie with me, or not? The bad news is, we won't have enough time."

Tanaka had a huge hit with *Eagles of the Pacific* a year earlier, in 1953, but only bad luck since. Two projects collapsed when rights he'd thought were in hand turned out to be too expensive, and the most recent production had been all set to go until the Indonesian government panicked in the face of all the anti-Japanese protests and canceled the cast and crew's visas. Tanaka said he spent the flight back from Jakarta bathed in his own sweat. Toho, poised to regain its market leadership, had seen its hottest young producer allow its biggest project of the year to blow up in his face. He'd telephoned from the Jakarta airport to ask Mori, the executive production manager, how soon he'd need to come up with a replacement for that spot in the production slate, and Mori had answered that he'd better have one by the time he landed. He spent the flight peering miserably out his window at the endless ocean and found his mind wandering to *Lucky Dragon No. 5*. He claimed he'd been so animated when his big idea hit him that the woman beside him had been startled out of her sleep.

In March the Americans had detonated a fifteen-megaton hydrogen weapon over Bikini atoll in the central Pacific, and *Lucky Dragon No. 5* was one of those little trawlers out for tuna that found itself inside the test zone. They'd been where they were supposed to be but the detonation was twice as large as predicted. They reported seeing the sun rise in the west and then being covered by a powdery white ash for the hour that it took them to retrieve their nets. Back in port it was determined that all twenty-three crew members and their entire haul had been heavily contaminated. And it turned out that the radioactive tuna had entered the Japanese market from other trawlers before the contamination was discovered, and the result was months of nuclear fear and anti-American hostility. Tabloids had called it the Americans' third atomic attack on Japan.

The year before Tsuburaya had forced Tanaka to go to see his beloved *King Kong*, which had just earned four times as much in its worldwide rerelease as it had originally, and Tanaka had also been impressed by the global numbers for Warner Bros.' *The Beast from 20,000 Fathoms*, the story of a dinosaur thawed from its hibernation by American nuclear testing in Baffin Bay.

The United States government estimated that 856 ships in the Japanese fishing fleet had been exposed to radiation, and that more than five hundred tons of fish had to be destroyed, and offered a settlement for the survivors that the Japanese government declined to accept. And Tanaka recounted that it struck him as he looked out over the Pacific below that the stories could be combined; and for the rest of the flight he scribbled on the back of a folder that his seatmate had lent him the outline of a story in which a prehistoric creature was awakened by an H-bomb test in the Pacific and then went on to destroy Tokyo.

When Tsuburaya finally returned home for dinner on the night of the Star Festival, Masano served soba noodles and mashed fish. While he ate, she was sober and quiet. He mentioned again by way of conversation a cough that wouldn't go away and she prepared for him without comment what she called her broth of the seven plants, which included shepherd's purse, chickweed, parsley, cottonweed, and radish. She sat with him while he drank it and, once he finished, told him he should smoke less.

For months his project was known at Toho only as Project G, for giant, but lately the staff had taken to calling it *Gojira,* a fusion of the word for gorilla, because of the monster's agility, and the one for whale, because of its size. Tanaka and Honda, the director, liked that as much as anything else anyone had come up with.

Upon leaving the following morning Tsuburaya noticed the telescope in the entryway and remembered to ask how the star-viewing had gone. Masano asked how he thought it could have gone, given that it had rained.

The rest of the morning was spent laboring through an interview with the *Weekly Asahi.* The reporter, a young man with goggle-sized glasses, seemed to prize his own skepticism and asked each of his questions as if jabbing a tied dog with a stick. Did Eiji Tsuburaya, the Master of Miniatures and head of Toho's Special Arts Department, *feel* the burden of his responsibility for the visual effects on which Toho's new flagship production would either float or sink? Tsuburaya assured him that he did. Was it true there was a nuclear subtext to the story? Tsuburaya admitted that there was. And would Mr. Tsuburaya be willing to favor the *Weekly Asahi*'s readers with an exclusive first glimpse of the movie's monster? Mr. Tsuburaya would not.

Eiji Tsuburaya was born in the village of Sukagawa, two hundred and twenty kilometers north of Tokyo in the Fukushima prefecture, and his grandmother and uncle told him every day of his childhood that he'd been delivered on a date propitious for creativity. His parents were Nichiren-sect Buddhists and as members of the rural gentry had been granted exclusive license to operate the local general-goods store, which remained the main clearinghouse, in that region, for sake, soy, and miso. His mother died when she was nineteen and he was three. In both of the photographs of her which remained, she appeared birdlike and consumptive and tilted him toward the camera much as a schoolgirl might display an examination on which had been scrawled a failing grade. In both she seemed to regard the photographer with a kind of pensive anxiety.

With his father subsequently forever at the store, he was raised by his grandmother Natsu and his uncle Ichiro. He and Ichiro were so close in age that his uncle seemed more like an older brother, and so people stopped using Tsuburaya's given name, which meant first son, and started calling him Eiji, or second son.

When he was nine Ichiro took him to see Tokugawa and Hino at the Yoyogi Parade Grounds. Captains in the Imperial Army, they were aviation pioneers who'd made the first successful powered flights in Japan. He spent the next four years teaching himself how to build model airplanes out of wood, especially Tokugawa's Henry Farman biplane. He'd wake each morning at four and light his lamp and work until he had to leave for school and then, when classes were dismissed, he'd rush home and pick up where he'd left off. Once he'd achieved the verisimilitude he sought, he began increasing the scale until he was working on aircraft so large their wingspans no longer fit into his room. His father disapproved, but Tsuburaya believed he was building something that would fly him away and around the world. The bigger models ended up causing enough of a stir with the neighbors that the local newspaper did a feature about him entitled "The Child Craftsman." And throughout his career Tsuburaya was teased about the fact that the first time he saw a motion picture, he found himself more fascinated with the projector than with what was going on onscreen.

Akira was their third child and second son, born much later than the other two. Their daughter, Miyako, had died in her sleep two years after her birth. She'd had a small fever and called out in the night to Masano, who told her that she would be fine and then fell back asleep after everything had quieted.

For three months afterwards Masano could not be induced to leave the house. Neither her family nor her friends had any effect. She came around only mechanically at first to the notion that they still had a son to raise, and Hajime, who was two years older, cried himself to sleep each night in terror and helplessness while his mother gently stroked his head.

Tsuburaya was then a camera operator and kept himself busy with his production schedule and with brainstorming apparatuses that would improve his work. He'd patented and sold the Auto Snap, a pedal-operated shutter cable that freed the hands for other tasks, and had also experimented so successfully with smoke pots for in-camera effects that he'd become known around the industry as Smoke Tsuburaya. When he came home, though, such news had to be left at the front door.

Hajime had finally regained his mother's attention by telling her he was collecting stones for the roadside Jizo image. According to the legend, the souls of all dead children went to the underground river where a she-devil got them to pile stones on the bank by assuring them that if they made their piles high enough they could climb to paradise, but then she perpetually knocked over their work. Jizo, a roadside deity, comforted them, and every stone placed in the lap of one of his statues was supposed to shorten their task. Each morning before school, then, Hajime and Masano would add one or two stones to the nearest statue's pile.

In this way, his wife had pulled herself along, moment by moment. She enjoyed it if her husband sat quietly beside her. She submitted to his ministrations but declined to touch him. She seemed to appreciate being put to bed at night.

That was the year *King Kong* came to Japan. Tsuburaya had seen *The Lost World* some years earlier, but this was staggering: Willis O'Brien had with his little figures and suitcase jungles transformed RKO Radio Pictures from whatever it had been before into a world power. Tsuburaya wrote him with questions but never discovered if his letters had gotten through. He saw the film six times. He took Hajime, who was so terrified that they had to leave in the middle. Without a response from O'Brien, his only recourse was to use his connections to obtain a 35mm print and break down its effects himself, frame by frame. One evening he brought Masano in from where she was sitting and situated her next to him beside the projector. The following evening he let her remain where she was.

A week after the Star Festival, Tsuburaya was beginning dinner at his desk when Honda telephoned with news of yet another logistical catastrophe, then caught himself in the middle of his narrative and said, "Oh, but today you have to be home. It's the Obon." And he was right: of all the days of the year, this was not the one to come home late. If the Star Festival for Masano was all about how exhilarated they'd once been as lovers, the Obon was the principal commemoration of her lost little girl. She had reminded Tsuburaya once, at the beginning of the week, and then had not mentioned it again. She'd be celebrating for the full three days, and on the first night she intended that as a family they would light the paper lantern and hang it on the grave to invite their daughter's spirit to come forth and visit their home. On the table for the dead her meal would already be set out, with tiny portions featuring her favorite dishes. Akira, as always, had been given charge of arranging the display.

Hajime, now nineteen, was invited, but had yet to indicate whether he would appear. Masano had requested it when they'd last seen him, on a school holiday, and he'd answered that he'd see what he could do. He then pointed out that he'd finished his technical training, and asked his father whether he might work with him as assistant camera operator on the miniatures team.

Tsuburaya discussed what that would involve, and Masano interrupted to ask if they could return to the subject of their daughter and Hajime's sister. Then Hajime said he would make every effort, and his mother told him he should see that he did.

That night she informed Tsuburaya that she considered their son's request a bad idea, at least for the time being; that he should stay in school; that he didn't need additional training in how to ignore his family. Tsuburaya felt the need to defend his profession.

"Well, at least promise you'll do nothing without consulting me," she finally requested.

"Who Toho hires is none of your concern," he reminded her.

"What you do with our son *is* my concern," she answered. And neither of them pursued the matter after that.

When Mori and Honda first approached him, he'd been thrilled at the prospect after all of those years of finally being able to work on the kind of stop-motion effects he had so admired in *King Kong*. But when Mori asked him to write up a projected preproduction and shooting schedule for his unit, even after every shortcut he could conceive, he was forced to report that to do the job right he would need a little less than seven years. On the phone he could hear Mori repeating what he'd said to the others in his office, and there was a general hilarity in the background. When Mori returned to the line he was still chuckling. He said he could give

Tsuburaya two months for preproduction and another two for shooting.

That left Tsuburaya's department with few options other than what they knew best: miniature building. Which was what everyone expected of him anyway.

His big break had come when Toho was urged by the government during the war to pour nearly all of its resources into *The War at Sea,* the epic charged with the task of persuading the public that the new war with the Americans was one the Japanese could win. Using photographs supplied by the navy, his unit had recreated Pearl Harbor on a six-acre outdoor set on Toho's backlot, and had done so with such persuasive detail that the footage of the attack on Battleship Row was confiscated by U.S. occupation officials after the war because they'd taken it to be real. The movie returned the highest grosses ever recorded in Japan, tripled his budgets and staff, and ensured that anyone in the country with a special-effects problem would seek out the celebrated Tsuburaya.

So if on this new project O'Brien's solutions were denied to them, it meant only that they had to approach the situation in a new way. This didn't dishearten them, since they already understood that whenever fixed rules were applied to a problem, only parts of it might be perceived. They operated on the principle that you weren't ready for a task until you admitted it was beyond you.

He came up with the idea of an entire 1/25 scale miniature set of the capital, detailed inside as well as out in order to be convincing when trampled. Breakaway walls would reveal entire floors with all of their furnishings when the monster sheared away the outside surfaces. Various aspects of the city's infrastructure, such as mailboxes or street lamps, would be rendered in wax and melted by huge offscreen heat lamps to simulate the monster's radioactive breath. Small and precisely calibrated pyrotechnic charges would be installed to reproduce the explosive destruction as fuel and automobile gas tanks ignited.

And 1/25 scale would allow a monster of the proper size to be generated by simply putting a man in a suit.

The simplicity of the plan held enormous appeal. He'd always been drawn to the handmade approach, and of course the studio appreciated the relative lack of expense. Something made from nothing was how he liked to put it.

Mori and Honda loved the budget and feared the plan. A man in a suit? Tsuburaya only shrugged at their unease. They either trusted him or they didn't. Proof was stronger than argument.

The day after the logistical catastrophe, Honda called to report that he'd handled it without Tsuburaya's help. Honda was probably Tsuburaya's closest friend, though at that suggestion Masano once responded that she would love to see Honda's face when someone told him as much. Honda was forever sporting an American's rumpled little fishing hat and was fond of walking great distances. He and Tanaka met when hiking the Diamond Mountains in Korea in the early thirties. Mori and Tanaka had both thought Honda would be the perfect director for this new project since he'd had so little trouble with all the visual effects in *Eagles of the Pacific*, and had worked so well with Tsuburaya. Having been a longtime assistant to Kurosawa, he was experienced in dealing with lunatic perfectionists. "Or, in other words, Tsuburaya," Mori had said at their first full staff meeting.

They also liked that Honda had no patience for storylines that dawdled. They'd handed a first attempt at the script to the mystery writer Kayama and what he'd produced was far too tame, involving a nondescript dolphinlike creature that attacked only fishing boats and only to feed its insatiable hunger. Most of the story had involved the poor thing swimming this way and that in search of food.

Honda had clear-cut Kayama's script, demanding something terrible enough to evoke both the fire raids on Tokyo and the bombings of Hiroshima and Nagasaki. He'd served three tours of duty as an infantryman, had been a prisoner of war in China, been repatriated near Hiroshima, and then had wandered the devastation three months after the surrender.

He thought much like Tsuburaya did: that the director, like a department head, had to include in his leadership the responsibility to protect the artisans under his umbrella. And, of course, to recruit those artisans. And where were they to be found? They had to have the right sensibility toward beauty, sufficient technical training and scientific knowledge, and a strong will, passion, and creative talent.

Honda claimed he drew his belief in himself from the soil of his life experience. His mother had also died when he was small, and his father soon afterward. He'd been left unable to attend school and had taught himself to read while carrying firewood for his neighbors. He knew that encountering the unfamiliar might involve many errors before a solution was found, and he had an intuition that seemed to draw on an extraordinary visual resourcefulness. When he loved something, he'd exclaim, "Oh, this is spring water!" Again like Tsuburaya, he knew that the craftsman worked with and for his world, but ultimately went his own way, not seeking praise. When *Eagles of the Pacific* premiered, Honda was on a little lake, fishing. Because the objects themselves were one's best signature.

As a young man, Tsuburaya had been struck by how different the Japanese hand was from the big, untrained hands of the other races. Masano had a calligrapher's hands, long-fingered and tapering, and he'd been seduced by their dexterity and sensitivity when watching her set out her simple gifts for him in the hospital. The daughter of a Kyoto engineering magnate, she was fond of movie stars and thanks to her father's influence, was touring the studio when the camera crane Tsuburaya had invented collapsed and he crashed to the floor in front of her. The shattered lens shield had slightly cut her forehead but even so she cradled his face and neck while his assistants came running. She later claimed he'd reached up to touch her injury, but he had no memory of that. On the same afternoon she'd appeared in his hospital room, bearing her gifts, and remaining behind after everyone else had left. They'd married a year later, when she was nineteen.

Their courtship had mostly taken the form of long-distance love notes, in which Tsuburaya found a courage of expression based on longing and the safety of isolation. *All of us,* he wrote later: *when we make a little progress, we're captivated by our cleverness.*

Their feelings were an act of faith, just as the sublimity of an artisan's pot was a gift and not a calculation. They gave themselves over to those feelings the way lips kissed the thickness of a tea bowl's rim.

They honeymooned in the old Okinawa, which was now gone. Its capital had been a dream city, its narrow streets mossy and hushed, over which dark leaves threw down their shade. Eaves on the ancient red-tiled roofs featured heraldic animals fired from clay.

But lately it seemed to him that their minds were bound by obsessions that deprived them of freedom. They each put in longer days, he in his innovations and his wife in her grieving. All the rituals that had solidified their happiness now reflected back its opposite. In Masano's photo albums of her loss, baby girls on their thirty-third day were taken to the shrine in thanksgiving by their grandmothers, who prayed for their welfare. As always, the tinier the tot, the more brilliantly it was dressed. Some photographs of these celebrations were prominently displayed on the family altar. Or, in the event of the child's death, on the grave.

Tsuburaya's experience was that one who was gone was forgotten, day by day. As his grandmother put it, "Destiny's in heaven, and rice dumplings are on the shelf."

But Masano knew spilt water never returned to the tray. And if she forgot, she said, Tsuburaya reminded her by going on with his life. She said that in the face of her unhappiness, he was like a blind man peeping through a fence.

"I'm sorry for my myopia," he told her after the Obon had concluded, and after she'd followed some late-night tenderness with despair. He once again had come home nearly at dawn and she'd risen to meet him, backing him across the room with her beautiful hands.

"I suppose it's like that old saying that the lighthouse doesn't shine on its own base," she'd remarked some hours later, while each still smelled of the other's touch.

Before getting fired, Kayama suggested that the comic-book artist Abe should design the creature. Abe had been the illustrator for *Kenya Boy,* a series about an orphaned Japanese boy who was lost in Africa and continually had to fight off prehistoric monsters. Why Africa was overrun with prehistoric monsters was never explained. Abe produced a month's worth of designs, each of which was less useful than the previous one. He was finally let go when he put forward a proposal that featured a giant frog's body and a head shaped like a mushroom cloud. With no time to hire another designer, Honda and Tsuburaya decided to simply hybridize a dinosaur of their own conception. Various illustrations were pulled from libraries and children's books and mixed and matched on the drafting table. Of course it would have a tyrannosaur's head, but an Iguanodon's body seemed an easier fit for a stuntman's requirements, in terms of operating the suit. And Honda added a stegosaur's back plates along the spine to ensure their creature would appear distinct from any recorded species.

During the clay-rendering stage they had his staff experiment with scaly, warty, and alligator skin before settling on the last. And with that decided, one whole unit was turned over to the suit's construction.

The first version was framed in cloth-covered wire, over which rubber that had been melted in a steel drum was applied in layers. The result was immobile and weighed three hundred and fifty-five pounds. In the next attempt, the cloth itself was painted with the base coat, so only two layers of rubber were necessary, but the result was still a staggeringly heavy two hundred and twenty pounds. But after a month of further futility, they had to concede that rubber applied any less thickly would crack at the joints, so the second version would have to do.

To minimize the length of time the poor stuntman would have to spend in the thing, another suit was produced and cut into two sections for shots requiring only part of the monster, waist-up or waist-down. For screen tests of the latter, Nakajima, the stuntman, galumphed around in his heavy suspenders like someone wearing clown pants or waders, his great rubber feet crushing the rough models they'd arranged around the stage.

They chose Nakajima not only for his height and physical conditioning but also for his dogged determination. To prepare for his role, he'd taken a projector home with him and worn out Tsuburaya's print of *King Kong,* and he told anyone who would listen that he'd spent two full weeks of evenings observing bears at the Ueno Zoo.

Another unit had successfully produced a smaller-scale, hand-operated puppet of the head that could spray a stream of mist from its jaws, for close-ups of the creature's radioactive breath.

"So is your monster ready to go?" Masano asked the night before shooting was set to commence, out of the dark, when Tsuburaya had thought she was asleep.

"I think he is, yes," Tsuburaya answered, surprising even himself.

One of the first recitations that he remembered from primary school involved the five terrors, in ascending order: "earthquake, storm, flood, fire, father." It surprised no one that "father" was judged the most dangerous. As preoccupied as their fathers were, when it came to their sons they still found time for disappointment and punishment. And waiting to see that disappointment coalesce on his father's face, during those rare occasions in which Tsuburaya spent time with him: those were some of his unhappiest memories.

His academic performance was always adequate but his father was particularly unhappy about his refusal to moderate the time he devoted after school to airplane building, and in the event of a harsh report on this from his grandmother, his father gave him the option of having his most recent model-building efforts reduced to kindling or having his hand burned. Like many before him, his father believed in the deterrent effect of burning rolled wormwood fibers on the clenched fist of a misbehaving boy. Once lit, the fibers lifted off from their own convection currents after a moment or two, but even so always left behind a white scar.

Afterwards his father treated the burn himself, with a cooling paste, and talked about the lessons his own father had taught him. He always began with the maxim that with either good acts or bad, the dust thus amassed would make a mountain. He had other favorites as well. When addressing elders or the opposite sex, the mouth was the entrance to calamity. Hard work in school had its usefulness, because what seemed stupid now might prove useful later. We should love our children with a stick. And it was always better not to say than to say.

His father reminded him that in the old days a child like Tsuburaya would be made to swallow a small salamander alive as a cure for nervous weakness. One rainy morning in a park, when his father thought he'd been too peevish, he held one up to Tsuburaya's mouth and said that a childhood classmate of his had reported he could feel it moving about his stomach for some minutes afterward.

Yet Tsuburaya also remembered him taking them on the hottest days for shaved ice with grape, strawberry, or lemon syrup, the syrup never getting down as far as the red beans at the base of the paper cone. He remembered a delivery in a downpour in which they sat in their wagon watching farmers in a field in the distance, in their raincoats woven from rushes looking like so many porcupines while they squatted to rest. He remembered insect festivals in the evenings when the autumn grasses bloomed and the singing insects they'd gathered in their tiny cages were, at an agreed-upon stroke, all freed, and how they waited—himself, his grandmother, Ichiro, and his father—for that moment when the cicadas would get their bearings, puzzle out their freedom, and let loose their rejoicing in song.

For the first day of principal photography, the visual-effects team was divided into its three units, one for location photography to shoot the plates for the process and composite shots, one for the lab work, and one for the miniatures. Tsuburaya called Hajime that morning to let him know that he could join the unit. Hajime was so excited, he claimed, that he ran all the way to the studio when the streetcar was late.

"Why didn't you take a cab?" Honda asked once he arrived. "You're sweating on our work," he added, when Hajime only grinned for an answer.

Tsuburaya told him that he had three minutes to get the film casings loaded, and the boy disappeared to cool himself off as best he could at the sinks in the washroom before returning with his hair askew and in a borrowed shirt.

It turned out that before they'd even gotten through a half a day, another stuntman, Tezuka, was needed to spell Nakajima, so exhausting was the part. The suit was stifling in the August heat even without the studio lights, but with them it was a roasting pan. Added to that were the fumes from the burning kerosene rags intended to simulate Tokyo's fires. Under the searing lights Nakajima was barely able to breathe or see, and could only spend a maximum of fifteen minutes in the suit before being too overcome to continue. Each time he stepped out of it, the supporting technicians drained the legs as if pouring water out of a boot. One measured a cup and a half of sweat from each leg.

The second half of the first day's schedule involved the destruction of the National Diet. Tezuka fainted and broke his jaw on the top of the parliament building as he fell, so they were back to Nakajima again. While awaiting his recovery, they repaired the damage to the building.

Upon Nakajima's return, everything went off in one shot. While he maneuvered his way down the row of buildings, crew members at Tsuburaya's signal heaved on the cable that ran up through a pulley in the rafters and worked the tail. When it crashed into the side of the National Diet, another technician detonated the pyrotechnics and plastic and wooden parts rained down on everyone in the studio. Honda said it looked even better through the eyepiece than they might have hoped. And they all felt at once exultation and disquiet. While the men extinguishing the fires sprayed everything down, the fastenings were undone and the top part of the creature was peeled from poor Nakajima's head and shoulders. While he was given some water it hung before him like a sack.

Tanaka came by to see the last part of the shot and reported that Mori had taken to calling what they were doing "suitmation."

"How'd the boy work out?" he asked Honda, half-teasing.

"I haven't heard any complaints," Honda told him in response. And Hajime pretended to be too absorbed in sealing the rush canisters to have heard what they said.

Masano was asleep when Tsuburaya was finally dropped off after the first day of shooting, and asleep when he left the next morning. Toward the end of the second day, an assistant informed him during a break that she'd telephoned to let him know that Hajime would be joining them for dinner that night.

His son was lugging film cans to the processing wagon while

Tsuburaya read the note. "You're dining with us tonight?" he called to him.

"That's what I'm told," Hajime answered.

They rode home together. It was still bright out and the dining table was flooded with a quiet white light from the paper windows. Masano collected Imari porcelain and had set out for the occasion her most prized bowls and cups.

Seeming even more grim than usual, she asked how their days had been. Tsuburaya told her his had gone well. Hajime smiled like a guest in someone else's home, and Akira seemed beside himself with joy at his brother's unexpected presence, though even he seemed to register the tension. For appetizers there were a number of variations on raw radishes, Hajime's favorite, including some involving three kinds of flavored salts. Masano had begun believing more and more fiercely in the purifying usefulness of salt.

There was a silence while they ate, except for Akira smacking his lips. When they finished, Masano cleared the table and served, for dessert, more radishes, pickled and sugared. She asked if they had anything to tell her.

"Do you have anything to tell your mother?" Tsuburaya asked the older boy.

Hajime seemed to give it some knit-browed thought. "It's nice to see you?" he finally offered.

She sat back with her arms folded and watched them exchange looks. "I've tried to give our son some direction; a little instruction," she finally remarked. "But you know what that's like. It's like praying into a horse's ear."

"I've taken Hajime on as my camera assistant," Tsuburaya told her.

"Yes, I thought that might be the situation," she answered, and even Akira acknowledged the extent of her anger by hunching his shoulders. "The Personnel Department called, needing information," she added.

He'd provided their oldest son with a job, and a good one, Tsuburaya reminded her. That seemed cause for celebration, and not complaint.

"As you say, I have no cause for complaint," Masano told him. But something in her shoulders once she'd turned away left him so dismayed that he found he no longer had the heart to argue. They sat facing each other like mirror images of defeat.

"Thank you for this excellent meal," Hajime told her.

"Thank you for coming," Masano answered. Tsuburaya put his hand atop hers, at the table, and she let him leave it there.

But she didn't speak to him again until later that night, when he threw off his covers in the heat. She said then that as a young woman she'd felt anxious about seeming awkward when she tried to express herself. And that until she'd met him, she'd feared it had something to do with being too self-centered. And that their letters—their feelings—had helped her understand that something else was possible.

"Remember how thrilled we'd be when we saw my name in the credits?" Tsuburaya asked her.

"I read some of those letters today," she told him. In the dark he couldn't see her face. "They're such strange things. So full of connection."

"Hajime can work for Toho and remain a loving son," he told her.

"I need to sleep now," she explained, after a pause. And after another pause, she did.

He departed earlier than usual for the studio the next day, and at his driver's horn-blowing, he raised his head from his work to find his car in a great migration of bicycles ridden by delivery boys, bakery boys, and messenger boys, some of them negotiating astonishing loads: glaziers' boys balancing great panes of glass, soba boys shouldering pyramids of boxed soups, peddlers' boys with pickle barrels, all weaving along at high speed. When a toddler in a tram window reached out to touch one, the cyclist veered away down a side street.

Honda greeted him that morning with Ifukube's score, which he played for everyone on the upright piano. No surprises there. Ifukube had spent the war composing nationalist marches, and what he'd presented to Honda was a mishmash of some of his favorites. Apparently he hadn't even looked at the rushes. "Close your eyes and you're back on the home front," Tanaka called acidly from the hallway while Honda was playing it.

That afternoon two full sequences were filmed. After Honda approved the second, he asked if Tsuburaya had come up with anything to conceal the wires for the attacking jets. Tsuburaya showed him on the Moviola the little test he'd conducted, and Honda was stupefied and overjoyed: what had Tsuburaya done? Where had the wires gone? Tsuburaya explained that he'd hung and flown the models upside down, then had inverted the image. The wires were still there, but no one noticed them *below* the aircraft instead of above. Honda wanted to call some others in and make a fuss about it, but Tsuburaya reminded him that if time and budget were the main walls around the moviemaker, it was his job to help punch through them. "So we can get on to other things," Honda agreed. And Tsuburaya could imagine Masano's response, had she heard.

Early in the war they'd brought Hajime to see the rare birds and animals that had been added to the Ueno Zoo after the conquests in the south. Tsuburaya remembered the days being perpetually sunny. Hajime had also loved the rooftop pool of the Matsuzakaya department store, where shoppers were treated to mock battles between electrically controlled models of the Japanese and Allied fleets while the store's customer service manager talked about the need for consumer restraint. Plaques bearing the phrase "Honor Home" were in the windows of every house that had a father or son off at the war, and Masano had joked to her friends that only her husband's age had held him back, and that national mobilization was never a problem if all that was asked of men was that they cast off parents, wives, or children before going off to war.

But by that point he was already working in the Special Arts Department at Toho. The ten major studios had been forced to consolidate into just three, all making mostly war films in order to promote national policy and strengthen the country's resolve. The rooftop display had given him the idea for the miniatures photography for Toho's first drama about the China war, *Navy Bomber Squadron*. And the climactic battle sequence had gone off so well that he'd then been given responsibility for the scene in which the Chinese primary school, once destroyed, turned out to have been a secret armaments depot. Those sequences had resulted in his first screen credit for visual effects, though the sight of the bombed Chinese school seemed to cripple Masano's enjoyment at the premiere.

Had they ever been closer, though? The ongoing national emergency had seemed to revive her sense of all that she still had to lose, and nearly every night her face found his in their bed once they had extinguished the light. Every family was urged to start the day at the same hour with radio calisthenics, and during the first six months after Pearl Harbor there were nothing but victories to report, so the radio made for good listening. Hajime found it hilarious to watch his parents huff and sweat. More and more disappeared from public life to exist only in private, the way before the war the censors had edited out of foreign films all instances of socialism or kissing.

Accounts of each battle were concluded with a rendition of Ifukube's Naval March. But then as the war turned, announcements of this or that territory's strategic importance were reversed, and its loss apparently meant nothing, whereas its capture had been wildly celebrated the year before. Hajime spent even longer hours in school undergoing mandatory vocational and military training. And Masano was further saddened at the eradication of neighbor-

hood birds by the heavy guns of an artillery training division bil-
leted nearby.

Tsuburaya told her one night that it was just like Japan to go to
war with the nation upon whom she was most dependent for the
raw materials essential to prosecuting that war. Modern warfare
began in the mine and continued in the factory, feeding on coal
and steel and oil, and ninety percent of the oil Japan consumed
before the war was imported, nearly all of it from the United States.
She seemed to find this point even more painful than he did.

They were told that Leyte was the battle that would determine
the fate of the nation. Once Leyte was lost, it turned out that Luzon
was the key. After Luzon, Iwo Jima. After Iwo Jima, Okinawa. "Well,
apparently the mountain moves," Masano answered, a little bitterly, when he remarked to her about it. She was especially demor-
alized by a newspaper account of the destruction of Okinawa's
capital, and the printed photo of their narrow and hushed streets
from all those years ago shelled into rubble.

By then there were no pleasures. Food was miserable, lovemaking was impossible, there was no time even for reading, and they
constantly feared that even at his age Hajime would be called up.
Dinners were rice bran, fried in a pan, which looked like custard
but made Hajime cry when he ate it. Movie production had come
to a halt due to a lack of nitrate for film stock. Workers at Toho
were serving as labor volunteers in the countryside, helping farmers and returning each night with a few sweet potatoes for their
work.

And then came the raids. Hajime demanded to be taken to a
public exhibition of a B-29 in Hibiya Park, where the bomber had
been reconstructed from the parts of various downed aircraft and
was displayed alongside one of Japan's latest interceptors. The
fighter looked like a peanut beside a dinner plate. Such was the
Americans' nonchalance by that point that they dropped leaflets
the day before detailing where and when they would strike. Aloft,
these leaflets resembled a small, fleecy cloud, but as they fluttered
down they dispersed over the city.

The fire raid on March ninth centered on the area hit by the 1923 earthquake, the trauma that had separated him forever from his father. The one on the tenth extended the destruction. The next morning they returned to acres of ruin where their homes had been. Block after block was burned flat, with lonely telephone poles erect at odd angles like grave markers, leaving only ash and brick and the occasional low shell of a concrete building. Where the desolation wasn't complete, the neighborhood associations were still holding air-defense drills and doing their best to resettle those bombed out of their homes.

The only topic of conversation by then was food, or the failure of the rationing system. Everyone spent their days foraging. They were told to collect acorns for flour because they had the same nutritive value as rice. They ate weeds and boiled licorice greens and bracken ferns. And then they heard that as the result of an attack by a very small number of B-29's, the city of Hiroshima had been considerably damaged. And that the Emperor would be addressing the nation by radio for the first time in history.

When Tsuburaya mentioned by way of offering encouragement that they'd completed the first month of shooting, Masano said in response, "You take as much time as you need to. Whatever your lack of interest, our routine is going to continue as it has."

He was taken aback. She'd caught him struggling into his rain shell and preoccupied with the problem of the high-tension wires the monster was to destroy on his way into Tokyo. She was at their kitchen table working on a gourd that was supposed to afford the sparrows some protection from rats. The gourd would hang from a nail under the eave outside their front door.

This wasn't how things would always be, he assured her. Soon the shooting and even postproduction would be over.

"I'll continue to maintain your household and raise your child, whatever happens between us," she told him.

"What does that mean, 'whatever happens between us'?" he

asked. He was shaken, the notion of yet more separation like a fear of the dark.

"Akira's very proud of you," she answered. "And his brother. Do you know what he said to me before he left for school? He said he understood why neither of you liked him."

"Do I need to stay home?" Tsuburaya asked her, and set down his work satchel. "Do we need to talk about this now?"

"He's nine years old and he sounded like me," she said.

He unbuckled his rain shell in contrition, pained at her attempt to keep her composure. "I'll talk to him this evening," he told her. "Hajime will talk to him as well."

"It's one thing if it's just myself," she said. "But I can't watch this happen to him, too."

"I'll go see him now," he said. He had his driver wait outside Akira's school, but the boy's classroom was empty when he finally found it. The instructor in an adjacent room said he thought the class might have gone off on a nature walk.

When Tsuburaya was twenty-two, his father took the train to Tokyo for business and left his grandmother and Ichiro in charge of the store. The idea seemed to be that he might partner up with a larger distribution chain. But he might also have been trying to exert some influence on his son.

Tsuburaya had by that point given up his dreams of aviation, and after serving in the Imperial Infantry had returned to the store, uncertain of his future. Before his call-up, a chance encounter had led to his training as a cameraman for Edamasa, the famous director, whom he'd worked for until his conscription notice had arrived. Back at home, he stocked shelves and took inventory. His father claimed his son's choices were his own, but his grandmother hectored him to give up dreaming about movies and airplanes and to give some thought to his family and especially his father and uncle, who shouldered the burden of the family business alone.

But when he heard from Edamasa again, the pull was too

strong, and when he was sent out to buy rice one morning, he left a note stating he wouldn't return until he'd succeeded in the motion-picture business or died trying. When he telephoned from Tokyo a week later to let them know he was safe and settled into a place where they could reach him, Ichiro came to the phone but his father and grandmother did not. Ichiro said his mother still hadn't recovered from the effrontery of the note.

So he was surprised to receive his father's invitation to lunch. They arranged it for the day of his father's arrival, but that morning the truck had broken down on some location shooting for which Tsuburaya had volunteered in the hills and he found himself stranded out of town.

The day his truck broke down and his father arrived at the capital was September 1, 1923, and a few minutes before noon his father was still expecting him for lunch when the Great Kanto Earthquake brought the Imperial Hotel's chandelier down onto the table before him. He said he'd just lifted his water glass away from his place setting when it was as if a giant had stamped it flat. He stood up with his pant leg open at the knee like a haversack. Something in the shattered and telescoping table had lashed open his lower thigh.

The moment before, he'd been peering over at the lunch room's little indoor pond, where dull carp drowsed in the tepid water. Then there was a rumbling and the first shock, a vertical jolt. At the second jolt, the chandelier came down, and the floor began to pitch and rock so that the heavy parquet snapped and ricocheted like fireworks, and after he'd stood he was unable to run and got thrown onto his side. From there he saw the office concern across the street collapse into a dust cloud so intense that it was as if the hotel windows had been permanently chalked with yellow.

Out on a side street, he managed to tie his tattered pant leg around his thigh, casting around for his son, and with every jolt the hotel and an adjacent bank flexed like buggy whips and cracks appeared along their walls, from which window casings and marble avalanched into the street. He said that with each shock it was as if the earth had been pulled out from under him. Where was Eiji? Where was his son? He ran, searching, as the concussions changed to undulations. And then it appeared to be over, though every few minutes the aftershocks were sufficient to knock to him to his knees.

He found himself in a little park, panting. Sparrows under a stand of orange trees seemed somehow to have been grounded, hopping about, for all the freneticism of their wings achieving only a few feet of altitude before fluttering back into the dirt. He was weeping, he realized, in fear for his son. Should he go back? All avenues in that direction had been blocked by massive slides of debris.

All of this he'd related to Ichiro the last time Tsuburaya saw him. Only the oval of his face had been spared the salve and the bandages. Tsuburaya had wondered if the doctors had applied the same cooling paste his father had used on his burns. He said hello to his father, who then directed him and his grandmother to wait outside the ward. His grandmother went off to berate the over-worked medical teams from the Relief Bureau, but he held his ear to the open door.

"Keep him away from me," his father said, and Tsuburaya couldn't fully register what he'd just heard. His father went on to tell his uncle that within a minute the city had been cut off from everything, the water and gas mains ruptured, the telegraph and telephone wires down. The trolley rails where he crossed them had sprung upward after snapping. He'd called for Eiji and in response heard cries in all directions. And then he noticed the rice-cracker shop already on fire, the smoke rising into the still, hot air. There seemed to be no one present, no one making an effort to put out the flames.

Later Tsuburaya thought that he'd probably heard more of his father's voice that day than he had for the previous five years. He was crying for his father's pain and because of his banishment from the room. Every so often Ichiro asked if the pain was very bad and never received an answer. When his grandmother returned, she whispered something and tried to pull Tsuburaya away from the door, but he tore his elbow away with such ferocity that she never tried again. *You should go back into that room,* he told himself. Instead he stood where he was and listened.

Everything had been destroyed and the gas mains shattered just as lunch fires were being lit in hibachis and stoves all over Tokyo, in hotels and lunch counters and apartments and factory work stations from Ota to Arakawa. All of those braziers scattered their coals onto tatami mats on crooked old streets and alleys just wide enough to provide sufficient drafts. His father saw firemen—their water mains now dry—trying to use nearby moats and canals. He said those not trying to pull the trapped from the rubble did their best to put out the fires, but there were too many of them, and almost no water. Then the wind picked up.

Because there was no single point of origin neither was there a single advancing front of fire, and no one knew where to go or what was safe. Everyone who could headed to the river, and along its banks the mobs were increasingly herded toward the bridges, where they were crushed or tipped over the side until the bridges themselves caught fire. His father struggled toward anyone who resembled his son until he was knocked into the water by a handcart, and there he stayed alive by keeping submerged until oil from ruptured storage tanks ignited upstream, the fire cascading at him along the surface. He scrambled out just ahead of its arrival.

Beside the Yasuda Gardens he pitched himself into a broad, bare lot that had been the site of the Army Clothing Depot, where uniforms were stored for shipment. Its size and location along the river promised more safety—across its twelve acres there was very little to burn—and thousands poured into it all through the afternoon, as everywhere else became more and more of a conflagration. They came singly and in groups, some pulling carts piled with outlandish goods, and found places for themselves. Patients from nearby hospitals were carried in on stretchers. Everyone was polite, settling down shoulder-to-shoulder to wait. They watched the fires surrounding them burn. The crush was so pronounced that he gave up the notion of hunting the crowd for his son.

Someone behind him complained that he'd forgotten his chess set. The bitter taste of smoke in the air intensified. He wished he'd had some lunch.

And then, across the river, starbursts of sparks and flame seemed to be climbing the columns of smoke high into the clouds. He asked the man beside him for the time, and the man told him it was a little after four. The wind was intensifying, and from the west they could hear the sound of a huge airplane flying low across the river. Was it a rescue mission? It was flying toward them, but in that direction the sky was enveloped in black. And then he saw it wasn't the sky but a column so wide it seemed to cover the horizon, and that it was spinning and shot through with fire. Debris crossed its face and reappeared again. By then they could hear nothing else.

It seemed to detonate everything on the other side of the river before it came across. It swept away the barges. It blew apart the School of Industry. It drew river water forty feet up into the funnel before it sheared off as steam. By the time it hit the Clothing Depot it sounded like gargantuan waterfalls crashing together.

Two policemen agape on a refugee's cart were blown away. Tsuburaya's father was knocked down and blasted along the ground until his hand caught onto something. A teenaged girl on fire flew by over his head. Human beings all around him were sucked into the air like sparks. He shut his eyes against the wind and heat. A tree was wrenched from the ground, roots and all, before him, and he crawled into the loose earth and was able to breathe. Some ruptured water mains there had created a bog, and he tunneled into the mud.

When he revived, the backs of his hands had been burned to the bone. Everyone was gone. The skin atop his head was gone. His ears were gone. Something beside him he couldn't recognize was still squirming.

At their store that evening, two hundred and twenty kilometers away, Tsuburaya's grandmother reported that the columns of smoke and cloud carried upward by the convection currents made everyone wonder if a new volcano had been born. An intense red glow spread across the southern horizon.

His father said he remembered only fitful things afterward. Someone carried him somewhere eventually. An army cart in one of the burned-out areas stopped to pass out cupfuls of water to refugees. A riderless horse stood in the road too badly burned to move. Bodies looked like black rucksacks except for the occasional raised leg or hand. He remembered a shirt like his son's under a cascade of lumber. A functioning well with a long queue beside it. He died soon after he mentioned the well, describing the water he so enjoyed from it.

In the years following his death Tsuburaya talked to historians and scientists and survivors. The historians informed him that over four thousand acres of Tokyo had burned, ten times the acreage of the Great Fire of London's, and that a hundred thousand people had perished, a hundred times the number consumed in the Americans' San Francisco fire. The scientists informed him that the updraft that produced the columns his grandmother witnessed had caused a gigantic vacuum near the ground and the surrounding air had swept in to fill it before being drawn upwards itself, resulting in a furnace four thousand acres wide and an updraft that generated tornadoes as it pulled the fire up into it: fire tornadoes. And the survivors told him stories like the ones his father had related. Though of course once Masano and Tsuburaya had endured the fire raids at the end of the war, he no longer needed to turn to others for that sort of understanding. "Smoke Tsuburaya," she'd said to herself one night as they'd hurried down the steps to a shelter. He'd had less trouble than others negotiating a safe route through the fires, since he knew from his father's experience which way to go.

"Do you think he knew I was listening?" he'd asked his uncle on the morning his family had returned home from his father's death-bed. He'd shamed himself by weeping so much on the train that his grandmother had finally taken a seat opposite him.

"I don't think he gave it any thought," Ichiro answered.

At the sound bay, everyone was very excited about the roar Ifukube had come up with. Tsuburaya had charged him with the task of creating for the monster's cry something melancholy and ear-splitting—"Try producing *that* combination," Ifukube had complained when given the instructions—and he'd spent two weeks sorting through recordings of wild animals before he'd finally given up and settled on drawing a heavy work glove across the strings of a contrabass and manipulating the sound in an echo chamber. The result was hair-raising. The entire production team was beside itself with happiness. He had also overlaid a recording of a taiko drum with an electronically altered mine detonation to produce the monster's footfalls.

Halfway through the shooting Honda told Tsuburaya that he was using many more close-ups of the monster's face than he'd thought he would, because its dilemma was becoming more real to him. Man had created war and the Bomb and now nature was going to exact its revenge, with tormented Gojira its way of making radiation visible. That's why he'd insisted that its skin be thick and furrowed like the keloid scars of the atomic survivors.

Tanaka was uneasy, in fact, with how often the movie referenced the war. And he worried that the long shots of the burned-out city would recall for everyone the newspaper images of Hiroshima and Nagasaki.

In the rushes of the final scenes, Honda noted how sad Gojira looked when he turned from the camera.

"That's the way I made the mask," Tsuburaya reminded him.

"No," Honda said. "The face itself is changing through the context of what we've seen him go through. By the time the movie ends he's like a hero whose departure we regret. The paradox of fearsomeness and longing is what the whole thing's about."

"I wouldn't know about that," Tsuburaya told him.

"It's like part of *us* leaving," Honda said. "That's what makes it so hard. The monster the child knows best is the monster he feels himself to be." After Tsuburaya didn't respond, he added, "That's why I love those shots of the city after the monster's gone. All that emptiness, like a no-man's land in which eloquence and silence are joined. If you don't have both, the dread evaporates."

That was true, Tsuburaya conceded. He volunteered that he was particularly proud of the shots of the harbor at night before the creature's eruption from the sea: all along the waterfront, silence. Silence like thunder.

Akira was turned to the wall in his sleep when Tsuburaya got home. One foot hung over the pallet, exposing an impossibly thin ankle. He left for the boy a little maquette that the team had used to model Gojira's head, standing it on the floor next to his mat.

Masano had apparently taken to mounting amulets throughout the house where their influence was desired, against pestilence at the doorway or against storms on the ceiling. The house was dark and still. Tsuburaya went through some old production notes at his desk. Atop one of the shot lists he found some gingko leaves and a note from Akira. His instructor at school had told him they kept the bookworms away.

"I'm a bad father," Tsuburaya told Honda before his unit got started the next morning. His friend seemed unfazed by the news, so he added, "A bad husband, too."

"Supposedly the cat forgets in three days the kindnesses of three years," Honda answered.

They shot the scene of the creature crashing through the rail yards at Shinagawa. The suit's rubber feet were continually torn up by even the thinnest steel of the model rails, and shot after shot after shot proved unsatisfactory. Some of their work was as repetitive as a carpenter's hammering. But the house still had to be built.

Tsuburaya repaired the feet himself with cotton swabs and a glue pot and a fine brush while Nakajima drank tea and enjoyed the break. Handcraftsmanship justified itself as an expression of intimacy with the world. Honda made jokes about the number of people standing around on salary, but Tsuburaya reminded him that the potter accepted long hours at the kiln with his body and soul.

"That's good to know," Honda responded. "But in the meantime, nobody gets to eat."

Mori mounted a publicity blitz four full weeks before the release, including an eleven-installment radio serial, and by the premiere their monster's face glowered down from every bus and tramway stop, and a nearly full-sized Gojira balloon swayed and bowed in the wind over an automobile dealership in the Ginza district.

It worked: *Gojira* recorded the best opening-day ticket sales in Tokyo's history and had a better first week than Kurosawa's *Seven Samurai*. "It's like a dream!" Akira shrieked at the showing his family attended, and Masano watched the destruction in respectful silence. Some of the older audience members left the theater in tears.

Mori had already begun to arrange the sequel. Since *Gojira* ended with the scientist's warning that if the world continued with nuclear weapons there would someday appear another such monster, the sequel would involve two: Gojira and his bitter enemy, yet to be designed. One possibility for the latter appeared to Tsuburaya in a dream the night after the premiere, a gigantic tussock moth rendered with enough scientific accuracy that its face and mouth parts were horrific. In the dream it was obsessed with two magical little girls. Tsuburaya even glimpsed the teaser line: "The Mightiest Monster in All Creation—Ravishing a Universe for Love."

American investors had already won the auction for *Gojira*'s international rights and decided to add new footage involving an American reporter trapped in Tokyo during the rampage, in order to give Western audiences someone for whom to care. They announced they were also going to tone down the nuclear references. They retitled it *Godzilla,* and added the subtitle *King of the Monsters.*

A month after the premiere, Tsuburaya walked home alone late one December night, bundled against the cold. In the fishmonger's shop the dried bonito looked like whetstones in the window. He stopped at a sushi stall for some boiled rice with vinegar.

The boy who served him had a bamboo crest motif on his coat and he asked why Tsuburaya was smiling. Tsuburaya nearly told him that in all of his work he'd always been looking for the patterns that were an object's essence, and that on the boy's coat the bamboo was an emblem of the living bamboo there inside it. The best patterns became the nation's communal property, like that bamboo or England's lion. Or his monster.

The boy suddenly asked why he was weeping. He said he was weeping for all that he'd been granted, and for everything he'd thrown away, then thanked the boy for his concern.

In his toast at the dinner following the premiere, Honda had noted that Tsuburaya's success was centered around his talent for developing a team and uncaging each member's skills. He joked that Tsuburaya led by example and cajoling and intimidation, that for him nothing was ever perfect and no one was ever finished, and he got a laugh by concluding that a day with Tsuburaya was like four with Kurosawa, in terms of consigning someone ever more irrevocably to misery.

For Tsuburaya on nights like that December night, a long walk meant an even later arrival. In his father's childhood, after sunset,

villages were dark and quiet and cold. A gong might call worship-
pers to the candlelit temple. A dog might bark. Otherwise what
one saw and heard was up to the moonlight and wind.

Masano hadn't spoken to him about the movie, though she had
told Hajime that by the end she'd been moved by how profoundly
it had affected the other patrons her age. That December night, the
moment Tsuburaya finally arrived at home, Hajime announced he
was leaving to work on a picture in Malaysia. Masano stopped
serving from her platter and looked at her husband as though all
had been fine before he'd come in. "There he is with his warm
smile," she finally said to Hajime. "Orchestrating his catastrophes."

"This wasn't his idea; it was mine," Hajime answered.

Akira stood up from the table and ran from the room, distraught at his brother's announcement.

"We'll be sorry to see you go," Tsuburaya told his son.

"The only thing you're sorry about is a production delay,"
Masano told him, and Tsuburaya remembered that crows supposedly couldn't feel the sun's heat because they'd already been
scorched black.

She went off to see to Akira, and Hajime finished his meal in
silence. Tsuburaya retired to his study and noted that the nowhere
in which he chose to dwell was the abode of perfect focus. He was
like the blind old teacher who never knew to stop lecturing when
the breeze blew out the light.

He told Hajime this story at the station the next day while they
waited for the train. That he had difficulty keeping his son's attention made him as sad as the departure. Hajime finally said that
he'd rarely heard Tsuburaya talk so much before. The train pulled
in, and they were silent while the arriving passengers streamed off.
They might both have been imagining Akira, back in his room
alone.

"Your brother's going to be very sad to see you go," Tsuburaya
finally said.

This seemed to irk Hajime. "When did I become the villain?"
he asked.

"No one's calling you a villain," Tsuburaya told him.

Hajime handed his bag up to the porter. "You know who you've always reminded me of?" he asked. "Prince Konoye. The two of you, actually." Then he climbed the steps to the car.

Tsuburaya was too surprised to respond. He did manage to ask Hajime if he had enough money, but the porter's departure call distracted them both and the train pulled out. Once it gathered some momentum Hajime waved, once, before his car passed out of sight around the curve with surprising speed.

Tsuburaya was left on the platform, where he remained after the other well-wishers had left. The wind swept a seed pod of some sort onto his foot.

Konoye had been Prime Minister before the attack on Pearl Harbor. He'd always understood what war with America would mean but with each new step toward destruction had lacked the will to insist that the nation do what was right. The joke about him had been that he was so perpetually unsure of his intentions he sometimes got lost en route to the toilet.

Tsuburaya and Masano had talked about Konoye more than once, especially after his death. She'd been very upset about it, in fact. He had poisoned himself before his arrest by the Americans, leaving behind in his room only his family seal and a book, the newspapers had reported. In the book, written by the Englishman Oscar Wilde, Konoye had underlined a single passage, as if he'd hoped to make his amends in pencil: *Nobody great or small can be ruined except by his own hand, and terrible as was what the world did to me, even more terrible still was what I did to myself.*

Boys Town

Here's the story of *my* life: whatever I did wasn't good enough, anything I figured out I figured out too late, and whenever I tried to help I made things worse. That's what it's been like for me as far back as I can remember. Whenever I was about to get somewhere, something would step in and block me. Whenever I was about to finally have something, something would happen to take it away.

"The story of *your* life is that you're not to blame for anything," my mother always said when I told her that. "Out of everybody on earth, you're the only one who never did anything wrong. Whatever happens, it's always somebody else's fault."

"It *is* always somebody else's fault," I told her.

"Poor you," she always said back. "Screwed by the world."

"Hey, Dr. Jägermeister's calling," I used to tell her. "Bottoms up." And she'd just go back to whatever she was watching.

"So what's the deal with dinner?" sometimes I'd say. "You have a busy day?"

"Go to Pizza Hunt," she'd tell me.

"That's *Hut*, you fucking idiot," I'd tell her back. And then she'd say something else wrong the next time, just to frost my ass.

I was thirty-nine years old and living with my mother. I hadn't had a good year.

"What was your last good year?" my friend Owen asked me. "Nineteen ninety-two?"

He wasn't doing too well himself, but he managed to come over once or twice a week to eat whatever we had lying around.

I made some comment about whatever it was we were watching and he said, "What do you like? Do you like anything?"

"He likes to complain," my mother told him. "He likes to make trouble."

I liked to complain. I almost choked.

What did I like? I liked my dog. I liked hunting in the woods. I liked target shooting. I liked my kid, when I was first getting to know him. I liked women who weren't all about money or what I planned to do with my future.

"It'd be different if you ever got laid," Owen said during a commercial. My mother snorted.

"Hey, you're the one with the hand in your pants," I said.

"Now he's going to tell us about Stacey," my mother told him. But I didn't say a word.

My kid was down there in Stacey's house a thousand miles away. I was supposed to send checks but otherwise not come around more than once or twice a year. I mean, try to cram a whole year's worth of family time into one week. Maybe it'd work for you but it didn't for me.

Stacey said the kid was asking where his dad was, and that if I wanted to see him I had to send money. It got so I let my mother answer when she called. They'd stay on the phone telling each other stories about me. "You think *that's* bad," my mother would say.

A guy in Basic told me that girls who weren't good-looking were the smart move because they were more grateful and weren't as likely to run off with somebody, and that made sense to me. I met Stacey at Fort Sill and liked her family better than her. I was a 71 Gulf, which is like a clerk, hospital stuff, administrative. She was, too. I'd be dropping off discharge batches and she kept her head down when I teased her, but I could see her smile.

We went out for a year and five months and then we got married and had a kid. She was always saying she was going to move out but she finally did the deed when I pushed her down the stairs. She was all like "You coulda killed me," and I was like, "Hey: you shoved *me* first, and there was a railing, and there was carpet." She said, "You don't shove somebody at the top of the stairs," and I said, "Well what did you do to *me*?" And the cop who showed up was a guy who had a crush on her in high school and he was all, "You can't be with this person. You want to press charges?"

He's standing over her while she's crying at the kitchen table and I'm in the den thinking, *Why don't you rub her fucking back?* And she was all Miss Generous: "No, just get him out of here. I don't feel safe."

Out here in the fucking sticks you don't meet anybody. I went to this singles' social in the basement rec room of the church. You had to fill out forms so they could match people up. These two women were running the thing. They asked if I could read and write. When they saw my face they said it was just a question on the form.

But then I always reminded myself I didn't have it so bad. Our next-door neighbor's nineteen-year-old had some kind of thing, muscular dystrophy maybe, and they told her kids like him only lived to be about twenty-one. When she came over for coffee with my mother, she told us to pray that his heart muscle stopped before his lungs, because that'd be a less horrible way to go.

I had all kinds of jobs. If it was some fucking thing no one else wanted to do, I did it. I worked in a hospital laundry. I washed pots and pans. I separated metals in a scrapyard. I drove a shuttle. That job had a little pin that came with it that said *Martin, for Comfort Inn.* Whenever I said stuff to my mother like I could see why my dad walked out, she'd go, "Where's your pin? Don't lose your pin."

I started thinking I should just go off the grid. You know, if I wasn't using anything or spending anything, I didn't need to make anything. I'd grow my own garden and shit. In the winter there'd still be rabbits and deer. I'd work out. Read a book. Improve my mind, unlike the other fucking imbeciles around here.

"Who says you're not using anything or spending anything?"

my mother said when I told her. "*Somebody's* cleaning out the refrigerator every two days."

"That'd be your friend Owen," I said. "Your TV pal."

"*My* friend Owen?" she said. "He doesn't come over to see *me.*"

"Well, I never asked him to come over and see me," I told her.

"So why's he come?" my mother said.

"Because he's a fucking *bum,* like me," I told her. " 'Cause he's got nothing else to do with himself."

"All right, all right," she said. "Don't get excited."

"Don't get excited," I said.

"Don't get excited," she said. "Put that down."

The Comfort Inn was my last job. I took two days off to go to my grandmother's funeral and they never let me forget it. The week I was back even when I did a good job on something all I heard was You never told anybody you weren't coming in, you didn't let us know we were supposed to cover for you, you left us holding the bag. I'm working and the supervisor's just standing there running me down instead of doing his job. I finally told him that kind of horseshit was all well and good but, you know, it was pretty unprofessional.

You get lonely, is what it is. A person's not supposed to go through life with absolutely nobody. It's not normal. The longer you go by yourself the weirder you get, and the weirder you get the longer you go by yourself. It's a loop and you gotta do something to get out of it.

There was this girl Janice who I saw a lot at the store. I started talking to her, because it seemed like she was always out, and I was always out. I went to the library a lot, or the store, and I'd see her. She seemed like a good person, and when I was with her I found myself thinking maybe I could do this or maybe that. Sit down at a restaurant with someone and eat like a human being. Take her back to my place and maybe watch a movie or something if my mother would ever fucking leave the house.

Naturally this Janice had an ex-husband who was a cop. But as far as I could tell she didn't see too much of him.

I didn't need to be near any cops. The last thing I needed was somebody running a check on me.

My mother and Owen didn't know about Janice. They didn't know I had a plan all worked out. That asshole here hadn't completely given up.

One of the times I saw her in the library she was taking out like three DVDs about Milo and Otis. I said to her, "So you like dogs, huh?" and she said she did. I asked if she had one and she said yes to that, too. I told her I had one and she asked what kind and I told her. She said when she was leaving that maybe she'd see me walking it and I told her that maybe she would.

I went over there twice with my dog and couldn't get myself to go up to the front door either time. The second time I was talking to myself and it still didn't work. And while I was standing there my dog took a dump on her sidewalk.

I walked the woods for however many years and know the area better than anybody. Down the end of the logging road where people went to park, on the edge of the state forest, I hid a bag, a big duffel, that had a sleeping bag and two knives and one of my rifles in it. One of the knives was really more like a machete and ax combined. I had some bug spray in there, too. I thought it would be like a survival bag, if it came to that. I had it all in a big plastic garbage bag to keep it dry. Then somebody stole the whole thing.

I got everything in Wichita Falls at a gun-and-knife show after I got out of the military. I still had the .308 and a .357 Desert Eagle and a lot of ammo, so I started another bag. This one I made sure I hid better.

Fifth grade we used to play this capture-the-flag game where anybody who got touched had to go stand on the base and there'd be fewer and fewer kids left after one side started winning. Fifth grade for some reason everybody decided it was boys against girls, and they'd pick out who they wanted to get caught by. You had to use two hands to touch and I would always tear free and so I'd be one of the last ones running around. This horrible cold day the girls were looking at their first win if they could just get me. Four or five of them boxed me in and everybody on both sides was going crazy. This girl named Katie Kiely was right in front of me and all she had to do was step forward. I remember not being able to stop myself from grinning. And her expression changed when she saw my teeth, and she couldn't make that last move. The other girls were shouting at her and then it was like they caught what she had and they couldn't step forward either. It was like I was a hair in their food. The teacher rang the recess bell and we all just stood there looking at each other. Then she rang it again and we all went inside.

My dad left the year before, or the year before that. I was in either third or fourth grade. Apparently when he and my mother could still joke around it was always about me coming to a bad end. At least that's what she said later. Like anybody could tell anything about anybody when they were nine years old. One Christmas she said that as part of the joke he gave her a VHS of *Boys Town,* the movie where Spencer Tracy's the priest and Mickey Rooney's the tough kid who goes straight because he gets a new baseball glove or smells some home-cooked bread or some fucking thing.

She watched it every year around Christmas. I think it might've been the only thing he gave her that she didn't throw out after he took off. She'd always go, "Your movie's on," after she put it in the machine, but she always ended up watching it by herself.

There was one scene in it I liked, where a kid at one of the big lunch tables at the home tells Mickey Rooney how easygoing the place is, and how if he wants, he can go on being Catholic or Protestant or whatever. And Rooney tells him, "Well, I'm nothin'." And the kid says back, "Well, then you can go *on* bein' nothin'. And nobody cares." And one of the other kids showing him around says that on a clear day you can see Omaha from there. And Rooney goes, "Yeah? And *then* what've you got?"

I didn't think I'd seen the movie that often but I got it in my head so I must've watched it a lot. There's this other scene where they're about to strap a guy who didn't pan out into the electric chair. And the guy goes to Spencer Tracy, "How much time have I got, Father?" And Tracy goes, "Eternity begins in forty-five minutes, Dan." And the guy asks him, "What happens then?" And Tracy goes, "Oh, a bad minute or two." And the guy's like, "After that?" And Tracy tells him, "Dan, that's been a mystery for a million years. You can't expect to crack *that* in a few seconds."

There were a lot of things I wanted to do about my appearance but only so much could get accomplished until I got certain things squared away. I recognized that. I had a lot of stress. That's what nobody understood. I was in the military and after that I was working two jobs, and trying to raise a family, and it seemed like even so, living at home and not doing anything, I had even more stress than I used to. Back then I never complained about it, I just did it, but people didn't realize that I did whatever the average person did times two. I took whatever shit the average person took times four. And I never said anything, never said a fucking thing. I did my job and worked my eighty-hour weeks and knew as sure as shit that whatever I wanted was going to get taken away from me.

And the kind of thoughts I started to have people had all the time. But it was like everybody said: thinking and doing were two different things.

After my dog took the dump on her sidewalk I didn't see Janice around for like three weeks. I thought maybe she was avoiding me. Or maybe she'd gone to Florida. Or maybe she was dead. I wrote a note, finally, and stuck it in her screen door: ARE YOU STILL INTERESTED IN DOG WALKING? And then when I got home I remembered I hadn't put my number on it. And then I remembered I hadn't put my name on it.

That third week, my dog finally flushed a turkey in the state forest and I blew its wing off. I took it home to my mother and she said, "I'm not cleaning that fucking thing." And I said, "I bring you a whole turkey and you act like all I'm doing is making work for you?" And she said, "I'm not gonna start up with you," and went back to her show. So I threw the turkey in our Dumpster. Then when I was walking the woods I thought that was stupid, so I hiked all the way back and pulled it out. I'd give it to some charity or church so some poor kid could have some decent meat. So somebody could get something good out of it.

The guy who sold me my Desert Eagle told me that it was the last of the Israeli ones and that no more were going to be imported. Somebody else told me later that that was bullshit. I got all the extras at the same time and taught myself how to change the barrel length, so the version I had in my new bag had the ten-inch barrel instead of the six. The guy at Gilbert's Gun & Sportsman kept telling me he wanted to see it again. He called it "the Hand Cannon." I joined an Owners' Forum on one of the USA Carry Web sites for a little while to get some tips and just talk to somebody. My user name was MrNoTrouble and somebody trying to be funny asked if that was the name my mother gave me and I said yeah. I met some guys online who seemed okay and some of them said they knew what I was going through. One guy, triplenutz, didn't live too far away and said we should meet up and go hunting together, but we never did. Another guy talked about taking his old toilet out back and letting fly at it with his Eagle from eighty yards. He recommended the experience for all Eagle owners. He said a piece of the flush tank broke the garage window behind him.

I got my dog from the stray facility at Fort Sill when I was leaving. I saw his photo on the Morale, Welfare, and Recreation Web site. The poor little fuck was just sitting there behind the chain link looking at his paws. The adoption fee was fifty-two dollars but that came with rabies and distemper-parvo shots, plus deworming and the heartworm test.

I stayed away a couple days after the turkey incident and when I got back I sat on the porch and cleaned my rifle in the cold. After a while the porch light went on and finally the door opened and my mother asked me to take her shopping. She had the door open only a little, to keep the heat in. "I need some things," she said after I didn't answer, like she was explaining.

"Why didn't you have Owen take you?" I said. She'd had trouble driving since she hurt her back. It didn't bother her to ride, though.

"He hasn't been around since you left," she said. "So you gonna take me or what?"

We went to the Price Chopper and the state package store. "It's not for me," she said when she told me about the second stop. "I'm getting stocking stuffers for Daryl."

I went up and down the AM dial while she was in there. Every single song I heard was what my father used to call a complete and utter piece of shit. "Don't ask me who Daryl is," I said to her when she finally came out.

"You know who Daryl is," she said. She dumped the bags on the seat between us.

"I thought this wasn't for you?" I said, looking at the Jägermeister.

"I was here, I figured I might as well get something for myself," she said.

The other bag was filled with little travel bottles of liquor. "I got an assortment," she said. "He likes those and Peppermint Patties."

"I think you got that thing they talk about on the news," she said when we were halfway home. "PTSD. Is that what it is? I think you need to talk to somebody."

"PMS," I told her.

"I think you need to talk to somebody," she said.

"I talk to somebody every day," I told her. "Believe me, it's no fucking picnic."

"Owen said you could file a claim," she said. "Everyone gets something from the government except my kid."

"That's because your kid's an imbecile," I told her. "We already know that."

"All I'm saying is I think you need to talk to somebody," she said. "And now I'm gonna drop the subject."

When we got home the poor fucking dog had wrapped himself around the tree with his chain. I don't know why we left him outside, anyway.

"You're not gonna help me carry stuff in?" my mother said when I left her in the car.

She showed up in the door to my room a few hours later after I was in bed. "There's phone numbers and stuff you can find," she said. "Owen told me."

"So have Owen call them, then," I said.

"Owen doesn't need them," she said.

"You got enough money," I told her. "And I been through worse shit in this house than I been through out of it." And that shut her up for like three days.

When she was finally ready to talk I went back to the woods. I took the dog but of course he ran away. I only found him again when I got back to the house. People like to talk about cancer or strokes but if I was going to get something I'd want to get cholera. I came across it on the Plagues & Epidemics website and they said that it killed 38 million people in India in less than a hundred years. It even sounds like nothing you want to fuck with: *cholera.*

After Basic at Fort Sill I was in for four-and-a-half active and then four in the Reserves. In the Reserves I trained to be a 91 Bravo, which was a field medic, but I washed out. When they gave me the news they said not to worry, they'd still find me something to do. I ended up working out at the Casualty and Mortuary Affairs Operations Center. "What'd you do there?" my mother wanted to know when I got back. "Oh, you know, a little bit of this, little bit of that," I told her. I think she was watching *The Farmer's Daughter*. Even Owen had to laugh.

You want to talk about sad: even after all I been through, one of the saddest things I ever saw was a year after I got home, when my mother pulled over at a stop sign, it must've been ten below, and she's got the window down and she's scooping snow from the side mirror and trying to throw it on her windshield to clean it. We'd gone about three blocks and couldn't see a thing before she finally pulled over. I'm sitting there watching while she leans forward and tosses snow around onto the outside of the glass. Then every so often she hits the wipers.

She did this for like five minutes. We're pulled over next to a Stewart's. They got wiper fluid on sale in the window twenty-five feet away. She doesn't go get some. She doesn't ask me to help. She doesn't even get out of the car to try and do it herself.

My hair started falling out. I found it on my comb in the mornings. I could see where it was coming from. Not that anybody gives a shit, but you put that together with the teeth and you have quite the package.

I came in from thirty minutes of sliding slush off the porch and there was my kid's voice on the machine. My mother was playing it over again and turned it off when I got inside. She went back to whatever she was doing at the sink.

"Were you gonna tell me he called?" I asked.

"You cleaned up all that ice already?" she asked me back.

"I didn't do the ice. I did the slush," I told her.

"What am I supposed to do about the ice?" she wanted to know. I left her and went into the living room. She said, "There's a message from his mother, too. She says she's gonna get a lawyer to hop your ass unless you start sending some money. And somebody else called," she added, once she was back in front of the TV.

I went out to the kitchen and played the machine. There was only one message and it was from the kid, saying he wanted to wish me a happy holiday. He said, "There was a thing about your unit in the paper so I sent it up to you." I could hear a little buzzing, maybe something in our phone, maybe something in his. "Let me know if you get it," he said after a minute, like he was waiting for someone to answer.

I'd been getting a headache that felt like lights going on and off and trying to crack my skull. "Who else called?" I asked. I was still standing there at the machine. The water from my boots was black from all the shit in the snow.

"How would I know?" my mother called from the living room. "She didn't leave a name."

"It was a woman?" I asked. "She wanted me? Was her name Janice?"

"I just said she didn't leave a name," she said. When I went back to the living room and stood in front of her, she said, "I can't see," meaning the television. "You got in *here* fast," she added, after I sat back down on the sofa. "What do you got, a girlfriend?"

I kept thinking this was my one chance, and then about how Janice could've found my number. Maybe she asked someone at the library?

"You're not answering me now?" my mother said.

"I'm trying to *think* here," I told her.

She shut up for a while. Then she finally said, "I don't know why anybody would want to give *you* the time of day."

I was thinking I should get the dog and go over Janice's house, but it was sleeting. I figured I'd do it when it got better out. But I couldn't sit still and my mother finally said, "You're shaking the whole floor," meaning with my leg, so I went up to my room. The dog came up to check on me and took one look and went downstairs again.

Then it got so bad I had to go out anyway so I hiked down to the creek and checked some of my traps. I was wearing my field jacket with the hood but I still got soaked. Two of the traps I couldn't find and there was nothing in the third because I don't even know if I'm setting them right but a month ago I found one snapped shut with some blood around it in the snow. When I got back there were police cars all around my house. I hid in the sand pit a few houses down and watched until they went away.

What is this *what is this what is this?* I was thinking. I was surprised how much it freaked me out. I had some tricks I'd come up with over the years to keep from losing it, and I used them all. I waited a half hour after the cop cars left and lay there banging my chin on my gloves. Who else did I know who'd be in a sand pit in the snow outside somebody else's house?

The sleet changed to rain. It was so cold my head was rattling. One of the medics supposedly training me in the Reserves used to call me TBI, for Traumatic Brain Injury. The first time he called me that I told him I hadn't had any brain injuries, and he said, "Well, maybe it happened when you were a baby."

Finally I stood up and came down the hill and circled my house on the outside. The backyard was like a lake. The light was on in my mother's bedroom and I went up to the window. On the dresser under the lamp there was a pamphlet that said, *Your Service Member Is Home!* The TV was going in the living room but maybe she was in the cellar. I waited until she came up the stairs and then pushed through the back door.

"They're looking for *you*, boy," she said when she saw me. Not, You must be fucking freezing. Not, how about a warm shower.

"What'd they want?" I asked.

"They said they had a number of things they wanted to talk to you about," she said. "They wanted to look in your room and I said, You got a warrant? I told them you'd be back tonight."

"What'd you say that for?" I asked.

"What was I supposed to tell them?" she said. "That you were out looking for a job?"

I went up to my room to think. There were some issues about prescriptions at the local pharmacy. Some bad checks back in Wichita Falls. There was a girl I'd scared by not letting her past me when we ran into each other in the woods. She'd torn her sleeve when she finally got away. It could've been a lot of things.

"I gotta go," I said when I came back downstairs. "I'm gonna do some camping for a while."

"Camping," she said. "In this." She put her hand out to the window.

"Don't tell them where I went," I said. "Far as you know, I never came home."

"I should be so lucky," she said.

I changed into dry clothes and put on like twelve layers and got together a rain fly and a cooking stove and a tent and a big pack full of cans of food and other shit and got out of there. "You taking your *dog*?" she called, but I never heard what she said after that.

It took me an hour to get to the end of the logging road because I was covering my tracks with a pine branch as I went, and then another hour to find the duffel bag in the snow, and from there I followed a creek uphill way into the forest. I found a spot I already knew they had good cover and visibility and got everything set up and then started going through what I had and just what it was I thought I was going to do.

There was a trail fifty yards below that did a hairpin, and snow-mobilers used it and cross-country skiers. Farther down was a waterfall and swimming hole and I remembered a notice on the library's Christian Outings bulletin board about a faith hike for teens called the Polar Bear Mixer.

I figured, Well, if I'm going to jail I might as well get something to eat first, so I made some stew. And while I was eating I started thinking that once the cops had me one thing would lead to another and I knew what went on in jail, I'd heard stories. So I emptied the duffel in the tent and got all geared up. I had stuff I didn't even know I had. A bipod mount for the rifle and a winter camo wrap for the stock and barrel and scope. Even winter camo field bandages. When I was finished I felt like this way I was at least ready for whatever.

But nobody came down the trail. It got dark. I got some sleep. Nobody came the next day, either. I had little meatballs for breakfast and sat around and waited and finally went out looking for rabbits but the snow was too deep so I had to come back.

I'd stepped in the creek and even with three layers of socks my feet were freezing. In the credits part of *Boys Town* right at the beginning there was a kid in an alley warming his hands over a fire in a bucket. I'd forgotten that.

The guy that gets electrocuted is the one who gives Spencer Tracy the idea for the orphans' home in the first place. When they're getting ready to take the guy to the chair the governor tells him he owes a debt to the state, and the guy goes nuts on them. He asks where the state was when he was a little kid crying himself to sleep in a flophouse with drunks and hoboes. He says if he had one friend when he was twelve he wouldn't be standing here like this. Then he throws everybody but Tracy out of his cell.

I spent the afternoon keeping the stove going and sitting on a tarp and squeezing my head with my hands. The difference between where I was and my mother's house was that where I was I didn't have to listen to TV.

I had everything I needed in front of me and I still couldn't let well enough alone. That night it sleeted again and the next morning my stove was covered with ice. I washed my face and changed my socks and got my Desert Eagle and hiked back down to the road and through the woods to the culvert that led the back way into town. It was sunny and I was sweating like a pig by the time I climbed out of the culvert at the turnaround at the end of Janice's street, but I didn't want to hang around for too long so I stood there for a few minutes with my field jacket open, flapping it to dry myself off, and then went up to her house and rang the bell. The

Eagle hung in the big inside pocket like a tire iron and I thought, *I don't know what you brought* that *for.* A guy swung the door open like he'd been waiting for me. He had to be the ex-husband. He looked me up and down and said, "What can I help *you* with?" But I let it go and just said, "Is Janice here?" And he gave me another look and I remembered how sweaty I was and that I was wearing four shirts under my field jacket. Collars were sticking up all over the place.

He said, "Yeah, she's in the back. What can we help you with?"

I stood there bouncing my leg for a second and reached under my coat like my Eagle might've fallen out. Then Janice came up behind him and I saw her get a good look at me. And I just said, "Nothing. I'll come back," and I left.

"Hey," the guy called from behind me, and I heard Janice laugh. Halfway down the block I cut through somebody's yard into the culvert. My heart was going so fast I was sure I was having a heart attack. She was probably still laughing. He was laughing with her. It was a comedy. I crouched at the bottom of the culvert and stepped around like a midget taking a walk. Even my outside shirts were soaked. I can never believe how fast I sweat through my clothes at times like that.

I worked my way up the culvert to Janice's backyard and then ran up to their window but it was too high to see in so I just reached up as far as I could and squeezed off four rounds. From that angle, I probably just hit the ceiling. The Eagle's so loud that at first your ears can't believe it. Somebody yelled something but I couldn't tell what. After the last round I was booking back through the yard for the culvert. I could hear somebody whooping from the next house over. They probably thought it was fireworks. And while I was hauling down the culvert to my path through the woods I got to hear sirens from every cop car in upstate New York.

The whole way back through the woods and up into the hills I thought, *You're* going to be hard to track. I mean, the snow was three feet deep. Even the town cops weren't going to be able to screw this up.

I had to rest on the logging road and again along the creek but finally got back to the tent. I pulled out my sleeping bag and threw my rifle and the Eagle and all the rounds I had on top of it. I could hear guys on the logging road already, the sound carried that far.

People talk about, Oh, this kid's sick and that kid's bipolar and this and that and I always say, Well, does he piss all over himself? And the answer's always no. That's because he *chooses* to go to the bathroom. Because he *knows* better. He *controls* himself. People *control* what they do. Most people don't know what it's like to look down the road and see there's nothing there. You try to tell somebody that but they just look at you. I don't know why people need to hear the same thing ten thousand times, but they do.

Guys are breaking through the brush down below to my left and right, which tells me they're not only coming but they're coming in numbers. I can start to see them even through the trees.

I haven't cleaned the rifle. Mr. Logistical Planning. Even when I try to make lists for myself I can't follow the lists.

At least I tried, though. I tried harder than most people think. But what I did was, in life you're supposed to leave yourself an out, and I didn't.

I can hear even more sirens, off in the distance. The cops down below have stopped short of the hairpin. They're keeping their voices low. They might be starting to catch on. I dig deeper into the snow, wipe my eyes, and put my face back to the scope, sighting back and forth. I don't even know if I'll open fire. I never know what I'm going to do next. They'll probably just come up here and pull me to my feet and push me all the way down the hill. Another scene that always got me in that movie was when the kids were waiting for Spencer Tracy to bring something home for Christmas. Of course he didn't have any money so all he can pull out and show them is a package of cornmeal mush. And this one little kid just stares at him. And then the kid finally says, like he wants to kill somebody, "What *else* you got in that bag?" And when Tracy has to tell him that he doesn't have anything else, the kid goes, "I thought you said that if we were good, somebody would help us."

Classical Scenes of Farewell

As a child who could barely hold myself upright without tottering, I was steeped in my mother's belief that our tumbledown farm was serried about and tumid with devils. In my mind's eye they stood in a ring and clasped one another's taloned hands and leered in at me while I slept. My fourth summer was the year that Sophie, the stonemason's daughter, was seized with a helplessness in her limbs until her father conceded her diabolic possession and took her to the Church of Our Savior, where the priest found five devils residing inside her, whose names were Wolf, Lark, Dog, Jolly, and Griffin. The devils confessed they'd conjured hailstones through her by beating the surface of well water with her hands and that they'd additionally concocted the tinctures and ointments she'd used to blight her neighbors' apple trees. They said they'd requested, and been denied, a special grease that would have turned her into a werewolf. When asked of whom they'd made their appeal, they said only "The Master."

When I was twelve, the man from whom we rented our pastureland—a lifelong bachelor whose endless mutterings were his way of negotiating his solitude, and whose imagination extended only to business; the sort who milled his rye without sifting it, so it might last longer—was found in the middle of our lane one winter morning, naked, his feet and lips blue. He said a demon had appeared to him on a pile of wood under his mulberry tree, in the likeness of a corpulent black cat belonging to the house next door.

171

With its front paws the cat had gripped him by the shoulders and pushed him down, and then had fastened its muzzle on the man's mouth and would not be denied. The man claimed that for nearly an hour he'd remained that way, swooning, speechless, and open to the cat's searching jaws, unable to make even the Sign of the Cross and powerless to diminish the urgings of its tongue. He had no memory of where his clothes had gone, or how he'd ended up in the lane.

My mother had long since taken to enfolding a crucifix in the bedcovers when she turned down my poor linens for the night. My chamber was in our barn's loft, attached to the back of the house, and from this, the highest point on the hill, I could view the Delorts' farm to the west. Their daughter, Katherine, was the continual object of my confused nightly agitations as well as the focus of my joy.

And then one sunstruck August afternoon when we were passing through the village, my mother and I investigated a disturbance on the church steps, a crowd squabbling over who had sufficient schooling to interpret the document posted on the doors before them. A sacristan emerged to provide assistance and to read aloud what he declared to be a juridical confession lately obtained through the harrowing of some of our neighbors. Said neighbors had been identified to the ecclesiastical investigators by other neighbors.

The confession stated that Marie Delort along with her daughter had for three years been giving herself over to a pair of demons, from Friday midnight through to Saturday dawn, and had assisted at a series of conjurings in the company of others. According to the deacon Katherine had testified that her association began when one evening, washing her family's linen outside of town, she saw before her a man with a curved back and pointed ears whose eyes were like emeralds in an ash pit. He called for her to give herself to him and she answered that she would. He then gentled her cheeks with both hands, his palms softly furred, and flooded her mouth with his breath, and from then on each Friday night she was carried to a gathering from her own bed, simply by willing herself free. At the gathering place she shed her night-dress and was approached, every time having been made to wait for a period alone in the darkness, by the same man leading a gigantic he-goat, which knelt before her, and to both apparitions she abandoned herself.

The sacristan then read her mother's corroboration of this account, which further detailed the strange trance during which she was also transported from her bed, and their mutual adoration of the goat and the man, and their not only bathing in but also taking in all sorts of offensive liquids, with satiation being the object of their every clutch and gesture.

I was born Etienne Corillaut of Pouzauges, in the diocese of Luçon, and am known as Poitou, and I am now of twenty-two years of age, and here acknowledge to the best of my abilities the reasons for those acts that have made this name along with my master's the object of hatred throughout the region. I here also address the questions that my kinsmen hear from every stable hand, every innkeeper, every farmer in his field: What transpired in his mind that allowed a young person to have acted in such a manner and then to have lived apparently untroubled among his fellows? What enabled him to have stepped forward into the sunlight and Nature's bounty for *six years* of such iniquity?

My master is Gilles de Rais, whom I have served as page and then bodyservant for these last six years; and for the past three, since he first offered access to the full chamber of his secrets, he and I with five others I will name have been responsible for the entrapment and mutilation and dismemberment and death of one hundred and forty-two children between the ages of five and fifteen. Coming in the Year of Our Lord 1440, this admission dates the full vigor of my offenses back to the winter of 1437. But even before he chose to sweep back the curtain on the full extent of his ferocity, I knew myself to be already standing outside the ring of salvation, having failed so signally as a neighbor and a brother and a Christian and a son.

My father failed no one, having been brought up in honesty and industry with a mild and peaceable disposition, and my first memory of my mother is of the two of us gathering into her basket rue and southernwood in bright sunlight. I remember her saying one sweltering morning that the forest, our edge of pastureland, and a hive of bees were our only livelihood. I remember her tears. Later there was a shed and a little tower with a dovecote. We raised rye and beans and pot-herbs. As I grew stronger I was given suitable responsibilities, my first being light weeding during the day and laying the table and filling the hand basin after sunset. Before that my contributions had been limited to fanning the wasps out of my little sister's sweet milk.

At that time I was devout. I retired each morning to pray and refused refreshment for a quarter of an hour afterward. And I displayed other singularities. My brother and sister avoided me, which I attributed to acts of stupidity that somehow had discredited me forever. I played alone, chopping at roadside weeds with my special stick. "Still fighting your cabbages?" my brother asked one day, having seen me thrash some wild collards.

My mother liked to claim that all she brought to the marriage was a bench, bed, and chest, and I first registered their sadness while hiding in the fields watching my father cut clover. My mother brought him soup, ladling it out in the shade of an elm, and he said, "Will you kiss me?" and she answered, "We all have our needs." He then told her to take back her soup, for he didn't want it, and scythed all the clover without eating and returned hungry to the house.

He complained later that it was as if his accounts were tallied small coin by small coin. She confided in my brother, her favorite, that she lived in dread of bad weather, during which his father would pass the hours in the kitchen, his resentment turning from the weather to her. We slept with pounding hearts when they fought.

And during a rainy October the day after my eleventh birthday my brother fell sick of a malady of the brain. We moved him to a room off the kitchen with a hearth that backed on to our stove, where during sickness or bloodletting or weaning, a greater warmth could be maintained. My mother made him an egg dish into which she chopped dittany, tansy, marjoram, fennel, parsley, beets, violet leaves, and pounded ginger. He was seized with convulsions and his writhing was such that she couldn't stay in the room. He died at cock's crow two mornings after he was first afflicted.

She afterward seemed so bereft and storm-tossed that our neighbors called her "the Wind's Wife." November imprisoned the farm with its load of ice, sheathing both sickle and hoe. In our little pond fish hung motionless and petrified with cold. My mother kept to herself in the kitchen, puzzled and drained by our questions, her smile gloomy and terrible in its simplicity. Our father sat on a stool drawn up near the door, a hermit paying his visit to a sister hermit.

And even after the winter seemed well ended it suffered a relapse, piling snow deeper atop our work. My sister and I offered ourselves to our mother without success. On this side and that, she seemed to find only sore constraint and bitter captivity. Her blood turned thin as water and she developed scrofulous complaints. When at her angriest, she wiped my nose, violently, and said it was oppressive to be looked at so reproachfully by children. If we asked for too much, her panicked response frightened us further.

Her own presence seemed to distress her. She fell endlessly behind in her work. She was found at all hours bent in half and rubbing her back. She couldn't warm her hands. One palm on the table would quiver, and, seeing us notice, she'd cover it with the other.

Our animals sickened as if bewitched. Our cat died of hunger. When the weather permitted my mother sat in the field as far as possible from the house. When storms drove us inside, on occasion I glimpsed her before she had composed her expression. One sleeting morning she taught my sister a game, based on the stations of a woman's life, that she called Tired, Exhausted, Dying, and Dead.

At night when I was visited by strange dreams and pleaded for her company, she told me she'd seen witches lying in the fields on their backs, naked up to the navel. She fixed on a story from a neighboring town of a man who'd confessed that he'd killed seven successive boys in his wife's womb by means of his magic, and that he'd also withered the offspring of his father-in-law's herd. She told us that lost girls were cooked in a cauldron until the flesh entire came away from the bone, from which the witches made an unguent that was a great aid to their arts and pleasures. She followed closely the sensational story of de Giac, the king's favorite, who confessed he had given one of his hands to the Devil, and who asked when condemned that this hand be severed and burned before he was put to death.

She took her life with a series of plants that my father said she had gathered from the most sinister localities. We discovered her early one bright morning. I remained in place near her bed, remembering her hand slipping off my inhospitable arm the evening before when she'd been trying to negotiate some ice on our doorstep.

I was fourteen. My sister was nine. We discussed what had happened as though it all belonged to a period now concluded. Our day-to-day world having fallen away, something else would take its place.

After that I paid only distracted attention to the ordinary round of life. If others came too close, I made signs with my hands as if to repair the harm I'd done them. At times during chores I would halt as if seized by my own vacancy. I saw very well how people looked upon me. I despised in my heart those who despised me. And when my father saw me in such torments, he thought: he loved her so much he's still weeping.

All I desired, morning in and evening out, was a love with its arms thrown wide. But the contrary is the common lot, everyone's family telling him furiously that everything hurts, always. The nest makes the bird.

This potter's wheel of futility and despair would have continued had our parish priest not singled out my voice for his choir, and detected in me what he claimed were aptitudes, especially for the sciences. What he offered as appreciation I took to be pity. It was suggested to my father that I be turned over to the monastic school at Pont-à-Sevre. But even before that decision could be made, Henriet Griart, having heard the choir, brought me to his lord de Rais's attention. He was then seventeen, and quick-eyed and enterprising in his service as steward.

Thus does this chronicle turn, harsh and bleak as it is, from one misfortune to another. I was presented at Tiffauges, which was so tall that its towers were cloud-capped when I first saw them, and orange in the setting sun. Out of its windows summer had never been so mild, dusk so vivid, or the surrounding hills so shady in their grateful abundance of streams and gardens. My sponsor, who'd refused converse during the carriage ride, provided some instruction on etiquette while we waited in the great hall, adding that if I behaved he'd see that my promotion was advanced with great ingenuity.

His kindness moved me. And when the doors opened for the castle's master and his retinue, tears sprang to my eyes. My interview was conducted through that blur of weeping. This was the lord whom even I knew to be one of the richest in France. Who'd fought side by side with Joan the year our country had pulled herself from her knees. Who'd drawn the bolt from the Maid's shoulder and in her vanguard had raised the siege of Orleans.

The sun was fully set. Boys in special surplices moved from candelabra to candelabra with delicate, whiplike tapers. All of the wall tapestries featured hunting scenes. His first words, seeming to come from somewhere behind him, were that I was a little angel. He had reddish hair and a trimmed red beard. A blue satin ruff. His face in the candlelight was like a half-veiled lamp.

Henriet was told to prepare me. I was pulled into an antechamber where my clothes were stripped from me and burned on a grate. I was fitted with a doublet of green and brown velvet and loose-fitting breeches and shoes, then taken through a small passageway bolted with an iron gate on either end and set with chevrons along its length to what looked like a side-chapel arranged with painted screens. Above the screens loomed the worked canopy of a gigantic bed. In the firelight the embroidered tigers flexed and clawed their mates. Benches with saw-tooth serrations above the headrests lined the walls. This seemed a secret room constructed where roof trusses converged from the projecting base.

A boy near the door was identified by Henriet as the aquebajulus: custodian of the holy water. He held before him a small bronze bowl. Upon entering, each of the lords dipped two fingers in it and made the Sign of the Cross, and then the boy departed.

Those present in that chamber besides myself, Henriet, and the lord de Rais were his lord's cousins Gilles de Sillé and Roger de Briqueville. That night while they took their ease on those benches and drank hippocras from a silver beaker that the steward had fetched, I was made to shed the doublet I had just donned and to lie across the billowy down of the bed's snowy comforter and to receive onto my belly the ejaculate of his lord's member. He knelt above me, having finished, attentive to my face with his head cocked as though listening for something, and then Roger de Briqueville handed him a jeweled dagger, the tip of which he pressed to my Adam's apple, and the sting caused me to squint before his other cousin cleared his throat and reminded him of my uncommon beauty, suggesting I be retained as a page. The lord de Rais turned his gaze to Henriet, who looked at me. In his eyes I saw my mother's gloomy and drained consideration. He shrugged, and nodded. With that shrug his lord returned his attention to my features. He set the dagger on the coverlet between us, touched his semen with a fingertip, and drew a line to my throat with it. Then he dismounted the bed. I was ignored through the conversation that followed.

Lying there, not yet having been granted leave to move, I experienced the ongoing impression that all this was inexplicably directed at me. The lord remarked that when he was three, his brother, René de la Suze, was born, upsetting the entire household, and that relations between them had never been cordial. He added that when at eleven he'd lost both parents, his father gored by a boar and his mother carried off by an inflammation of the brain. That same autumn had brought the disgrace of Agincourt, with the loss of his maternal grandfather's lone son and heir.

When he stopped the only sounds were the logs on the fire. Henriet caught my eyes with his but I couldn't tell what he hoped to communicate. And the lord de Rais, as though he'd already asked more than once, bade everyone to leave. When I rose, he instructed me to stay.

The firelight shimmered because I was weeping with terror. He asked my age in a gentle voice and, when answered, exclaimed "Fifteen!" with a kind of graciousness, as if at an unexpected gift.

He asked if I had heard of the emperor Nero. When I could not stop my tears, he went on to inform me that Nero never wore the same clothes twice. That he almost never traveled with a train of less than one thousand carriages. That his mules were shod with silver and his muleteers wore coats of Carnusian wool.

He said that at my age he knew already the men who were to influence the entire course of his life. That these great souls had taught him that to venture little was to venture much, and the risk the same.

He returned to the bed and eased himself down beside me, sympathetic to my shivering and heaving. While touching me he explained that balked desire, seeing itself checked as if by a cruel spell, undergoes a hideous metamorphosis. And steep and slippery then became the slope between voluptuous delight and rage. He said he was still undecided as to whether he was of a mind to let me rest and that only a straw turned the scale which kept me there. He lay beside me in silence for some moments while I regained custody of my emotions. Then he made me swear I would reveal none of the secrets about to be entrusted to me, prefatory to the oath

administered a few hours later before the altar in the Chapel of the
Holy Trinity. In swearing so I understood I was gathering to my
heart the secrets of sins both committed and to come. This oath
was taken in the presence of the same gathering that had witnessed
the initial events in the secret room. And following the oath I was
seated at the lord de Rais's right hand for a dinner of roast goose
with sausages, a stew of hares, white leeks with capons, plovers,
dressed pigs, a fish jelly, bitterns, and herons in claret, with rice in
milk and saffron afterward.

My account proceeds by gaps, not unlike my life. The castle at
Champtocé was an apparition out of a fairy story: black and grave,
sprouting crooked tall towers with battlements like broken teeth.
Grimly flattened fields surrounded it. But everything inside was
transformed by braziers of light and furniture of gold leaf, by
statues and bound manuscripts of worked silver. My sponsor
explained the tumult of passing men-at-arms by informing me
that our lord kept a personal army of two hundred and fifty, each
equipped with the finest mounts and armor, as well as complete
new liveries three times a year. He traveled, Henriet explained,
from residence to residence and kept an open house at each, so
that anyone, high-born or low, could stop for food and drink. As
for the low, it was well-known that this invitation was extended
only to young and beautiful children, either unaccompanied or, if
not, left behind to dine at their leisure.

He unlocked a curved black grate guarding access to a spiral
stairwell ascending the north tower, and led me up the stone steps
and at the top we paused before a room, also locked. The smell was
startling. Henriet held a small cloth soaked in cloves over his nose
and mouth. He did not offer to share it. Jean de Malestroit, Bishop
of Nantes, was to take possession of the castle in forty-eight hours,
he said, so this work had to be completed by then. We were joined
by Gilles de Sillé and another servant who did not give his name.
Inside the room we found the skeletons, heaped in a colossal

faggot-box set near the hearth, of forty-two children. The skin was shrunken and dried about the bones and flaked off to the touch. The box was the height of our chins and the jumble of bones inside as high as our chests. A stool was brought to help Henriet and myself climb up and in, each of us using a staff to clear space for our legs. This disturbed the beetles and flies and other insects to which the bones had been abandoned, as well as a kind of powdery dust that settled in our mouths and eyes. No one spoke except about how best to bundle the loads into large coffers bound with iron and already waiting in the middle of the room. When filled, each was to be double-bound with rope as a proof against the failure of the iron bands. Eight in all were required. I distinguished the number of children by counting the skulls. Our purchase on everything was increasingly complicated by hands turned white and greasy with a slimy ash.

We became aware of noises at the door's peephole, though none of my co-workers seemed troubled. I heard a woman's soft laughter. Henriet warned me to keep guardianship of my eyes. He later explained that Roger de Briqueville at times invited noble ladies of the district to watch such operations in progress.

We swept the last bits into the faggot-box, and a layer of resin-wood and ground aromatics was spread to mask the smell. The coffers were carried down the spiral steps at nightfall to waiting wagons, which were driven to a quay on the Loire and loaded onto barges to be poled down to Machecoul. There, before sunrise, they were hauled up to what Henriet revealed was our lord's own bedroom. And there they were emptied and the bones burned in his presence. And when each pyre cooled, it was our task to dump the ashes into the moat.

Henriet lost patience with my periodic torpor. When I complained about his anger, he widened his eyes and affected a fool's expression as though imitating someone. I was quartered near his wash basin and chamber-pot stand, and told not to touch his things. We took our meals together. After some weeks we began conversing at night once our chambers were dark. He said that from his earliest childhood he'd felt himself an affliction to those around him and had banished himself to the woods, where he couldn't be spied and only answered after having been called many times. Sometimes he hid in caves. He remembered asking his father if a hermit could live on plants and roots. One day during the harvest they found him looking in the hedges and hayfields for wild saffron bulbs to eat. He'd made a bow with which to kill birds, but hadn't managed to hit any. He was nothing like his younger brother, who in January ran beside the plow with a goad until he was hoarse from the cold and the shouting. At my age he had frightened his mother by pointing into the fireplace and claiming to have seen old Mourelle grinding her teeth. Mourelle was their mare, and of her he was deeply afraid. He also feared hens. But he was a lesson, he thought, for at some point he had applied himself diligently to discover what he should do to cease being reclusive and live among men.

He was given charge of my instruction. I learned to bear my head upright and to keep my eyelids low and my gaze four rods ahead without glancing right or left. To scatter our lord's room with alder leaves for the fleas. We set out bowls of milk and hare's gall for the flies. We strewed the floor around his bed with violets and green herbs. We cared for the smaller birds in his aviaries, prepared sand for his hourglasses, dried roses to lay among his clothing, and found boys to replace the boys who continued to disappear in his secret rooms.

Girls were sometimes accepted if slender and beautiful and as red-haired and fair-skinned as our lord. Each of his castles was thronged about by children made homeless by a hundred years of war and brigandage, begging where they could and stealing where they couldn't. Henriet and I spent an hour each morning sheltered in our aerie above the portcullis, selecting from those at the gate. For children of particular beauty we roamed the villages and churches. If a boy was of more respectable means, Gilles de Sillé or Roger de Briqueville would ask the father to lend the child to take a message to the castle. And later, if asked what had become of the boy, they said they didn't know, unless he'd been sent on to another of the lord de Rais's residences, or thieves had taken him.

Children were also provided by an old woman who came to be known along the Loire as "the Terror."

One Sunday after Mass we were cornered by a mother so agitated she refused to let us pass. Her husband was embarrassed by her fervor. Her other children shrank from her voice. Henriet told her he had seen her boy helping our lord's cook, Cherpy, prepare the roast, and that perhaps he'd since been apprenticed elsewhere. She answered that she'd been told twenty-five male children had been provided as ransom to the English for Messire Michel de Sillé, captured at Lagny. Henriet pointed out that she knew more than he, then, and forced his way past. She tore my sleeve as I sought to follow.

We were summoned to the secret room to meet a boy named Jeudon, indentured to the local furrier. He curtsied before us, comically, and steadied himself. He breathed over us the sour wine and cinnamon smell of the hippocras. He had beautiful, hay-colored hair and a fondness for candied oranges. He seemed happily confused by our little gathering.

His face changed when the lord de Rais, standing some feet away, took his member from his breeches and stroked it until it was erect. Henriet and I were instructed to hold the boy's arms until the lord de Rais, moving closer, lifted the boy's shirt and took his pleasure upon his belly. Then he looped a silken cord around the boy's neck, whispering assurances all the while, and hung him from a lantern-hook high on the wall.

The boy kicked and thrashed and spun on the cord. The sound he made was like someone spitting. The lord de Rais released the knot and slid him to the floor, savoring his expressions of panic and relief. He had the boy carried to the bed and freed from his clothing but bade us not release his limbs. "Please," the boy said to me, and then to Henriet. The lord de Rais sat without his breeches on his naked chest, leaned close again to whisper something soothing and, with the boy's eyes on his, produced his jeweled dagger from the bedclothes and carved a line across the center of his throat. The fissure welled and then fountained with blood. The boy's hand jerked in mine. The lord de Rais, spattered, pulled back and then leaned forward in his work, again taking the boy's gaze in his own eyes and sawing with a drowsy languor through windpipe and bone and then into the bedding.

The blood pooled faster than the bedding could receive it, so when he finally shifted his weight from the boy's chest a stream filled the indentation formed by his knee.

That night neither of us spoke until it was nearly dawn. Then Henriet used the chamber pot and, laying himself down again, claimed that even the pillars of heaven were based in the abyss. When he received no response, he wondered angrily who among us had not had the poisoned air lay its dead hand upon him. What did I know of Original Sin? He had to repeat the question. I finally told him I knew nothing of Original Sin. He said he believed in it, this dogma that taught all were lost for one alone, not only punished but also deserving of punishment, undone before they were born.

Was he weeping? I asked him, after debating the question myself. By way of answer he rose from his bed and struck me.

The disappearances whenever the lord de Rais was in residence were no secret, but there were always orphans, and parents to bring their children forward in the hopes of making their fortune in a great noble's service. Some sent their children in pairs that they might be safer in one another's care. If such a pair was to our lord's taste he had the more beautiful one's throat cut first so he or she might not pine overlong for the other. At all inquiries the herald of arms was to say that peradventure the boy was now with some upstanding gentleman elsewhere, who would see that he got on. Now in the secret room heads would line the window seat and the lord de Rais, once they were thus arranged, would ask each of us to choose the most comely. He had us each kiss the mouth of the head we chose, and then he hoisted his favorite, lowered it to his gaze, and kissed it with abandon, as though initiating it into the pleasures of the flesh.

The heads were kept for two or three days. Then they followed the bodies into the great fireplace, their ashes ferried from there to the cesspits or the moat.

Much is forgotten, and much will fall out of this account. My education in language and figures, set in motion by the parish priest, was continued under the auspices of one of the teaching friars responsible for the pages. I invited Henriet every so often to test my newfound knowledge, and he refused.

The seasons pulled us through our shifting duties while the fields around us displayed the lives from which we'd been plucked. March was for breaking clods. August was for reaping. December was for threshing and winnowing. The freemen brought their rents, their three chickens and fifteen eggs, to the tenants' tables for their accounting. Courtyard cats feigned sleep before blinking half-shut eyes at them. For a little while longer, the world of treasures that consoled us and softened woe seemed in place. But like toads crossing our path in the dark, the balance reasserted itself.

We saw a girl of seven on her back, shod only in one stocking, her head bare, some of her spread hair pulled out and lying at her feet. We saw a five-year-old with beautiful eyes and a filthy face whom I at first held and then released at Tiffauges's gates, watching her disappear like a bolt from a crossbow. We witnessed our lord beheading poppies with a rod and heard him remark that the world had been empty since the Romans. He spoke also of Joan, and how she entered Orleans armored in white at all points and carrying a standard depicting two angels holding a fleur-de-lis over an Annunciation. We heard him marvel at the magical world in which she lived, and the way, just like that, English resistance collapsed before her. As the months went on, he took an increased interest in selecting boys himself. He came to favor kneeling on the torso after the head had been removed but while some warmth still remained in the body. Henriet said that I developed so gloomy, wrought, and unforthcoming an aspect that passersby sometimes drew him aside and wondered if I was his lord's imbecile. I asked what I should do and he said that he hauled his necessities about with him, like someone shipwrecked. The world had abandoned him and he had returned the favor. His claim frightened me. I took to closing my throat with my hand as I lay beside him in the darkness, experimenting with various pressures. One night he took my hand from my neck and reminded me that insanity was a master's privilege. Later he emptied three full basins trying to clean his eyes after a boy's brains had bespattered them. Afterwards he lay on his pallet unmoving, and I was sorry for someone so young and so far from his father and mother and brothers, and for whom all comfort was a bed of stones when compared with his home.

Chasms opened beneath me, as if the earth would swallow my sin. I wept. I fell to the ground. I regained my feet. One morning I lay in a wheat field and some farmers saw me and were astonished, but said nothing. We were bound to our lord from the crowns of our heads to the soles of our feet. While he looked down from his heights of Pandemonium. And we fell under the spell of the slaughter with its reddish-brown eyes: ushers kept the doors, clerks added the accounts, squires dressed the dishes, and serving maids swept the halls and beat the coverlets, all while our souls, at their own bidding, flew headlong into dreadful extremity.

Our lord announced he was going to take a hand in our education. For two straight nights he appeared in our chambers and read to us from Suetonius. Then without explanation he stopped, growing increasingly agitated and impatient. Henriet in our more private moments explained why: he was spending over fifteen hundred livres per day. His family's wealth consisted of land and property, but what was needed, perpetually, was accessible money. For him wealth no longer counted as such unless it had wings and admitted of rapid exchange. In Machecoul he had founded his own chapel, the Chapel of the Holy Innocents, with a Collégiale of the finest voices and most beautiful faces he could find. Of the chapel itself it was said that even visitors from Paris had never seen the like: great glittering cascades of ornament engraved and set with precious stones and gold and silver, with all deacons, archdeacons, curates, and choirboys robed in vermilion and white silk with tawny furs and surplices of black satin and hooded capes. One wall was a towering organ, and he additionally commissioned a portable one it took six men to carry so he should not be deprived of music when obliged to travel. When the chapel was completed he had himself named Canon of Saint-Hilaire de Poitiers so he might wear the multihued ecclesiastical robes he himself had designed. He found a boy who resembled him so powerfully that the boy was designated Rais le Héraut, and dressed more magnificently than anyone, and given a place of honor in the cortége whenever the household rode out. So that everywhere our lord went, he could see himself preceding himself: our lord in white, Rais le Héraut in the deepest black.

When we traveled, our procession might take two days to fully pass through a town. When we halted we filled every tavern and lodging house. When we moved on, local innkeepers and tradesmen displayed the stunned and dull-eyed satisfaction of overfed cattle. And in addition to all this he was preparing to mount the mystery play he had commissioned, which at its climax depicted him at his moment of greatest glory. *The Mystery of the Siege of Orleans* was to be presented in that city upon the tenth anniversary of the raising of the siege, and featured twenty thousand lines of verse, one hundred and forty speaking parts, six hundred extras, and three specially built revolving stages. Each costume was to be made from new material. Even beggars' rags were to be created by slashing and defacing fine cloth. No costume could be worn twice. And unlimited supplies of food and drink were to be available to all spectators.

It seemed inconceivable that our household would find itself short of gold, but any number of estates and properties were mortgaged. And Henriet and I would be sent to retrieve bodies from our lord's bedchambers. He mortgaged properties twice and then refused to abandon them. He ransomed merchants and travelers. And finally he had to sell off estates. He sold two great crucifixes of pure silver. He sold his manuscript of Valerius Maximus and his Latin *City of God* and his parchment *Metamorphoses* of Ovid bound in emerald leather and secured with a golden lock. He sold the silver reliquary enclosing the head of Saint-Honoré, his most precious relic.

He sold so much that finally his brother and his extended family wrote to the Pope asking His Holiness to disavow the foundation of the Chapel of the Holy Innocents, and to the King requesting an edict forbidding the sale of any further family property. Both petitions were granted. Soon after, word came from his brother that his nephews had discovered a pipe full of dead children in the keep at Chemillé. Nothing came of it. In his family's eyes, once their property was safe, whatever else our lord did was his affair.

It was logical, then, that our lord would employ someone to manufacture more wealth. Joan had had secret knowledge and had put it, while he watched, to kingdom-shaking use. And now he, too, needed to appeal to secret powers. The world was an epistle and every scholar's dream was to unlock its hidden instructions. Most did so by searching for the philosopher's stone, which would transmute base metals to gold. Cold water could when heated be turned to hot air. In the same way other bodies could be similarly transformed. It was a matter of discovering the correct agent of change.

This was explained to us in a meeting convened in the secret room at Tiffauges. While our lord addressed us I looked over at the bed where he first held the jeweled dagger to my throat.

We were being taken into this confidence because we would all be a part of the great search about to begin. The sibyl foretold the future, but the conjurer made it, by recruiting Nature itself to fulfill his designs. There was an old saying in war that our lord had never forgotten: "Is there a chance? Where Prudence says no, the devil says yes." There were demons who had the power to reveal hidden treasure, teach philosophy, and guide those boldest of men who sought to make their way in the world. Years ago he'd received from a knight imprisoned in Anjou for heresy a book on the arts of alchemy and the evocation of devils. Gerbert, later to be Pope, was said to have studied astrology and other arts in Spain under the Saracens and to have summoned ghostly figures from the lower world, some of whom abetted his ascension to the papacy. Sylvester II was said to have been taught to make clocks and other infernal devices by wraiths he had summoned. We would each now put our energies into locating alchemists. I would accompany Gilles de Sillé, as Henriet would Roger de Briqueville. The latter pair would travel to Italy, the center of alchemic knowledge, accompanied by a priest from Saint-Malo whose presence would make such inquiries less dangerous.

With my lord's cousin I traversed much of France, without success. We found a goldsmith who claimed he could heal, prophesy, conjure, cast love charms, and transmute silver into gold. We gave him a silver coin and locked him in a room, and he got drunk and fell asleep. Others stepped forward as conjurers. One drowned en route to Tiffauges. Another's face was of such frightening aspect that our lord refused to be shut in the tower with him. But the other group returned from Italy by the year's end with a youth named François Prelati who'd received his tonsure from the Bishop of Arezzo, having studied geomancy and other arts and sciences. He had sapphire eyes and ringletted blond hair. He wore shells from Saint James of Compostela and a holy napkin from Rome. He'd been to the East, where he claimed to have witnessed the blasphemous Marriage of the Apes, after which the celebrant cleansed his hands in molten lead. He spoke Latin and French and as a test in Florence had invoked twenty crows in the upper story of his house. He claimed he regularly conjured a demon named Barron who usually appeared as a beautiful young man. Our lord immediately had him installed in the bedchamber across from his own, and provided with everything he needed.

Experiments commenced the night his laboratory was ready. Henriet and I watched from beyond the door and outside a ring drawn into the floor with the point of a sword. Our lord and Gilles de Sillé waited just outside the circle, the latter holding to his chest his figurine of the Blessed Virgin. The conjuror's face was jacklit by the green glow from his athanor, but it was unclear from the smell what he was burning. He spoke in Latin and when he stopped a cold wind blew through the tall and narrow window behind him. He drew ciphers in the center of each of the four walls. Then he poured a glittering powder into his little fire, from which a stinking smoke drove everyone from the room.

Our presence was commanded throughout the sessions that followed, in the event there was assistance the conjuror might require. The following night our lord brought with him a pact written in his own hand and bearing his signature. When it was burned in the athanor a great clattering rose above us, as though a four-legged animal was cantering on the roof.

More nights followed with the demon manifesting himself yet not appearing. The conjuror spied him and conversed with him when we could not. This progress made our lord wild with success and impatience. What else did the demon require? A week of conjurings passed before he answered. Then he said, through the conjuror in a changed voice, a soul.

Beside me in the doorway, Henriet's respiration shifted. This was the awful bargain we'd each expected.

"Well, he can't have mine," our lord told the conjuror. And in the silence that followed he added that he would get him the next-best thing.

The next morning I was told to convey a bolt of strong cloth and four loaves of bread and a sester of good milk to Henriet, who was going back to the village after having negotiated that price for an infant. That night our lord passed us in the doorway to the conjuror's room holding a vessel covered in linen, the way a priest holds a ciborium. He told the conjuror to tell the demon that he had come to offer this holy innocent's heart and eyes, and the glass when he uncovered it was smeared and the contents inside were ropy and bulbous and filled only the very bottom.

And again the demon did not appear. Henriet and I were charged with wrapping the remains in the linen cloth and burying them before daybreak in consecrated ground near the chapel.

The conjuror suggested a new method of invocation that involved a crested bird and a dyadrous stone. The latter could not be procured. Attempts were made with serpents' hearts and with the conjuror wearing a thin crown fashioned from pitch and umbilical cords.

Our lord spent more time in solitude. His aspect around those children we produced was more melancholic and distracted. He talked without explanation of his allies' desertion. He remarked during the disposal of one girl that he had been born under such a constellation that it seemed to him no one would ever comprehend the things he did.

He moved to Bourgneuf, where he stayed in a convent. He had another boy brought to him there. On All Saints' Day he informed us that Gilles de Sillé and Roger de Briqueville had gone abroad without explanation. The Dauphin announced a visit to Tiffauges, and Henriet and I were sent back at a gallop to ensure that all of the conjuror's vessels and furnaces were hidden or smashed.

In the villages even the poorest parents now flew at our approach. It was openly asserted that the lord de Rais was writing a book on the black arts and using as ink the blood of the children he'd butchered, and that when it was complete he would have the power to take any stronghold he wished. We still managed to deliver two boys, ten and seven, and then two others, fourteen and four. When he was in his cups he would lie back on his bed in the secret room, mottled in gore from the waist down, and lament that his world was disintegrating for yet a third occasion. During the first, the death of his parents, he'd had his grandfather for support; and during the second, the death of his grandfather, he'd had his wealth. Now what did he have? he asked us.

"I'm sure I don't know," Henriet told him.

He attended Easter service and received the sacraments among the poor, waving them forward to receive before him when they tried to stand aside out of respect for his position. He spent three days alone in his chambers in fasting and prayer. Then he decided to repossess the castle of Saint-Etienne-de-Mer-Morte, which he'd sold to Jean V's treasurer. Having done so, he held at sword point in the chapel the officiating priest, the new owner's brother, whom he then pitched into the castle's dungeon.

He had violated ecclesiastical property, attacked a member of the duke's household, and transgressed against the rights of familial possession. That night the conjuror and the priest from Saint-Malo did not respond to his summons, and sent no word of where they might be located. He spent the next days consumed with his design for a velvet doublet waisted in silk that was embroidered along its length with Saint John's Gospel in golden thread, which he presented to a new page whom he then murdered and incinerated before us.

We alone stayed, our only home now the mad ostentation of his cruelty. Perhaps we imagined that since devils were only as active as God suffered them to be, no one would undertake to punish His instruments. I stopped eating. Henriet fell into greater and greater silences. One night he said only that he knew when my upset was at its most extreme, because I then crossed my arms and held my hands to my shoulders. He refused to add to this insight. On another occasion while we lay there on our pallets in the dark, he wondered what there was for us to do, now, but to low and bleat and wait for the culling.

It was not long in coming. On the fifteenth of September a body of men under the command of Jean Labbé, acting in the name of Jean V and Jean de Malestroit, Bishop of Nantes, presented themselves at Machecoul and demanded that the lord de Rais constitute himself their prisoner so he might answer to the triple charge of witchcraft, murder, and sodomy. Our lord had taken particular care dressing that morning, as though he expected them. We were arrested with him, and taken to Nantes.

We rode together in a covered carriage, Henriet with his head in his hands. The lord de Rais held forth the entire journey. He said he was praying to Saint Dominic, to whose order the powers of the Inquisition had been conferred. He said he had heard of a man in Savenay who, despairing of cure, had amputated his foot and then, having fallen asleep praying to the Virgin, had roused himself to find his foot restored. He said no one, rich or poor, was secure, but waited day to day on the will of the Lord.

Henriet kept his head in his hands. The lord de Rais ignored him and addressed me. He noted that I once again had nothing to offer in response. But he said he'd seen my soul. He knew it by heart. He'd noted my hours of discouragement and been present at my yielding.

I had no response for that, either. The lord de Rais stopped speaking. His single other comment, before we arrived, was that he was glad that his François, the conjuror, had escaped.

. . .

The lord de Rais was summoned to appear before the ecclesiastical judge appointed by the Bishop of Nantes on the Monday following the Feast of the Exaltation of the Holy Cross, 19 September 1440. Our presence was commanded as well. We were seated in a small dock beside the notary public. He was first charged with doctrinal heresy which violated divine majesty and subverted and weakened the faith. He was next charged with sacrilege and violation of the immunity of the Church related to his having threatened with a sword a cleric standing on holy ground. He was then charged with sodomy, the Inquisitor, from the Order of Preaching Brothers, reminding the assembled that the act of depositing semen anywhere other than the vessel for which it was intended was a sin so fundamental that self-abuse was a more serious crime than rape. The Inquisitor cited the prophet who cries out and chides, "Sons of men: how low does your heart sink?"

We were advised that those of us mindful of our salvation should undertake to set forth an extrajudicial confession. When I asked Henriet upon our return to our cell if he intended to attempt such a document, he said that he looked forward to a time when the whole globe was scoured of inhabitants, with houses left vacant, towns deserted, fields too small for the dead, and crows on the highest branches shouldering one another in their solitude. He said we were like those rough countrymen during the years of the plague who were persuaded despite all to carry the corpses to the pits.

He agreed to read my account as I set it down. Having done so to this juncture, he remarked that he found it impossible to assert which was the more astonishing, the author's memoir or his crimes. When I questioned his response he wondered with some irritation if I'd been struck by the oddity of the author's having felt so acutely for the raptors, and not their quarry.

"I've felt remorse for all of those children," I told him.

"You wrote that he had this or that person's throat cut," he answered. "But you neglected to indicate who sometimes did the cutting."

At the hour of terce on Saturday, 8 October, the lord de Rais refused to take the oath on the Sacred Scripture and, having declined to respond to the articles of indictment, was excommunicated in writing. On 15 October he consented to recognize the court's jurisdiction and admitted to many of his crimes and misdeeds. On 20 October, in order that the truth might be more fully elucidated, it was proposed that the question of torture be put to the defendant. On 21 October he petitioned that the application of torture be deferred, and on 22 October offered his full and public confession.

He spoke for four full hours. He offered the assembly a diptych of Paradise and Hell with himself as the central figure in both panels, in the former a paragon of the highest ideals of Christian knighthood, and in the latter evil's conscienceless servant. He said he believed his acts to have been halted by the hand of God, and that by the same hand he expected to be granted salvation. He freely related all of his crimes in luxurious detail and admitted he had offended our Savior because of the bad guidance he had received in his childhood, and he implored with great emotion all parents present to raise their children with good teachings and virtuous examples. He requested that his confession be published in French for the benefit of the common people. He exhorted everyone in the court, especially the churchmen, to always revere Holy Mother Church, and added that without his own love for her he would never have been able to evade the Devil's grasp. At the end he fell to his knees and tearfully asked for mercy and remission from his Creator and for the support of the prayers of all those, present or absent, who believed in Christ and adored Him.

The civil court found him guilty of homicide, but the canonical court condemned him for heresy and sodomy alone, the latter being known as the cause of earthquakes, plagues, and famine. On 25 October he received pronouncement of sentence: he would be hanged, and then burned. His two accomplices, Henriet and myself, would be burned and then hanged. Afterward the Inquisitor asked if he wished to be reincorporated into the Church and restored to participation in the Sacraments. He answered in the affirmative. He requested of the court that since he and his servants together had committed the crimes for which they were condemned, they might be permitted to suffer punishment at the same hour, so that he, the chief cause of their perfidy, could console and admonish them and provide an example of how to die well, and perhaps thereby be a partial cause of their salvation. This request was granted. He further asked for a general procession, that the public might view their contrition, and, when this was agreed, that on the sides of the wagon transporting them would be hung paintings he'd commissioned of late, depicting classical scenes of farewell. And the court, in concluding its proceedings, was pleased to grant this final request.

We ask all who read this to judge us with the charity we might not otherwise deserve. We were brushed by our lord's divine impatience and, like driven horses, risked in his wagers. Now our share is only the lash. Tomorrow's morning has been chosen for the consummation of our sentences, the site a meadow close above the main bridge over the Loire, where the trees are often adorned with the hanged.

Where is the region of that law beyond the law? No one makes his way there with impunity. I've filled sheet after sheet in a box at my feet. I conclude a final page by candlelight while Henriet weeps and will not speak and refuses my consoling touch. He rubs his back as my mother did. He will not read any further pages I put before him.

But I write this for him. And my eyes will be on only him as our arms are lashed around the heavy stakes to our back, and his gaze remains on lord de Rais. He will hang his head and close his eyes as he does when the greatest extremity is upon him. And lord de Rais's final moments will manifest themselves before us. He will die first, and in view of his contrition the court has decreed that his body be taken from the flames before it bursts and buried in the church he has chosen. In his last moments he will be a model of piety, exhorting us to keep faith throughout what follows. Barely burned, his body will be laid out on the finest linen by four noble ladies, two of whom watched us through that peephole so many months ago, and carried in solemn procession to his interment. We will watch the procession go. We will be isolated in our agonies as the bundles are lit below us. We will be burned to cinders and our ashes scattered.

And God will come to know our secrets. At our immolation He'll appear to us and pour His gold out at our feet. And His grace that we kicked away will become like a tower on which we might stand. And His grace will raise us to such a height that we might glimpse the men we aspired to be. And His grace like the heat of the sun will burn away the men we have become.

Poland Is Watching

We haven't spoken in three days and haven't stretched out in two, and that's forty-four hours we've been braced back to back, holding our tent poles, one hand low and the other high, to keep them from snapping in the wind. They're supposed to be titanium but at Camp 3 they went off like rifle shots in the night and these are jerry-rigged spares. The winds are topping 130 kilometers an hour. The temperature has dropped to 49 below. We're wearing three layers of fleece, one of Gore-Tex, down bodysuits, insulated climbing shells, and even our overgaiters, with gloves inside gloves inside mittens, and headcaps inside balaclavas inside hoods. I've been unable to interrupt the clatter of my teeth. Jacek's breathing sounds like someone blowing bubbles through a straw. Bieniek has long since given himself over to a kind of stupefaction. We store the radio batteries in our underwear and load them only when we need to call Base Camp. Once we're finished, getting them back through all the layers takes ten minutes. Then we just grip one another and hold on until our testicles warm the battery casings. The casings conduct the cold with exceptional efficiency.

We're at Camp 4 and only 1,000 meters below the summit, but the summit's 8,126 meters high and in the winter at this altitude everything is sandblasted by the jet stream and the cold.

Because of that, the peak is called Nanga Parbat: Sanskrit for "Naked Mountain." When the sky is not storming, it sounds like a giant's flapping bed sheets as hard as he can. When it is, the turbine sound of the howl makes even shouting pointless. During those periods we're reduced to hand signals with mittens.

We've been on the mountain for twenty-seven days. Our sponsors have shelled out big money not for attempts but for results. Our team members, strung out along the various camps below, are spent. Our wives back home are miserable. Our children are frightened. Poland is watching.

If we descend we won't have the physical reserves to return. If we continue upward we'll be ascending without being able to make out our hands at arm's length. If we decide to wait out the storm, they'll find us once it's over, like everything else in the tent, from our sunscreen to our cameras: frozen solid and cascaded with frost.

This mountain is a widow maker in the summer, when the weather's as good as it gets. It's famous for the kind of ice and rock slides that in 1841 were big enough to dam the Indus, sitting at its feet. The first great mountaineer to set foot up here, the Englishman A. F. Mummery, along with his entire expedition, was never heard from again. Twenty-six climbers were killed before even the first *summer* summit was achieved. There have been twelve winter attempts since. None have succeeded.

There's a song we sing in bars: "Who does winter mountaineering? We do winter mountaineering!" We are the Poles. The first winter attempt here was a joint Anglo/Polish expedition in 1988. Then the Brits came to their senses and dropped out. The Italians partnered with us for a little while as well, and have the casualties to prove it. Only the Poles have persevered.

And attempt number 13 is in deep trouble. For the last three days we've been hunkered down in an air raid of wind. Camp 4 amounts to a small trench for the tent, chopped into a cornice of snow as hard as concrete. We're now in the seventh day, and we need to be back in Base Camp by the middle of the month, after which, as Kolesniak likes to put it, the winds *really* get going.

Kolesniak got started like the rest of us, as a schoolboy running around local crags and picking up whatever he could in terms of technique here and there. Afternoon larks turned into weekend excursions and then long holidays away from home. Now he's so famous that kids can buy a snakes-and-ladders board game of his K2 climb. He's one of the central figures in the golden decade of Polish Himalayan mountaineering, having summited ten 8,000-meter peaks, including Everest twice. Once everyone and his brother started climbing such peaks, he began proselytizing for what he called a true Alpine style, which involved refusing to benefit from the work of other teams, even if it meant ignoring ropes that lay fixed beside your route or declining to take shelter in unused tents. On Gasherbrum IV he forbade his team to follow a Japanese expedition's footsteps in the deep snow. It was a short transition from that to winter mountaineering.

Soviet restrictions on travel throughout the postwar period ensured that Poles missed out on the first ascents of all the highest peaks, leaving us with mountains so small they lacked even year-round snow, but we solved the problem by resorting to the unthinkable: climbing in winter. In 1959 Zawada electrified everyone by ascending a staggering number of connected peaks in nineteen days of continuous climbing. Kolesniak, still a boy then, snuck into one of his lectures in a packed five-thousand-seat auditorium, and Zawada displayed a slide of a towering rock face in a sleet storm and told the audience, "Show me how you climb in this and I'll tell you what you're worth."

It was Zawada who first conceived of attempting Everest in winter, once travel restrictions were lifted, and Zawada who led the expedition that succeeded. He lived to see Lhotse and Annapurna and Dhaulagiri fall as well. By then the world was calling us the Ice Warriors and the Pope was sending him climbing advice. Industries hired top climbers during the summers to paint their smokestacks: easy work that paid like state ministries.

And Nanga Parbat remained the reef on which all Polish shipping ran aground. In 1997 Pankiewiez and Trzymiel clawed to within three hundred meters of the top before their frostbite became so dire they could no longer press on. Duszkiewicz in 2008 reached through a blizzard what he thought was the summit only to find once back in Base Camp that he'd stopped to celebrate on a rise eighty meters lower.

And now here we are. For three years each of us has hoarded and sacrificed and trained for the right to earn this chance. We have flown five thousand kilometers and caravanned by truck and foot hundreds of kilometers more and ascended seven thousand meters in altitude and squandered tens of thousands of euros on permits and porters' fees and equipment. "Let's go, girls," Kolesniak has shouted whenever anything has gone wrong. "You're not going to grow the balls you need sitting around complaining."

And as Agnieszka never tires of pointing out, we're not the only ones who have sacrificed. Her father, on the occasion of our daughter's seventh birthday, sat me down and walked us both glumly through the state of my finances, and once he finished her mother, waiting beside him, then asked how on earth, if I loved her daughter and granddaughter as much as I claimed, I could justify what I was doing. In the other room Agnieszka made a loud snorting sound.

I answered that I didn't justify what I was doing. Nine expeditions in the course of a seven-year marriage meant that I'd been away more than at home. For five consecutive years I'd missed my daughter's birthday. This birthday I'd been able to make because our climbing permits had fallen through.

And each time I returned with a body so devastated it never fully restored itself. Agnieszka told her girlfriends that she called my first weeks back the Famine Zombie Weeks. My vertebrae and hipbones were anatomy lessons. I was able to focus on emotional issues only when she put a hand on each side of my face and redirected my gaze into her eyes.

At our airport reunions, after her relief and joy, I'd see her anger at what I'd done to myself flood through her like a third revelation.

I'd met her at a faux-English pub in Warsaw. Most of us met our wives at one climbers' drinking hole or another. But I'd had good timing: it turned out she'd just come from a co-worker's retirement party at which she'd heard him joke about the number of years he'd worked at his bureau—more than she'd been alive—and then estimate the actual number of staff meetings he'd attended and evaluations he'd filed. A horrified silence had settled over the party, she said, and she'd decided then and there to quit. The pub had been the first one she'd encountered. When she asked what I did, I told her I climbed the highest mountains in the world in the winter. We went home together that same night.

She had some idea what she was getting herself into, she told me that first night while we spooned and she smoothed her hands together along my erection. Her brother had been a rock climber and mountaineer.

I'd failed to pursue the subject because she'd by then fitted me into her with a tenderness and calm I'd previously associated only with the afterlife. "Shhh," she whispered at the force of my response. "Look." And she brought her mouth around to mine. She meant, "Look how comprehensively we've merged." She didn't have to tell me: I was already so confounded that for an hour after she fell asleep I perched naked on her chest of drawers peering down at her like a traveler who'd found water on Mars.

As a child I'd been such an aberration in inwardness and appearance that my classmates had christened me the White Crow. My first years of schooling had been traumatic and I withdrew from any social situation in which I felt maligned. Climbing had been my way out. My aptitude for math and science had won me some recognition and I'd been invited to join the geology section of the Young Pioneers, and the field trips to the mountains had begun there. There I learned about rope and free climbing, about weather and snow conditions. But I still was valued only for what I could *do:* my mentor on those trips used to say that our relationship thrived on my achievements.

I'd been three hours late for our first dinner together and Agnieszka had already eaten and gone about her evening. She warmed up my portion after I arrived. "You aren't angry?" I asked. "You've already eaten?"

"Why would I be angry?" she answered, looking up from her book. "And why wouldn't I have eaten?"

She told me the first time I left for an eight-thousand-meter mountain that she wasn't going to become one of those women her brother's friends used to pity: the climber's girlfriend, left moping at home. On the radio telephone from Annapurna I complimented her on her poise when we'd kissed goodbye. She said, "You should have seen me once you were out of sight."

And now what does she have? She and Wanda are home alone most of the time in Mielec. Mielec is famous as the place in southern Poland where hope goes to expire. "Is it *so* bad?" her mother asked, before she first came to visit, and Agnieszka found she couldn't bring herself to answer. "It's astonishing that you grew up here," she likes to tell me. "Or maybe it's not." At town meetings, after the first three hours on economic growth we sometimes get to the fouled water table or the air pollution.

Mielec had a big Jewish community, which of course was wiped out in the war. It features the largest aviation factory in Poland, where we both work. For tourists, there's the minor basilica of Matthew the Evangelist, which is ugly. For football we have FKS Stal Mielec, a perennial third-division also-ran. We have a sister city in the Ukraine that I'm told is every bit as demoralizing. There's a water park. Potholes aren't the problem they used to be. And around our three-room house, we have enough land fenced off for a kitchen garden and a pygmy orchard.

In Islamabad we were informed about the extra expense of the bond that had to be posted for the possibility of a helicopter rescue, which was particularly maddening since we'd be operating nearly the entire time above a helicopter's ceiling. It's no wonder so many teams press on for the summits even in insanely dangerous circumstances, given that each year the cost of climbing in the Himalayas becomes more and more prohibitive. The highest mountains are now lucrative commercial concerns. On our last day in the city Kolesniak showed us our expedition's revised bank account, which was a disheartening sight. We now had enough to get to the mountain and climb it, though not enough, technically, to get back home.

We'd chosen the Kinshofer Route on the mountain's Diamir Face, which meant a longer trek across the glaciers to our Base Camp. At the little town where we hired our porters the usual gaggle assembled outside our hotel, some having walked from villages fifty kilometers away, and Kolesniak did the selecting by eye. He said he used to check all candidates with a stethoscope but then discovered that most had blood-curdling noises coming from their lungs and others apparently had no hearts in their chests. From there we all jounced for six hours along a muddy and narrow road through brilliant light. At curves along the Indus Gorge the lead driver would stop and beckon us all out to look over the edge, down the cliffs to the river below. At one hairpin he kept gesturing into a ravine whose drop was so severe that none of us would look.

Besides Kolesniak, Jacek, and myself, Poland's banner is held aloft by Nowakowski and Leszek, two old campaigners, and Bieniek, a late replacement none of us know very well. Nowakowski's the sort of legend who on one seven-mile hike into a Base Camp stunned all of those who hadn't been able to maintain his pace by producing an entire watermelon from his backpack to share upon arrival. They call him Filthy N because he refuses to wash even weeks after an expedition has ended. A woman he once tried to pick up in a bar at first refused to believe the smell was his. Only the year before Leszek had all the amputations on his right hand, and with his damaged toes couldn't entertain hopes of a summit, though he thought he might get as far as seven thousand meters, depending upon how his older frostbitten areas held up at altitude. He claimed that nearly all of his preparation was psychological, by which he meant last-minute parties, all-night binges, and as much sex as the women around him would allow. On his last night in Warsaw he threw up over the balcony onto a pizza delivery boy and then tumbled over the railing to follow. The boxes broke his fall.

Poor Bieniek seems not to know what to make of us. He's a quiet young man whose wrist alarm features a digital recording of his son's voice, wishing him a good morning and exhorting him to come back safely.

Jacek I got to know in the Young Pioneers. We both suffered from childhood asthma, not unusual for climbers, perhaps because lungs stressed by the affliction become better conditioned to process oxygen later in life. We instantly became adept at egging each other on when it came to risks. On one of the field trips we celebrated his sixteenth birthday by abandoning the bus that was supposed to return us to the city, to see if we could walk back through the forests. We arrived five days later, having survived on berries and two loaves of bread. We'd asked a friend to tell our poor parents we'd gone camping.

Above eight thousand meters in winter everyone needs to be technically proficient and emotionally unflappable. Jacek started climbing chairs and tables when he was fifteen months old and is ingenious with gigantic spatial puzzles like ice falls, and once totaled his brand-new car in a drainage ditch and simply climbed out and continued to the party on foot. His friends noticed the trauma only when they realized at the end of the night that he couldn't lift a broken left arm.

His wife, Krystyna, was even less happy than Agnieszka about having been relocated to Mielec. The official story was that he was taking a position as coach for the local ski program, which, though the pay was miserable, would allow him to maintain his training schedule, but she knew better. "Mustn't split up the boys," she often groused when the four of us met at a pub. The night before we flew to Islamabad, she complained that he had commitments everywhere and, to top it off, had just agreed to serve as a cameraman on an expedition immediately after Nanga Parbat, despite having no experience whatsoever with high-end video cameras. "You know what his motto is?" she asked. "'No time no time no time.' If you ask him if he wants some eggs, he'll answer, 'No time no time no time.'" She said he'd given so many interviews across the country for the last two weeks that after he finally got home and fell into their bed he told her he needed to go on this expedition as a *rest*. She'd thrown all of his clothes out into the street.

"It was raining, too," Jacek added, holding up the sleeve of his sweater. "This is still wet."

"Wanda complains that they come back a wreck and we have to fit our lives to their schedules," Agnieszka said. "She always says, 'Why should we? He never fits his into ours.'"

"And first they're unbelievably full of themselves—they *did* just conquer the world—and then they're depressed," Krystyna said. "At parties I'll hear the women with their big eyes asking them how they do it, and I want to grab their faces and say, 'The question is, how do *I* do it?'"

"Who wants another drink?" Jacek asked.

She went on to say that she'd begun to realize how many people this mountain had killed only by listening to our other friends talk about it. Then she'd broken down and done some Internet research, after which she wished she hadn't.

"High altitudes aren't as dangerous as everyone makes them out to be," Jacek told her. "You could just as easily get killed crossing the road."

"Yeah," Krystyna said. "If you painted yourself black and crossed on moonless nights."

"I liked the old days when they were out of touch for weeks," Agnieszka said. "At least then you could manage your anger and fear and go about your life."

"It's not like we don't take every precaution," Jacek told her.

"Well, there's a relief," she answered. "That should prevent the avalanches and blizzards and oxygen starvation and cold."

Jacek reminded his wife that he'd shown her the entry he'd made in his notebook on Annapurna: *"It's high time that I stopped this kind of Russian roulette and starting thinking of someone other than myself."* And then she pointed out that after finishing that entry, he'd left for the summit.

Locating the Polish tents in a large encampment is always easy: they're the ones still lit and noisy at four a.m., the ones rising up out of a sea of bottles. At this time of year, though, we had the glacier to ourselves. We set up next to the windblown remains of an unsuccessful Japanese expedition from the summer before. At 3,500 meters there was already sixty centimeters of new snow. Inside the main tent, Kolesniak hung smoked meats and salamis he'd brought from home. As the interior warmed up the salamis dripped fat on whoever was beneath them.

The camp was centered on a glacier forested with ice towers. Every so often we'd kick up out of the snow an old tent peg or film canister. In the areas surrounding our doorways, cleared down to the ice, crevasses opened and shut slowly, like giant clams. The whole assembly was drifting away from the mountain a few inches a day with the movement of the glacier.

The shortened days made everything harder. By three the sun was behind the ridge and the temperature fell off the scale. Fingers became wood blocks and noses clogged with frost. We huddled in our tents eating pasta and salami, with loaves of chapati that were full of sand that the local monopolist leavened into the flour to increase its weight. The sherpas requested the water we drained from our pasta and drank it from small wooden bowls they pulled from their coats. When not working Kolesniak read to us aloud from something entitled *Reign of Blood,* about Idi Amin's dictatorship. From this we learned that Amin kept his ex-wives' severed heads in his kitchen freezer in order to keep his current wife in line.

We believe in acclimatizing by working hard and stressing the body. Only multiple ascents at these altitudes can teach you how you're really doing; the first few times, every sensation feels abnormal, and the body is sustaining such a beating that it's hard to judge how poorly it's adjusting. To get to Camp 1, at 5,500 meters, we had to negotiate a maze of ice falls. We left on schedule at midnight, the advance team having already pressed on ahead, with Kolesniak, as leader, bringing up the rear to better follow the progress of the entire group spread out ahead of him.

Telephone reception is now much better than it used to be, so even in the high valleys blackout periods last days rather than weeks, and Agnieszka had managed to get through to me at the Base Camp before our first acclimatizing climb. She worked me like a strop while I turned to the tent wall and strove to ignore the jeers and jokes from Kolesniak and Nowakowski.

She said she was happy it had gone well so far, but I could hear in her voice the steeliness that derived from the extent to which she'd already disappointed herself. I asked after everything at home and she said that the night before she'd been to a dinner party at which all of the wives had wondered what it was *like* to love someone so often away and always at risk of never returning. She said she got so fed up that she finally started answering, "Why? Have people *died* doing that?" She said it was worse than when she met climbers and they asked if *she* climbed, and then seemed to believe she couldn't register the change in their expressions when she answered.

"Are you there?" she asked.

"*Oh, you left me at home with the baby and the dishes and the window sash that needs fixing,*" Kolesniak sang out in his stupid falsetto.

"The boys are having a time of it, are they?" she asked.

"We're going up to Camp 1 in a few hours," I explained.

"So you need your rest," she said.

"I'm fine," I told her.

She said that after we'd said goodbye this time, upon leaving the airport she'd merged onto the highway in the wrong direction and then had thought to herself, Who cares? She'd gone thirty kilometers before Wanda's complaining had allowed her to summon enough energy to turn around. When I didn't respond, she added she sometimes felt superfluous and uninvolved with my concerns, but then realized that was only because she was superfluous and uninvolved with my concerns.

"We were talking about this maybe being the last trip for a while," I told her. "Jacek and me."

"You're addicts," she said. "Krystyna and I decided that the night you left. A trip like this is about the loss of your ability to control the dose."

"*I'm lonely,*" Kolesniak sang while he stripped excess weight from his pack. "*Here in my bed with only my zucchini.*" He opened his hood and stretched wide its collar to show me again the tattoo on his neck in English: *Love Is Pain.*

"I'll think of something," I told her.

"Oh, you're resourceful when it comes to things like raising money for climbing," Agnieszka said. "It's in everyday life that you're not so clever."

"I never claimed I was clever," I told her. "I only know I want to be with you."

"Who in their right mind tries to build a relationship with a high-altitude winter mountaineer?" she asked. "I mean, when you're *with* me you seem to understand words like 'love' and 'commitment.'"

"They mean more to me now than they ever did," I told her.

"*I* signed up for this," she said. "But what about people who didn't? Like Wanda?"

"This trip's different," I finally told her.

"I know," she said. "The more people a mountain's killed, the bigger deal it is to climb it."

"That's not what I mean," I told her.

"What would happen in Formula 1 racing if one out of every twenty-five drivers *died*?" she asked. "How long would it take people to put a stop to it?"

"If you can't live with what I'm doing, then I won't do it," I told her. "If it comes to that."

"Let me lay it out for you so you can think about it," she said. "If you felt about me the way I feel about you, you would stop climbing. Period."

"Let's go, Chief," Kolesniak said, giving my shoulder a shove. "Coffee klatch is over."

"I have to go," I told her.

"Of course you do," she said. "Listen to me: you come home alive."

"I will," I said.

"I love you," she said. Then she hung up.

Nanga Parbat is the world's ninth-tallest mountain, its summit at nearly the cruising altitude of commercial airlines. Passengers on flights from Islamabad to Beijing fly past it, not over it. It appears as a pyramid in the sky above an ocean of cloud. It has three faces: the Rakhiot, the Diamir, and the Rupal. The Rupal features the highest known precipice in the world: an ice wall of some five thousand meters. The Diamir, considered the climbable face, involves an ice fall known as Death Alley and, above that, a couloir pitched at seventy degrees and rising one thousand meters to the crest of a northwestern ridge. We dug Camp 2 into the top of that ridge before clouds and snow reduced visibility to zero.

Inside the tents with the stoves operating the temperature was twenty below. We could only imagine the temperature outside. It was so crowded that everyone had to lie still for one of us to accomplish anything. In that kind of storm everyone bunked with whomever they found themselves beside in line, and so Kolesniak, Bieniek, and I took turns every few hours to go outside and loosen the heavy accumulations straining the sides of the tent. Once he was settled Bieniek struggled with his camera, which was refusing to work because of the cold. Kolesniak told stories of the catastrophic Central Peak expedition of '75: the immeasurable winds that shredded their tent from around them and blew melon-sized rocks into the air, the same windstorm that on the other side of the ridge severed their teammates' tent moorings and swept their entire camp off the edge of a drop that fell a vertical mile.

Bieniek's wrist alarm went off and his little boy wished him another good morning. He then mentioned he was lucky to be here, having on his last trip overreached on a belay and fallen thirty feet and landed on his side on rock. He'd impacted with such force that his heart had come out of its casing.

"You know what they say," Kolesniak said from the darkness on the other side of the tent. "Good judgment comes from experience, and experience comes from bad judgment."

Bieniek went on to add that at first his boy told him he was the only one in his grade with a cool dad, but before the last two trips he'd been inconsolable at the airport and Bieniek had finally told his wife that maybe if these trips were injuring someone he loved, he should stop them.

"What'd she say to that?" I asked.

"She blew up," he answered, a little sheepishly. "She said they'd *already* been injuring someone I loved."

Kolesniak said his gesture toward family responsibility had been to buy a life-insurance policy from Lloyd's of London. He said his wife had told him now that he had a grandchild, he'd finally find out what it was like to hold a baby.

The snow's weight made the tent's sides an embrace. We augered out more space by crossing our arms and twisting our torsos. Then Kolesniak enforced some quiet, since we had to be up at two a.m. for the next push. Before I fell asleep I could hear him eating jam from a little jar with a spoon.

Mielec is known as the Aviation City mostly because of the factory the Germans built during the war. It cranked out Heinkel 111s and 117s until the Allies bombed it flat. Then the Soviets rebuilt it and it cranked out MiGs. When you played in the vacant lots you were always finding unexploded artillery shells. You'd set them on a wall and try to detonate them by banging their firing pins with a rock. I only heard of it working once, and the triumphant artilleryman lost both his hands and his eyesight. The unexploded ordnance from the Allied bombers was buried more deeply, but was live enough that kids for blocks around would show up and watch when the town was digging a utilities line.

Whenever he heard the construction equipment, my father knew where to find me and would come from work to pull me out of the crowd. He repaired clocks in a street kiosk and everyone said he had golden hands when it came to fixing things. He gave me tasks, too, repairing simpler mechanical objects like rat traps or hand drills, and when I succeeded our time together went smoothly and when I failed it seemed to color the rest of our day. He told my mother that his impatience with his own children bothered him. She told him that she had enough to worry about. And when I somehow stripped the gears of a coffee grinder, he spent an hour trying to undo the damage and then gave up. On the streetcar home he remarked to himself that he wished he lived in a climbing hut in the Alps, one of those tiny shacks with a bed that lowered from the wall, where you saw another human being only on the occasional weekend.

For people like me, winter mountaineering is just ordinary life with the polite layers shorn away. Jacek likes to say that reunions like this with old friends are the only way to recharge our spirits.

No one sees you with greater clarity than your teammates above eight thousand meters. And *still* they risk their lives to bring you safely down.

They say whatever your worst memory is, you see it again most often right before sleep. I climb because once I go back down, the world while I recover is easier for me. Agnieszka's eyes and mouth become again my garden and our entangled sleep my chair in the sun.

Kolesniak had us up by two and under way by three. The expedition climbed in siege style, with fixed camps en route stocked with bivouac gear and food and fuel. Each climb to set up a camp and return was itself a mini-expedition and furthered our acclimatization. We stepped out into darkness and blowing snow and fell into line, and up above could see bobbing lights and black figures already ascending a steep belt of rock. Above the rock the route was hard ice under unconsolidated snow that by dawn had gotten very deep: Jacek, in the lead, was up to his chest in powder, working his arms in a breast stroke to clear the space ahead. At sunrise Nowakowski took over, leading us up a serac of blue opalescent ice and then tunneling into a mass of overhanging snow that pummeled down on the rest of us. By the time my turn came I had to kneel into the deep drifts above me on the slope in order to compress them to provide traction for my crampons. In the sun and working hard we were almost warmed. We were grateful for the relative calm. Even the plumes from the summit crest were diminished.

On a flat spot atop the Kinshofer Step we erected Camp 3 and collapsed and ate. Most of us could barely move. From above, Camp 1's orange tents in the snow looked like something in a petri dish. The wind picked up. Cirrus clouds traversed to the northeast, a reliable sign of approaching trouble. When at a distance of forty kilometers Masherbrum was curtained by dark clouds, that was our meteorological alarm bell: at the speed the storm was moving we'd have just enough time to get down to Camp 2. We descended in a stew of white with snow crystals spiraling up around us.

I rode out the storm with Nowakowski and Leszek. Condensation froze into ice sheets on the tent walls and then shook off onto our heads. Leszek discussed what a bitch it had been to lose a third of his toes and four of his fingers. He'd tried to cook breakfast for friends and kept dropping the frying pan. A young woman had exclaimed to him at a party, "You're still *climbing*? With no *fingers*?" and he said he'd told her to go back to her television: that was her life. His was a little different. While he spoke he organized and reorganized each of our packs. His unhurried attention to detail made him intolerable at sea level but at altitude kept him alive.

By late the next morning the storm had passed and another was blowing in. We left Leszek at Camp 2 and ascended back to Camp 3. By the time we arrived powder avalanches resembling cumulus clouds were being blown off the mountain at right angles by the wind.

We used our knives to cut chunks of snow for tea. The snow fell continuously all day with increasing intensity. We peered out of doorways into what looked like a milky vapor. In the lee of the wind, the snowbanks rebuilt themselves with alarming speed. We were all suffering variously from the cold. Nowakowski's toes were dark blue. The nail of Kolesniak's index finger was missing but he said the finger hurt, which was a good sign. Everyone was queasy, the fluid loss through breathing at altitude having wiped out our body salts. Our heads were metal doors that somebody was kicking with hobnailed boots. We shared our last big meal, a banquet of sardines and powdered potatoes and soup. Kolesniak poured the sardine oil onto his split fingertips to soothe them. Leszek reported by radio from below that his tent was getting buried so deeply that when he went outside there were no traces of the guy lines.

We were at that stage of the expedition in which home had begun to seem imaginary. Trying to plan meant wading in one's head through a murky and drugged marsh. If some of us were going to press on to Camp 4 and then the summit, we would have to go soon. Our luck, such as it was, wouldn't hold out much longer. A mountain like this was the apex of however many gigantic river valleys, all of which in winter were storm machines, sending their masses of evaporated water up its slopes at high speeds. The next morning made our decisions for us. Kolesniak's headaches were so bad he could barely see. Nowakowski reported that he'd started to spit up blood. They both had to shed altitude, and quickly. They'd wait for us at Camp 2 or maybe even Camp 1. Jacek, Bieniek, and I would be the ones going up.

The four of us husbands and wives had stayed at that pub until five in the morning. We hadn't even had enough cash to pay the bill, so Agnieszka and Krystyna promised to return the next day to settle up. "Where we're going to get the money, I don't know," Agnieszka complained once the unhappy bartender finally left us alone.

The flight to Islamabad was leaving at eleven. Krystyna had taken to drawing patterns in the condensation rings on the table in order to manage her frustration, and Agnieszka every so often ran her hand through my hair, feathering it back and holding my eyes with hers.

"It's just so weird to watch the world celebrate their selfishness," Krystyna said. "I can't tell you how many times some interviewer has said that there's not an ounce of compromise in him."

Jacek raised a glass in a bittersweet toast to himself.

"They all believe some version of 'Hey, I'm doing something unbelievably dangerous here; all *you* have to do is look after the house and kid,'" she went on. She seemed so worn out with sadness that she was unable to look at him.

"At some point, the wife begins to get it," Agnieszka said, her arms at her side. I could feel the absence of her hand from my hair. "Being away all the time just *isn't* that hard for them."

"Leaving you is the worst thing I do," I said.

"Is it?" she said. She sounded genuinely touched that I thought this might be the case. "You know, you sign on for the ride, but then you wonder how long the ride can continue."

"I have to piss," Jacek said morosely.

"I never thought we'd be together this long," Agnieszka explained. "I thought we'd either separate or you'd get killed."

"Teresa Nelec always used to tell me that being a winter mountaineer's wife meant always being ready for the funeral," Krystyna said. "She told me that when her daughter was three, she asked why so many women came over to stay with her and cry. That was her reward for all the weeks he was off in Chad or the Himalayas and she was home with a baby and no car and no money."

Jacek staggered off to the bathroom. The three of us just sat there. I helped Krystyna with her condensation rings.

"You always say you want to stop climbing, but on your own terms," she told him once he returned. "And those terms always turn out to be one more gigantic mountain."

"You know, when climber friends ask what you're up to, everyone says, 'Oh, I'm leaving for this' or 'I'm getting ready for that,'" Jacek said. "If you tell them, 'Oh, I'm getting a job' or 'I'm just going to spend some time with the wife,' you can actually *see* the respect leave their faces." He looked at Agnieszka, who looked back.

"And it's not an experience you intend to repeat," she said.

Krystyna drove us home since she seemed the least drunk. I thought but didn't say that the mountains seemed to us another chance, our attempt to understand ourselves and exorcise those aspects we detested. To become the sort of person we could begin to respect.

Back in our house we looked in on the babysitter, asleep with Wanda, and I negotiated my way to the bathroom with my pants unbuttoned and soon found myself on my back in the tub, where I conceived of other insights it would be important to impart to Agnieszka. Mountaineering was the only life for which I was fit. I understood her despair: we spent every particle of energy we had to get off the mountain alive and return to our homes, then couldn't wait to go back. We returned to be nursed back to health so we could dally in our marriages and resume our fund-raising. The difference between us and addicts was that you never got us to admit that anything was wrong with what we loved to do.

Agnieszka appeared and shut the door behind her as if she'd heard me. She'd thrown on her gray sleeping shirt and shed her pants. She put a hand on each side of the tub and leaned over me. "Every morning when you were gone, Wanda and I would take down the calendar and cross out the previous day's date," she whispered. "Until we got to the day we were going to the airport."

"You're not wearing any bottoms," I said. I sounded appreciative.

"I would cry, too, if I were you," she whispered, and she pushed me back when I tried to get up and climbed on top of me in the tub. "When I think of the ten million things that could have happened instead of my meeting you," she whispered, and I grew in her hands and she put me inside her. In her bedroom Wanda cried out in her sleep, and we both stilled for a moment. Then Agnieszka started moving again. "I can't live without being part of the debate," she finally whispered, easing us up and down. "With my options being either to support the team's decisions or leave."

"I love you so much," I told her.

"I know. We should talk about that more," she said. And then she lowered her face to me. We woke an hour before we had to get to the airport, only because Wanda was stirring in her bedroom again and calling for us.

After any prolonged stay above five thousand meters, the body begins to consume itself. Conditioning deteriorates. Fat disappears and muscle tissue follows. With each moment of acclimatization at altitude, strength decreases. Waking in Camp 4 is like waking in prison after having done something awful the night before. The wind seems to be ramming the tent's nylon walls. I struggle to my knees and Jacek follows. We step out into the maelstrom.

The tent is buffeting as furiously as white water rapids. The sky is clear but to the south the clouds form a wall rolling slowly toward us. When all of that air and moisture hits the base of the mountain it will have nowhere to go but up. And as it does so it will accelerate.

Back in the tent we take final stock of the situation. We've now been on this mountain for twenty-eight days and have endured winter storms for twenty-two of them. Water vapor has begun to freeze solid even among the down feathers of the sleeping bags. At some point we lost the will to keep clearing the entrance, and snow has been slowly pouring in like sand through an hourglass. Every so often one of us takes a gloveful and eats it. A filling in one of my molars has cracked. But a needling pain in my fingertips suggests that my capillaries are still functioning.

Jacek loads his batteries back into the radio and calls the other camps. There's no answer from Camp 2, and from Camp 1 Kolesniak sings out *"I'm so lonely without my zucchini!"* and then goes silent. The batteries are already coated with frost. The moisture's probably done the thing in.

Bieniek has not moved since we awoke and we decide to consult with him later. Our thinking has slowed down. At altitude you imagine you're thinking clearly, but you're not. Urgency disappears. Sometimes you mistake the intention of acting for the act itself. Climbers have had the notion of hooking on to a belaying rope and then have stepped free-fall out into space.

Above us we can hear the white noise of the gigantic air masses splitting around the peak. Crystals continue to spatter on the nylon over our heads. We try to work it out: the tendency when this close to the summit is to expend your last bits of energy to get there. But once on the summit you still have to climb back down, with only the shortest of pauses in which to recover.

"I can do it," Jacek says. And it's as if he's speaking for me. The plan becomes to go up and get back to the tent by nightfall. We'll leave at three the next morning to get as far as possible before daybreak. We immediately set about trimming gear weight, so desperate to lose ounces that we tear labels from our clothing. We even leave the foil space blanket, which hardly weighs a thing. This activity exhausts us and after two or three actions we have to stop for a count of ten to draw some breath.

We need to wake at one to get out of the tent by three. The wind is gone but we're still shocked by the cold. Night and winter this high are like outer space. The other mountains below look like whitecaps on the ocean.

After so much time in the tent, it's like learning to walk again. Jacek takes the lead on ice so hard our picks ring off it as if it were a bell. We pant in the insubstantial air. For eight hours we traverse pinnacles and chop through cornices. On the ice walls we get our feet secure with the front points of the crampons and then move the ice axes and reverse the process. Every few minutes we rest, leaning into the slope, heads on arms.

Then Jacek gives out a cry up ahead and I see that there's nothing above him; he's swung a leg over a summit crest so narrow that he has to straddle it like a horse. I climb up behind him and we pull ourselves forward with our hands, right legs dangling down the mountain's north face and left legs the south. My boot punches through a cornice to provide a porthole view six thousand meters down. Jacek's babbling something but I can't make out what. I'm just relieved the wind is manageable.

Even at this time of day—is it noon?—the sky above is indigo, fading into a pink upper atmosphere.

We have to descend nearly immediately if we're going to reach the tent before sunset. It takes some minutes to communicate that to Jacek by shaking his shoulder and shouting into his ear. We dismount the crest and belay one another downward as if negotiating a ladder, taking turns as anchors with our ice axes. If we start sliding in the shape we're in, we won't be able to stop. At some points the slope is so steep that we can't see the wall below us from above. Spindrift burns our faces. A cloud mist leaves us in a half-light, like a waking dream. But an hour after darkness we manage to grope back into the tent and fall asleep instantly, one atop the other.

We wake to Bieniek's alarm. His little boy is muffled under all of the layers. The boy repeats his good morning until we dig out his father's wrist and turn him off.

We shake Bieniek and ask how he's doing but he doesn't answer. There are ice crystals in his hair. His nose and cheeks are brown. We ask more questions and he follows our movement with his eyes, though otherwise no longer seems present.

Once we're sufficiently revived we make some tea with the last of the gas in the stove. There's so little air in the tent that the flame is a small blue halo above the burner.

We shouldn't start this late in the day, but we have to leave nonetheless. We assemble what bivouac gear we can for the likelihood that we'll spend the night out in the snow. Jacek climbs from the tent as I put a farewell hand to Bieniek's shoulder. His half of the tent is caved in. I touch a glove to his face and he doesn't stir, but when I remove it he asks for water. While I pour him a cup, he says, "It's quiet out. You could go down." I ask if he can stand and he doesn't answer. He no longer seems to be breathing. I lean in close, and listen, then set the cup on his chest and climb out myself.

Jacek leads on the way down. During a rest break in an ice gully he tells me to keep an eye on him, because he's starting to hallucinate again.

The storm blows in while we descend. Every few feet I'm surprised to find I'm still moving. It's impossible to belay each other in these conditions but the alternative is to sit down and die. On less steep stretches I'm frightened by momentary blackouts from which I emerge after apparently having proceeded five or six paces.

During another rest break Jacek informs me he can't breathe properly and asks if his lips are blue. Our boots hang out into space off the ledge on which we're sitting. The wind is such that it looks like we're kicking with them.

I tell him not *so* blue. The process begun in the tents is accelerating with the strain of all this agonized work: his lungs are filling with fluid, drowning the alveoli that absorb the oxygen.

We keep plodding downward. Finally in the starlight I can feel how close we've come to the edge of a giant balcony and I force us to stop. We dig a shallow snow cave in a languid stupor and then spoon inside it, taking turns on the warmer side. Even only this much lower, the air feels richer and full of oxygen, a pleasure to breathe.

The storm gets worse. A dull thundering rolls down from the summit pyramid. One of Wanda's gestures sticks in my memory and I worry it like a puzzle. As my way of rejecting the notion that no more messages will get through, and that home has become an imaginary thing, I compose what I'm going to say to Agnieszka by way of apology.

The morning after our first night together, she told me that her brother had died climbing. When she went through his things, his assets turned out to be his equipment, most of which was left on the mountain. He'd always told her not to worry about the trip they were discussing; the *next* trip was the one that was going to prove dangerous. She told me this on the living room floor, her legs still wrapped around me. She was weeping and I was inside her. I analogized the intimacy in electrical terms, thinking we formed a complete circuit. After she pulled away from our kiss she said she still didn't accept that he was gone. That she'd told herself, toward the end of his memorial service, he still had five minutes to turn up.

We should have been talking about all of this. But there'd only ever been time to discuss what had happened since I was gone, and where I was going next.

The hand that was clutching Jacek to my chest seems to have disappeared. I hold the glove up to the darkness but the fingers refuse to move.

He asks for some water and then doesn't drink what I pass him. He recites my name and then, some hours later, Krystyna's, until we pass beyond words some time during the night. We doze and wake and the difference seems hard to parse. When my eyes refocus there's a strange shimmer all around us, as if the light is coming off the surface of the snow itself.

Agnieszka! I want to tell her. The mountains have brought us together, as well. They've always been the authors of our development. They've allowed us to see what no other human beings have ever seen. They've siphoned away the warmth, down to our core and beyond, as payment. They've left you and our child the notion, never correct, that you were alone all along. They've ensured that we've progressed this far, and no farther, when constructing our connections to this wild and beautiful earth.

Acknowledgments

Most of the stories in this collection could not have existed, or would have existed in a much diminished form, without critically important contributions from the following sources: the Municipality of Rotterdam's *Waterplan 2 Rotterdam;* the Royal Netherlands Embassy's *Pioneering Water;* Deltapark Neeltje Jans's *The Delta Project: Preserving the Environment and Securing Zeeland Against Flooding;* Rotterdam Climate Proof's *The Rotterdam Challenge on Water and Climate Adaptation;* Leo Adriaanse and Tjeerd Blauw's *Towards New Deltas;* the Netherlands Water Partnership's *Climate Changes and Dutch Water Management;* Hans van der Horst's *Rotterdam Discovered;* William Z. Shetter's *The Netherlands in Perspective;* the Ministerie van Verkeer en Waterstaat's *Storm Surge Barrier on the Nieuwe Waterweg;* Stadshavens Rotterdam's *1600 Hectares: Creating on the Edge;* Dutch Delta Solutions' *Made in Holland;* the Dutch Research Program's *Knowledge for Climate 2008–2013;* the Port of Rotterdam's *Maasvlakte 2: Space for the Future;* Elizabeth Kolbert's *Field Notes from a Catastrophe: Man, Nature, and Climate Change;* Jan de Hartog's *The Little Ark;* Colin White and Laurie Boucke's *The Undutchables;* Willem Elsschot's *Cheese;* Jules Archer's *Jungle Fighters;* Eric Bergerud's *Touched with Fire: The Land War in the South Pacific;* John Ellis's *The Sharp End;* George H. Johnston's *The Toughest Fighting in the World;* James Jones's *The Thin Red Line;* E. J. Kahn's *G.I. Jungle;* Samuel Milner's *The War in the Pacific: Victory in Papua;* Ian Morrison's *Our Japa-*

nese Foe; Peter Schrijvers's *The G.I. War Against Japan;* Stephen R. Taafe's *MacArthur's Jungle War;* and the Historical Division of the War Department's *Papuan Campaign;* Richard Ellis's *Sea Dragons;* Eileen Powers's *Medieval People;* Jules Michelet's *Satanism and Witchcraft;* Reginald Hyatte's *Laughter for the Devil: The Trials of Gilles de Rais, Companion-in-arms to Joan of Arc (1440);* Jean Benedetti's *Gilles de Rais;* Marjorie Rowling's *Everyday Life in Medieval Times;* Michel Foucault's *I, Pierre Rivière;* Gareth J. Medway's *The Lure of the Sinister: The Unnatural History of Satanism;* Frances Winwar's *The Saint and the Devil;* Peter Handke's *A Sorrow Beyond Dreams;* G. R. de Beer's *Early Travellers in the Alps;* Edward Whymper's *Scrambles Amongst the Alps;* Colin Fraser's *Avalanches and Snow Safety;* Fergus Fleming's *Killing Dragons: The Conquest of the Alps;* Ronald Clark's *The Early Alpine Guides;* Nicholas and Nina Shoumatoff's *The Alps: Europe's Mountain Heart;* McKay Jenkins's *The White Death: Tragedy and Heroism in an Avalanche Zone;* Betsy Armstrong and Knox Williams's *The Avalanche Book;* Brian Greene's *Fabric of the Cosmos;* Lisa Randall's *Warped Passages;* Ben R. Rich and Leo Janos's *Skunk Works;* Trevor Paglen's *I Could Tell You but Then You Would Have to Be Destroyed by Me;* Philip Taubman's *Secret Empire: Eisenhower, the CIA, and the Hidden Story of America's Space Espionage;* Freya Stark's *The Valley of the Assassins, The Southern Gates of Arabia,* and *The Zodiac Arch;* Lieutenant-Colonel P. M. Sykes's *A History of Persia;* Marshall G. S. Hodgson's *The Order of the Assassins;* Bernard Lewis's *The Assassins;* Jane Fletcher Geniesse's *Passionate Nomad: The Life of Freya Stark;* Calvin Trillin's "At the Train Bridge"; the Marinette County Jail transcript of the interview with Scott J. Johnson; Kurt Diemberger's *Spirits of the Air* and *Summits and Secrets;* Anatoli Boukreev's *Above the Clouds;* Maria Coffey's *Where the Mountain Casts Its Shadow* and *Fragile Edge;* Greg Child's *Thin Air: Encounters in the Himalayas;* Mark Jenkins's "Ice Warriors"; Noel Busch's *Two Minutes to Noon;* Charles Davison's *The Japanese Earthquake of 1923;* Frank Stewart and Leza Lowitz's *Silence to Light: Japan and the Shadows of War;* August Ragone's *Eiji Tsuburaya: Master of Mon-*

Acknowledgments

sters; Thomas R. H. Havens's *Valley of Darkness;* Masuo Kato's *The Lost War;* William Tsutsui's *Godzilla on My Mind;* Soetsu Yanagi's *The Unknown Craftsman;* and the Fujiya Hotel's *We Japanese.*

I'm also grateful for the support provided by Williams College and the Oakley Center for the Humanities and Social Sciences, as well as for the inspiration and expertise provided by Elizabeth Kolbert, Rich Remsberg, Milton Harrigan Jr., David Tucker-Smith, Susan Coby, Kerry Sulkowicz, Margreet van de Griend, Karin van Rooijen, Monique Somers, Rebecca Ohm, Christine Ménard, Arnoud Molenaar, Jaap Kwadijk, Jos van Alphen, Pavel Kabat, and Djeevan Schiferli. I'm equally indebted to the saving editorial intelligence provided by Peter Matson, Jim Rutman, Frances Kiernan, Max Winter, Eli Horowitz, Michael Ray, Jordan Bass, Emily Milder, and especially Gary Fisketjon.

Other readers and friends like Lisa Wright, Steve Wright, Gary Zebrun, and Mike Tanaka have been even more constant in their support. But I need to single out for special praise the contributions of those readers who encounter my stuff at its earliest stages—Ron Hansen and Sandra Leong—as well as the person who'd be the first to say, with complete accuracy, that she improves me in just about every other way, as well: Karen Shepard.

ALSO BY JIM SHEPARD

PROJECT X

In the wilderness of junior high, Edwin Hanratty is at the bottom of the food chain. His teachers find him a nuisance. His fellow students consider him prey. And although his parents are not oblivious to his troubles, they can't quite bring themselves to fathom the ruthless forces that demoralize him daily. Sharing in these schoolyard indignities is his only friend, Flake. Branded together as misfits, their fury simmers quietly in the hallways, classrooms, and at home, until an unthinkable idea offers them a spectacular and terrifying release. From Jim Shepard, one of the most enduring and influential novelists writing today, comes an unflinching look into the heart and soul of adolescence. Tender and horrifying, prescient and moving, *Project X* will not easily be forgotten.

Fiction

LOVE AND HYDROGEN

The stories in this dazzling array of work in short fiction from a master of the form encompass in theme and compassion what an ordinary writer would take several lifetimes to imagine. A frustrated wife makes use of an enterprising illegal-gun salesman to hold her husband hostage; two hapless adult-education students botch their attempts at rudimentary piano but succeed in a halting, awkward romance; a fascinated and murderous Creature welcomes the first human visitors to his Black Lagoon; and in the title story, the stupefyingly huge airship Hindenburg flies to its doom, representing in 1937 mankind's greatest yearning as well as its titanic failure. Generous in scope and astonishing in ambition, Shepard's voice never falters; the virtuosity of *Love and Hydrogen* cements his reputation as, in the words of Rick Bass, "a passionate writer with a razor-sharp wit and an elephantine heart"—in short, one of the most powerful talents at work today.

Fiction/Short Stories